I0601261

Open Wounds

A Harbour Bay Novel

Camille Taylor

Open Wounds

Copyright © 2015 by Camille Taylor.
All rights reserved.
First Print Edition: December 2015

Limitless Publishing, LLC
Kailua, HI 96734
www.limitlesspublishing.com

Formatting: Limitless Publishing

ISBN-13: 978-1-68058-403-5
ISBN-10: 1-68058-403-0

No part of this book may be reproduced, scanned, or distributed in any printed or electronic form without permission. Please do not participate in or encourage piracy of copyrighted materials in violation of the author's rights. Thank you for respecting the hard work of this author.

This is a work of fiction. Names, characters, places, and incidents either are the product of the author's imagination or are used fictitiously, and any resemblance to locales, events, business establishments, or actual persons—living or dead—is entirely coincidental.

Dedication

For mum.

Chapter 1

Detective Sergeant Darryl Hill parked his unmarked red Holden SS Commodore outside the small one-storey house. With its neat garden, mowed lawn and clean gutters, it was the last house anyone expected to see with blue and white chequered police tape around the perimeter. He half-expected to see a couple of kids run out of the house squealing in delight, tossing around a football.

It was mid-morning, so most of the neighbours were already at work. A few lingered outside the tape with obvious interest at what had occurred on their quiet street in the early hours of the morning. Darryl climbed out of the car and made his way toward the front door, following his partner, Detective Inspector Amelia Donovan.

His last partner, Matt Murphy, was currently on leave with his wife Natalie and adopted daughter Hallie, taking a much needed break in Port Douglas. Before he'd left on his trip, Matt had, with a smile on his face, suggested there might be a new addition to the Murphy family in the coming months.

Darryl couldn't believe Matt had settled so easily into married life, although at first it had been hard for him. Both he and Natalie worked long hours and they'd had to deal with being a readymade family when they had decided to adopt Hallie, who had been institutionalised for the past five years after witnessing her parents' gruesome double murder.

It had been Darryl's first homicide case since passing his detective's exam and both he and Murphy had been assigned to finding the man who the newspapers dubbed the Butcher due to fact that he butchered his female victims until they were almost unrecognisable.

He had been Harbour Bay's first and thankfully only serial killer. They still had the occasional homicide, of course, but it was nothing like the carnage left in the wake of the Butcher. Residents could once again sleep easy.

Harbour Bay, a city of about three hundred thousand on the southern New South Wales coast, was nestled against the harbour it had been named for. It had its share of good and bad, a blend of white and blue collar neighbourhoods and one large section spanning several blocks notoriously known as Coleani's territory. The area was also the city's central hub for crime.

Besides the state run rehabilitation centre, Paradise Valley, which specialised in the mentally unbalanced, the city also boasted a beautiful bay, a golden sand beach and marvellous breathtaking views. It also housed Harbour Bay's Local Area Command—LAC, which sat on an outcropping of cliffs overlooking the harbour, as well as the Tasman Sea further out.

Thankfully, despite its recent bad press, people from all over the country still flocked to one of Australia's best tourist locations.

Donovan showed her holographic Warrant Card—her official Police ID—to the uniformed officer standing guard at the front door and introduced both herself and Darryl for the record. The guard nodded, took note of their names on the crime scene log, and opened the door for them. She entered first, her light brown gaze sweeping over the interior of the combined kitchen, dining and family room. Darryl tried not to gag when he was assaulted with the aroma of dead bodies.

There is nothing like the scent of decomposing flesh to get you going in the morning, he thought grimly, as he followed her inside to the crime scene.

Two dead bodies lay face down in the centre of the room. Darryl barely glanced at the victims before moving to assess the scene. He liked to see the crime scene as his victims had first and noted there were no personal effects on the walls or on any of the surfaces. Had they just moved in? There were no boxes littering the room, so it wasn't as if they'd just finished unpacking. People of few means, perhaps, which would explain the shabby furniture that looked to be mismatched op-shop cast-offs. This was at odds with the expensive wall-mounted flat screen TV and gaming system. A game was frozen on the LCD screen where someone had paused it and the dialogue box was prompting the user to 'resume' as if they had been interrupted by an unexpected guest.

Friend or foe?

The room showed no signs of a struggle. The house was as tidy on the inside as the exterior. Darryl's gut told him that was important. He never knew men as young as his victims who kept such a clean house. Hell, he still didn't despite being in his thirties. It appeared they had no money to pay for someone to come in and tidy up. Was it an attempt to keep neighbours from discovering something they shouldn't?

The lingering scent of garlic and onion that warred with the smell of death had him turning to the coffee table near the bodies where two open pizza boxes sat beside the controllers for the Xbox. Most of the pizza had been consumed with only a few pieces left. A half-empty glass of flat Pepsi rested on the cardboard flap of the pizza box. He wrote down the name of the pizza company in his notepad so that he could interview the employees and verify the delivery time.

The forensic team buzzed about the room dusting for fingerprints. Men and women in white latex gloves snapped photos while collecting and methodically cataloguing evidence.

Darryl blocked out the hum of voices as he allowed his gaze to wash over the scene again. He had already seen all there was to see but a second look didn't hurt, and he memorised the scene so that he could recall it later.

Blood and brain matter had splattered against the furthest wall, indicating that both victims had been standing at the time of death. The deep crimson had soaked into the beige carpet around the two bodies. Each body had three bullet wounds—one in the head, two in the chest, execution style.

Donovan bent down, producing a pair of latex gloves from her pocket and expertly put them on as Doctor Eric Stone, the LAC's coroner, arrived with his liver thermometer.

"Large calibre weapon. A forty-five would be my guess, judging by the damage," Doctor Stone told them as he knelt down beside one body.

Donovan waited until Stone nodded his permission before searching through the pockets of the closest victim. She found a wallet, flipped it open, and slid out the licence. "Carl Benedict."

Darryl did the same for the other man. "Kevin Butler."

A young uniformed officer stopped beside Donovan and cleared his throat, trying hard to look her in the eyes. It was common knowledge to all uniforms that Amelia Donovan was a hard woman. If you stuffed up in her presence, you were blacklisted on further assignments. Darryl figured she got some perverse pleasure out of scaring the green officers.

"Detective Donovan, a neighbour from across the road witnessed a car leaving this address at about midnight last night," the officer said.

Amelia glanced at the young man, her gaze hard. The young rookie sweated nervously and shifted on his feet under her scrutiny.

"Where's the neighbour?"

The rookie turned and pointed to an older gentleman standing beside the sign-in officer at the front door.

"Over there. His name is Albert Carter."

She nodded briskly. "Thanks."

Darryl followed her as she made her way to the neighbour.

"You know you could give him a little more encouragement. A little 'good work' or 'well done' goes a long way," he pointed out as he saw the rookie's crestfallen face. "They may fear you but they also idolise you."

She gave him a sidelong glance. "Why should I be the one to pat them on the back? That's what they've got supervisors for."

Darryl sighed loudly, his point lost on her. It wouldn't kill her to acknowledge work that had been done well. She could easily make their day by remarking on their jobs. But she wouldn't be Donovan if she did. Amelia Donovan had to do it the hard way. She saw no reason why others couldn't do the same.

The neighbour, Albert Carter, looked at them as they drew near. His bushy eyebrows knitted together as he waited for his tale to be heard. His portly stomach strained at the buttons of his linen shirt and his hair had been well oiled and combed.

"Mr. Carter?" she asked.

Carter, who appeared to be in his late sixties, nodded. "Yes?"

"I'm Detective Donovan. This is Detective Hill," she introduced, pointing first to herself then to Darryl.

"How do you do?" Carter asked politely.

"Better than these guys," Donovan replied

casually, but Darryl saw Carter pale at her comment. "Mr. Carter, I just want to ask you a few questions."

"Sure."

She produced a notebook from her pocket. "At what time did you say you saw the vehicle speed away last night?"

"Around midnight. I'm on the neighbourhood watch committee, so it's my job to record strange circumstances."

She made some notes, her hand moving speedily across the page.

"And what made you think that was a strange circumstance?"

Carter raised an eyebrow. "The car skidded away. Like the person was in a real hurry."

"You didn't hear any gunshots or loud bangs?" Darryl asked. "A car backfiring maybe?"

Carter shook his head. "No. I thought it was strange, yes, but I had no idea illegal stuff went down in the house. The owner seemed nice enough. You know the type. Kept his garden clean, brought in his garbage bins. It came as a real shock to wake up to the police across the road and to hear that not just one person but *multiple* people had been murdered. My property value just went down."

Donovan nodded as if she gave a damn about his property values.

"Did you happen to catch the make or model of the car?"

Carter's dark eyes twinkled. "I did better than that." He handed her a piece of paper. "I got the number on the licence plate."

"Thank you, Mr. Carter."

Darryl turned away from Carter and spoke to the nearest officer.

"Put a BOLO out on this vehicle."

The officer nodded. "Yes, sir." He relayed the request into the radio that rested on his shoulder.

Darryl turned back to his partner. "Gotta love nosey neighbours. They make our jobs so much easier."

Donovan stared out at the picture perfect street with its green lawns and painted houses. The place resembled a cover for *House and Gardens*.

"Yeah, although I wouldn't like to live in this neighbourhood, what with every move you make being scrutinised."

"Got something to hide, Donovan?" he teased.

"Hardly." She scoffed. "But I wouldn't want some joker with no life telling me how many times a week I 'entertained' or if I forgot to mow my lawn this month."

He agreed. There was little privacy to be had these days, let alone your neighbours keeping tabs on you. It was no way to live life, being inside a fishbowl—which was clearly the case for everyone on this street. However, no privacy was good for solving cases.

He and Donovan moved back to the crime scene, just as Stone finished zippering the last body bag closed.

"Give me a couple of hours and come see me. I should have some answers by then," he told them.

"Thanks, Doc."

He watched with interest as Donovan bent down

to examine the tiny, almost invisible mark of white powder on the floor where the bodies had once been. It was clear the body had protected the powder after it had fallen.

"Looks like I found something."

He kneeled beside her as she placed the powder into an evidence bag.

"Is that cocaine?" he asked, narrowing his eyes.

She shrugged one shoulder. "One way to find out."

Darryl handed her a drug testing sachet and she deftly added a little of the powder into the clear plastic sachet and broke the vial inside the bag. The liquid inside turned a blue colour, indicating that the powder proved positive for drugs.

"Murder and cocaine. I'm guessing they were having themselves a party," she said flippantly.

The mobile phone attached to her belt chirped from its perch beside her gun holster. She yanked it off and answered, listening to the voice on the other end. Once she had the information she needed, she pressed the disconnect button and faced him.

"They found the car. It's downtown."

He nodded. "Let's go."

"I'll drive," she said.

Darryl rolled his eyes and exhaled his breath heavily. "I hate it when you drive."

Normally he had no issue letting his colleagues drive but Donovan was a mad woman behind the wheel of the car. She didn't slow down for anything or anybody, usually weaving in and out of traffic at about ten kilometres an hour more than the sign dictated. He had witnessed a few near misses and one in particular that he wasn't too proud to say scared the shit out of him. But he wasn't about to argue with her. His lovely partner could get a bit touchy and his number one rule was to never piss off an armed woman.

He climbed into the passenger seat and secured his seatbelt as she started the car. "What's wrong with my driving?"

Where should I start?

She suddenly grinned, changing her whole heart-shaped face. She was an attractive woman, not graceful, but she had a quality that certainly made every man give her a second look. Strong and fit, with mocha tanned skin, she kept her raven hair short and pulled back into a severe ponytail.

She never wore makeup, and never needed to, having the type of skin which looked good under any circumstances. Other than her obvious good looks and lithe body she was intelligent, hardworking, a damn good cop, and had the respect of her team.

"I thought you took tactical driving," he complained.

"Twice," she said.

Chapter 2

An hour later, Darryl sat with Donovan in their car, watching the grey Saab parked across the road. The council pretended neighbourhoods like this didn't exist. Litter blew across the road, graffiti lined every wall and surface, going from the brightly coloured to the explicit and crude.

Several of the city's homeless sat huddled in corners or begging for change outside the local grocery store. Even during the day the drug pushers worked the streets, unfearful of being harassed by cops.

The smell emanating from the street was enough to make a man's eyes water and the sun beating down on the concrete wasn't helping. Stakeouts were never like in the movies. It was a lot of sitting and waiting. Most times leaving with what you came with—nothing. Darryl resisted the temptation to turn on the air conditioner. It was summertime, and they were roasting in the car with the windows rolled down. The owner had better show up soon, otherwise they were sure to fry, which would no

11

doubt put his partner in even more of a foul mood.

He turned in her direction as she began tapping her fingers impatiently against the interior of the car. Shifting in her seat, she stretched out her five-foot-seven frame in the small confines, then glanced at him with sympathy etched on her face. Being six-foot certainly wasn't helping matters and he was squished uncomfortably in his seat. He consulted his watch with impatience.

"We've been here over forty minutes," he told her.

She nodded and turned to the old model Saab. It was probably older than him, but had been kept in fairly good repair. The grey had faded with time and there was rust over the front wheel where the paint had been scraped off when it had collided against something.

Donovan grunted and twisted the cap off a bottle of water and took a sip. "If he's not out in five minutes I'm going in after him. I don't care if I have to drag him out of a whorehouse mid-screw, he's coming with me."

That was one thing he liked about working with Donovan. If she had an opinion she let him know it. Not that his previous partner Matt wasn't a good cop—he was, and one of the best—but she tended to be less diplomatic about getting answers and that seemed to work for her.

It was no secret she had her eye on Superintendent Alec Harris's job when he retired in the next year or so. If it was a democracy, she'd have his vote. The detectives of Harbour Bay's LAC were a dedicated bunch. Other than Donovan and Murphy, there were two others in their unit—Dean Matthews and Nicholas Doyle—who usually partnered up. It was rare when they were all called to work the same case. The last time had been the previous year when the Butcher was loose.

A young man of about nineteen, covered in tattoos and scars, exited the nearby red brick office building and walked towards the Saab. Darryl sat up in his seat, becoming alert when he realised this could be their guy.

"That's him," he said with absolute assurance.

"He doesn't look too imposing," she commented, as she too watched the young man, her body tense with anticipation. "I've dated men creepier than him."

Darryl glanced at her. "I worry about you."

She shrugged. "What can I say? I always fall for the bad guy. Leather and motorcycles get me going."

"That would be the worry part."

She flashed him one of her rare smiles. "I'm a big girl. I can look after myself."

The man stopped as he reached the door of the Saab and suddenly, as if aware that he was being watched, searched the area, his gaze immediately falling on him and Donovan. He stared at them for a moment before taking off on foot.

Donovan opened her door. "He made us."

They both exited the car at the same time and started chasing their quarry down the street. Darryl cursed, knowing they were at a distinct disadvantage. Their suspect knew the area, knew the places he could get lost in, people who would hide him…and it wasn't as if they were welcoming toward cops. He and Donovan would have to watch their backs. It wasn't just the suspect they had to worry about now.

"I knew I should have driven," he said as he tried to suck in breath. Running in blistering summer heat in a suit was not the best idea.

"Oh, this is my fault?" she wheezed beside him, easily keeping up with his much longer strides.

They rounded a corner and found themselves moving through a maze of side streets and back alleys, some residential and others commercial. Large dumpster bins overflowed behind restaurants and rats ate the discarded garbage hungrily.

For a moment they lost sight of their fugitive and savagely cursed when they found themselves at a T-junction. In silent communication, they split up, each taking a separate direction, hoping the one they picked would prove lucrative.

***

Amelia found herself on a path which led back to the main road where both the police Commodore and the suspect's car were parked. She was determined to find the driver in time and stop his getaway. He would pay for his crimes.

The faces of her victims flashed in her mind.

She took a leap and quickly scaled the chained fence which closed off an old driveway beside what appeared to have once been a warehouse. She jumped down, landing on her feet, stumbling slightly as she made contact with the ground.

She barely avoided the blow that came out of nowhere, rolling to safety as her attacker hit the fence in the exact spot she'd been standing. Her skin burned from where it made contact with the rough concrete.

She went for her sidearm, her hand gripping the butt of the gun and within seconds the weapon was out of the holster.

The kid launched himself at her, slamming into her arm hard, causing her to drop the gun before she had a chance to use it. She cursed silently at her ineptness. She had been trained better than that. Her only excuse was that she had been slightly disoriented from the landing. She hated excuses just as much as she hated incompetence. The truth was she just hadn't been prepared for him. He was quick on his feet, a teenager with high energy. She would need all her wits with her during this fight, should she have a chance of overpowering him.

He sent his large fists into her abdomen. She forced herself to ignore the pain as she fought to protect herself, using her arms to block further hits. His bulky mass pushed against her, sending her lighter weight backwards. Her ankle turned and she fell hard against the pavement, the action stealing her breath and jarring her body, only managing at the last moment to protect her head. Knowing she would be bruised and battered tomorrow, she lithely shot to her feet in one swift movement. Her body was already beginning to protest against the beating.

But her attacker wasn't done yet. He extracted a knife from his pocket and with a flick of his wrist, the cool stainless steel serrated blade popped forth from within the grip. He slashed at her, the blade swished deadly in the air, nothing but a blur. She jumped back as his hand crossed back and forth in front of her as he advanced on her, leaving her with no choice but retreat.

He went at her again and she was thankful she kept her hair short, just long enough to be pulled into a stumpy ponytail. She'd heard of plenty of female officers who had been injured over the years because their attacker had grabbed their hair and used it to immobilise them. She wasn't about to let some dirt-bag slice her up because of something as simple as vanity. She was nothing if not practical.

Amelia deflected each attack, her gaze following the fast movements of the blade as it came dangerously close to cutting her. She moved on her feet nimbly, her only chance of disarming him to be faster than he was.

She caught his arm as he moved in for what he hoped to be the first and final blow and applied pressure to his wrist as she brought up her knee, hitting him in his thigh, when he moved. An inch to the left and he would've been done. He cried out but refused to release his weapon, his only way of escaping without handcuffs.

Amelia stamped hard on his instep, eliciting another cry of pain from him and pushed him into the wall, applying more pressure to his wrist. Annoyed, no make that pissed off, her body taut with anger as she thought about this kid going at her with a knife. It was about time someone taught him a lesson. A slow fire beginning to burn beneath her skin as she fought her attacker. Punches landed wherever she could reach before she threw her body weight into him. He grunted, his movements becoming panicked as he realised she'd not been as beaten as he'd thought.

He relinquished his knife, dropping it to the ground. Immediately, he pushed back at her with all his might, his flight or fight instincts kicking in. He may have been a kid, but he had the strength of an adult male and he managed to throw her away from him. He moved towards her, his eyes wild, his breathing harsh.

She pivoted her foot, and swung a back-kick in his direction, hitting him square in the stomach. He dropped to the ground, winded and beaten. The blow sapping what was left of his energy.

Amelia tried to catch her breath, her body aching and tired, calling out for rest. She produced a pair of handcuffs from the small of her back and proceeded to restrain her captive as she read him his rights.

Darryl moved slowly towards her, his gun aimed, his finger poised over the trigger. He searched the immediate area for unseen danger as she yanked her prisoner to his feet. She wiped the sweat from her forehead and regarded her partner seriously.

"Like I said, I've dated creepier guys than him."

Chapter 3

Kellie Munroe increased the speed and incline on her running machine. Her heart was racing and she could feel the stitch on her side. She was breathing fast and sweating profusely, her long blonde hair pulled back into a tight ponytail.

Her body protested every step, every breath, telling her she wasn't as fit as she should be. For twelve years, Kellie had prided herself for being as physically fit as possible although due to her current workload she had become slack with her visits to the gym. She continued to run until she could no longer keep going, her legs jelly. She turned off the machine and took a deep drink from her water bottle, swallowing half the contents as she wiped the sweat from her brow with a small towel. She glanced at her watch. Her lunch break was long over. She would have loved to spend some time lifting weights, building her physical strength, but she knew she had to get back to work.

She stretched her aching body on the yoga mat nearby as her heart rate slowed down.

"Looking good, Munroe," a voice said from behind her.

She looked over her shoulder to find Detective Sergeant Nicholas Doyle grinning at her. She realised her position, her behind up in the air as she reached out for her toes.

"You'd better not be thinking what I think you're thinking, Detective. It could be viewed as sexual harassment, and I would hate to report you," she informed him, knowing full well he wasn't. Nick was friend.

His grin got bigger and he gave her a wink. "You know me."

"Yes I do, Nick." She sat down on the mat, changing the angle of the stretch, the muscles in her thighs tingling as she held the position.

She and Nick often bantered. He was the only one she felt comfortable enough to tease. Neither of them ever took any offence to what the other said. Some days she needed his teasing barbs. It helped push her past her endurance while training.

"Haven't seen you around lately," he commented.

She studied his hard body and tight muscles, black hair and piercing blue eyes. It was unfair to the rest of the male species, Nick having taken more than his share of good looks and charm.

"You obviously haven't been missing a session."

He shrugged and flexed a muscle. She refrained from rolling her eyes. Nick was a decent guy and much to the disappointment of the female officers never dated anyone he worked with, however remotely. He was the only son in a family of five, and had been instilled with strong, protective, and tender feelings towards the fairer sex. He was an 'unofficial' big brother, having taken all his fellow female colleagues under his wing. If anyone messed with them, they'd be messing with him.

"I could get you in real good shape, Munroe, just let me know when you want it."

She nodded. "I will thanks," she said sincerely. "We'll get right down and dirty."

Nick grinned, showing his white teeth as he reached down and brought Kellie to her feet in an easy motion. She knew she wasn't heavy, weighing the right amount for her body type, but Nick could make even the heaviest woman feel no more than a feather. "Right."

They were of course talking about self-defence, which Nick taught once a week at the LAC's internal gym. He made sure that every female officer attended his classes and that each walked away with the tools and confidence they needed to defend themselves.

Nick Doyle was a good guy. She could see why the women all flocked towards him. If he had been so inclined, he could easily play the field, but Nick was the monogamous type. He loved being in a relationship but had yet to find the right woman.

"Well, I've got to hit the shower," she said. If she rushed she could be dressed and back at her desk in ten minutes. If she was lucky.

"Sure. I'll see you later, Munroe."

In the shower room, she washed the sweat from her body, careful not to get her hair wet. She dried herself off and dressed in her dark navy blue skirt that stopped at her knees. She tucked in her white short-sleeved blouse and carefully applied some blush and clear gloss to her lips, then coated her long blonde eyelashes with mascara. After pulling out her ponytail and brushing her hair, she let it fall to the curve of her breasts, her bangs blending into her hair. She put on her shoes—a pair of three inch black heels—and got into the elevator, making her way up to the top floor of Harbour Bay's LAC building where the office of Special Crimes and Internal Affairs—SCIA—was housed.

She exited the elevator and started toward her work station directly ahead, the first cubical on the floor. Her boss dumped a file on her slightly disorganised desk and started to walk away.

"Hey, you can't just dump and run," she announced, and sped up her pace as fast as she could, hindered by her skirt and heels to catch up to him.

Kellie picked up the folder and waved it in front of her boss's face.

"What's this?"

Her boss, Lewis Carlisle, ran his fingers through what was left of his hair. He was one of the unfortunate men whose hairline receded far too early. "New case. A complaint was made that one of the detectives downstairs was being a little rough with the crims."

Her eyebrow shot up as she opened the folder. "A little rough?"

Kellie's breath caught in her throat as her gaze found the official police department's photo of Detective Inspector Amelia Donovan. She read the name on the file in case by some accident it had been misfiled. It hadn't.

Amelia's file was thick, filled with recommendations and what seemed like a matching amount of complaints that had been filed against her for rough handling.

Detective Donovan was ambitious and it was no secret she took no shit from anyone, least of all the criminals she brought in. She commanded a lot of respect from her colleagues and worked hard for it. She didn't let the fact she was a woman deter her, nor did she ask for preferential treatment. She gave it as good as she got.

Kellie glanced up at Carlisle. He watched her closely.

"Sir, you know I can't take the case."

Lewis exhaled loudly as if she purposely went out of her way to make things hard for him. "You're the only one I can spare at the moment. Both Holly and Fitzsimmons are buried deep in their cases."

Clark Holly and Frank Fitzsimmons were the two other high ranking officers within the SCIA. While both were fine men and good cops on their own, Holly was an anal son-of-a-bitch who took the hide out of anyone who so much as dared to borrow his stapler. Fitzsimmons was more laid back, a veteran of thirty years who went home to his wife and children every night.

"And the personal history?" she asked.

"It shouldn't be a problem. After all, you're a professional and I have the upmost respect for your opinion. I know you'll not let personal entanglements sway your decisions."

If only she had his confidence. It had been some time since she had seen Amelia. They no longer ran in the same circles and neither had sought the other out. Even though they worked in the same town, on different floors of the same building, they never spoke. She wasn't certain this would go over well. Even without the past between them, she was IA and automatically despised by most cops, some seeing her as something lower than the criminals they arrested and Mia was sure to be no different.

Kellie believed in what she was doing, and the truth was somebody had to do it, so why not her? Someone had to police the police. Cops were not above the law and they needed to know they still answered to someone.

It would be difficult, and Mia wouldn't help the situation.

The next few weeks were not going to be easy, and not just because of the present situation but because of the past as well. The past which hung over them like a dark grey cloud, forever threatening a storm.

But there was a difference between personal and professional. Now all she had to do was act the part. She gave hear boss a curt nod before turning her attention to Mia's file, reading the complaint that had prompted the IA investigation.

Twenty minutes later she was on her way to the second floor. She tried to calm her knotting stomach as the ensuing confrontation filled her mind.

Chapter 4

Superintendent Alec Harris's face burned. His voice was a tenor below shouting as he spoke to the two detectives standing in his office. The vein in his temple throbbed from the restraint. He felt like he would blow a gasket, and he couldn't believe the suspect Hill and Donovan had brought in was all black and purple—the result of a fine beating courtesy *a la* Donovan.

This was not the first time he had been in this position and until he retired it wouldn't be the last. The date, only a year and half away, felt like forever.

Alec ran his hand through his blond hair with its streaks of white—the only thing that showed his true age—and took a steady breath. When he spoke again, his voice was a deep baritone. "The guy looks like he was in the ring with Mike Tyson."

Internal Affairs was going to be all over this, and he'd already had a long chat with Lewis Carlisle up in the penthouse suite. He knew he'd be sending one of his own down here. That's all his command needed, a goddamn IA investigation.

He shook his head. "You can't just go round beating the suspects to a bloody pulp."

Donovan didn't look remorseful at all. "In my defence, he had a weapon and my back-up was nowhere nearby."

Alec stared at the ceiling as if he'd receive some divine answer. He almost asked the Almighty, *Why me?*

It was never ending. At home he had the joys of dealing with his very stubborn, headstrong, troublesome teenage daughter, Sophie, who was too much like him for his liking. Sometimes he wished she'd be more like her mother, but then he shuddered. Caitlyn hadn't come without her problems and bad habits, either. At the thought of what it had taken to ensnare her, he felt somewhat relieved his daughter took more after him than her mother.

He loved Caitlyn with all the world, but the woman was trouble. Sometimes he didn't know whether he wanted to kiss her or strangle her, and now he was dealing with a stubborn subordinate. It seemed to him he was always dealing with the fallout of female hormones. He'd been lucky to survive his twenty-year plus marriage.

An ulcer burned in his gut. "It's just not today, but every goddamned day."

Darryl obviously felt the need to intercede on behalf of his partner, which only angered him more. "Boss, in certain cases sometimes it's necessary to—"

Alec cut him off. "Shut up, Hill, I haven't started

on you yet."

"Yes, Boss," Darryl said, chastised.

Alec brought his gaze back to the current pain in his arse. Donovan was almost always causing him problems. "You can't keep doing this, Donovan. You can't beat up the suspects. It's not your place to decide what punishment they get."

Donovan's eyes narrowed at him, and her mouth parted to say what he assumed to be a smart arse remark, but she was cut off when another voice— one not belonging to any of the three in the room— spoke.

"But that has always been your M.O. hasn't it, Mia? Act first, think second."

Alec turned towards the speaker. Kellie Munroe stood in the doorway with one hand on the doorframe and the other on her hip. Surprise momentarily registered on Donovan's face before she stiffened, her expression darkening. Interesting. He glanced from one woman to the other.

"You two know each other?"

Donovan stared hard at Kellie. The same look, he noted, that often made a hardened criminal squirm in his seat but seemed to have no effect whatsoever on the blonde in the doorway. Again, his interest piqued.

Donovan nodded and spoke through her perfect white teeth. "Yeah, we grew up together. We were friends once."

"I guess Mia doesn't share the same fond memories."

"I have one: your back walking away. What are you doing here?" She watched Kellie with a mixture of wariness and pain. He easily read his detective. She and Munroe were not on friendly terms, or at least Donovan wasn't. He'd yet to suss out the other woman.

Christ, this was all he needed—more female hormones. The tension inside the room had gone up several notches and he could feel the temperature plummeting. He rubbed a hand over his face.

Kellie's blue eyes turned frosty and her jaw clenched at Donovan's words. She stepped inside his office, her hips swaying enticingly, and Alec wasn't the only one who noticed. Darryl's body had tensed and his hungry gaze swept over her womanly figure as if she was a banquet he planned to dine on.

Had his desire for Cait been so obvious all those years ago? God only knew, he'd tried to hide it, even ignore it. But some things were meant to be.

"I think you know the answer to that, Mia," Kellie told her. "Michael Lambert filed a grievance against you for excessive force and bodily harm and from what I hear, he has the bruises to back it up. I've been assigned to watch you, every move you make."

Donovan's face turned red and her hands clenched into fists. He quickly moved between the two women before blood could be spilled and gave Darryl a steely warning that told the younger man his thoughts had not gone unnoticed. Darryl blushed and looked away.

"Like hell you are," Donovan spat.

Kellie stepped closer to Donovan, seeming oblivious to the waves of pure fury emanating from her. "You have two options, Mia. Deal with me or you're suspended without pay until my investigation is complete."

Donovan stepped threateningly towards Kellie, who stood her ground. Alec's respect for her went up a notch. Darryl started to move forward to intercede but he placed a quelling hand on the man's arm. Darryl shot him a questioning look but he ignored it and focused on the women.

"You're playing a dangerous game, Kellie. I don't take threats lightly."

Kellie laughed humourlessly. "It's not a threat, Mia, it's a promise. One I will make good on if you fail to include me in every facet of this case. That pain in your arse that you're feeling right now— that's me, and it isn't going away until I do."

Alec's mouth twitched up at her choice of words. Hadn't he just been referring to Donovan as *his* pain in the arse? It was a nice change of pace.

"Now that you ladies are reacquainted," Alec said in a voice that told them he'd had enough, "let's work together amicably for a positive resolution."

He saw his tone register in the bodies of the two women and their backs both straightened at the reprimand and turned to him. Both were composed but the emotion swirling in their eyes told him this was far from over.

Kellie stepped away from Donovan and bumped into Darryl's chest. She spun around sharply as if burned from the contact. "Sorry," she mumbled.

Darryl grinned. "No worries."

Alec let out a resigned sigh. "Darryl Hill, Kellie Munroe. If you haven't already figured it out, she's

IA."

Kellie obediently raised her hand for the perfunctory shake. Darryl wrapped his much larger hand around her and gently shook it.

"Detective," Kellie acknowledged before turning back to Alec.

"Now," he said, weariness creeping into his bones. "Are you going to be able to play nice together, or do I have to separate you?"

Kellie raised a blonde eyebrow at Donovan as if daring her to admit she had a problem with her. Donovan moved past Kellie, her shoulder grazing the other woman's before taking a seat in one of the chairs by his desk designated for visitors.

"I don't have a problem. One IA rat is the same as another in my book," Donovan replied.

He growled. Alec swore he spent more time acting like a kindergarten teacher than a superintendent. He supposed that was the best response he would get from his insubordinate detective and turned back to Kellie. She reminded him a lot of his wife, but where Cait was soft, Kellie had a hardness about her. He wasn't used to seeing that look on someone so young.

Kellie kept her gaze on his, not bothering to respond to Donovan's barb.

"I expect Detective Donovan," she began formally, "to make an effort to include me so that I may observe her actions in real situations and have the opportunity to interview her colleagues as to her character."

Alec nodded and turned to Donovan and gave her a hard stare. "You will abide Sergeant Munroe."

"Yes, Boss."

"I mean it, Donovan. You close her out and you're off the case. Am I understood?"

He could see his words hit home. A vein in her temple throbbed. Being kicked off the case would mean she could kiss any further career advancement goodbye. Alec studied Kellie. Was he making the right decision by allowing her to remain on the case? What had Carlisle been thinking when he'd sent her down? Had she not made him aware of her past with Donovan? Whatever had happened, it was as raw and painful as if it had been yesterday, and Kellie had the power to destroy Donovan's career with a flick of her pen. Would she take advantage of that power to harm the woman who'd once been her friend?

Alec hoped not. From what he'd seen today, Kellie Munroe had a good head on her shoulders, and while she might allow her temper to get the better of her, she had also shown great restraint. Not everyone could remain passive on the receiving end of Amelia Donovan's harsh tongue.

Either way, he would talk with Carlisle to ensure his detective received a fair assessment. Donovan may be a pain in the arse to one and all, but she was one of the best detectives he'd ever worked with despite her many behavioural and personality issues. She would make a damn good boss one day. If only she grew up before the decision was made and realised that sometimes diplomacy is best no matter how she felt about it.

He'd been in her shoes, full of ideals. He'd been adamant when he'd taken the position as superintendent that he wouldn't bow down to bureaucratic bullshit. But a good leader knew how to get what they wanted, being devious enough to obtain it without pissing anybody off. He'd become a pro. He didn't care about bottom lines. He cared about results and the protection of the men and women beneath him.

Donovan took a deep breath and most likely bit off the torrent of words that were on the tip of her tongue. She flicked a glare at Kellie before turning back to him.

"Understood, Boss."

Chapter 5

Nick watched Amelia storm past on the way to her desk. She would've knocked him over, had it not been for his lightning quick reflexes. She was in a mood, darker than usual, and he itched to stir her up. He just loved watching her eyes spit fire at him.

Of course she was an easy target, with a chip on her shoulder and so much to prove. Who she wanted to prove herself to, he didn't know. She had long ago earned their respect and nothing beyond that mattered. But Amelia Donovan didn't know when to quit, just like him, which was what made them such good detectives.

Darryl followed at a more leisurely pace and shook his head when their eyes met.

"Don't do it, Nick. You'll regret it," Darryl warned him.

Nick grinned. "Look out, everybody. Hurricane Donovan is in full swing, ready to take out the coast."

He spoke with his usual jovial manner and just as he expected, he was rewarded with a death glare from Donovan. Nick flashed her a winning grin that caused women of all ages to melt, and waited for her sarcastic comeback. None was forthcoming.

Nick had the feeling it would be a long and painful day, and he'd be lucky to live to see the end of it. He had a natural ability to antagonise people and rub them the wrong way. His team had learned to get used to it and of course return whatever he did tenfold, so it was a win-win for all. Everybody knew he was the class clown.

He turned his attention to Kellie who stood beside Darryl and sent her a wink.

He'd known Kellie for years and remembered the first time she'd been a student in his class. She'd only known the basics of self-defence. Nick had taught her the rest. He'd shown her how to defend herself, and how to inflict the most damage possible. If his students ever needed the skills he taught outside the gym, there was a damn good reason and he wanted them to be safe. He wanted them to be able to put their attacker down.

Kellie had been wary of him at first. He didn't pull his punches and his students went home with bruises until they learned to block his attacks. Kellie had almost drawn blood the first time he'd pinned her to the mat and it wasn't a mistake he made twice. He was a patient man and had given her the power over him that she needed to get her out of the darkness she'd been drowning in. She fought her demons and when she understood what he'd done to help get her there, she began to trust him and could now knock him on his arse with little to no effort.

"Nick," Kellie acknowledged, smiling at him.

"Twice in one day. Lucky me."

Darryl stiffened. Interesting.

Nick sat on the edge of his desk. "How are you?" he asked Kellie. "You were up and out before I had the chance to talk to you."

Kellie's eyes widened and he replayed the words and realised how they sounded. He winced. "At the gym today…you were up and out so quickly. I missed our chats," he rephrased.

"Tomorrow then. Don't be late or I'll kick your arse," she said with a twinkle in her eye.

"You already do that. So what are you doing down here? I thought your kind stuck together."

She accepted his dig at her job with good humour. "I'm on a case."

Nick frowned. "Really? And you needed Donovan's help with that?"

Kellie gnawed on her bottom lip and Nick glanced at Darryl before sliding a covert glance at Donovan who was busy ignoring them.

"Kel, no," he said, his voice full of agony. "I know what I said about your kind, but we're all cops here and Donovan's one of the best."

Her face showed a mixture of anguish and determination. "It's just a formality, Nick. A complaint was made. It has to be followed up."

"Shit." He dragged a hand through his hair. "You know this could be a career ender," he charged, anger evident in his voice.

He understood the need for Internal Affairs, but he didn't have to like it. He hated the fact that Kellie was investigating one of their own—one he worked closely with. He hadn't meant to sound so harsh. She had a job to do just as he did, but it had slipped out before he could censor himself. Her face paled at the harsh recrimination and he wondered if their friendship would survive this.

"Jesus, sorry, Kel. I didn't mean to sound like such an arsehole."

He reached over and pulled her gently to him, giving her an apologetic hug. The tension in her body was like a punch to the gut. He would give anything to go back and unspeak those words. Kellie didn't need that shit from him. Her job was hard enough as it was.

He kissed her forehead, then stepped back. He withered beneath the look Darryl shot him.

"I know the deal, Nick," Kellie said softly. "I'm not out to ruin careers."

"I know that, honey. I'm sorry for opening my mouth."

Amelia snorted. "I swear that's the best thing I've heard all day."

Nick grinned light-heartedly at her, happy to be made fun of. He was sure that one day he would end up with his mouth duct-taped shut.

"Me too," Darryl said as he brushed past him. Hill looked about ready to pack it in for the day. His once crisp shirt was now rumpled and had come loose from his pants. His tie had been jerked, causing the tails to be uneven and there were also lines on his face that hadn't been there earlier.

Darryl rubbed the back of his neck with his hand and small sweat marks showed on the fabric under his armpits. He offered silent sympathy for his colleague. There was nothing worse than getting stuck between two furious females.

He loosened his own tie, the atmosphere in the room getting sucked out as the electricity crackled between Amelia and Kellie. He crossed his arms against his chest.

"Are we good?" he asked Kellie, determined to make it right before she left.

"I'd make him suffer," Darryl told her.

She smiled and squeezed his arm gently. "Oh, he will, there's no question about it. But it will be in the boxing ring."

Her gaze drifted over to Darryl as the man bent to secure his firearm in his desk drawer. He unabashedly cleared his throat and Kellie's gaze darted to his. She blushed profusely when he grinned at her and waggled his eyebrows. He saw the gleam in her eye that she got whenever she prepared to take him down, and was thankful they weren't alone. He would pay tomorrow.

Catching sight of his partner, Dean Matthews, he gave out a loud wolf-whistle. Dean growled, or at least what Nick took for a growl since he couldn't quite hear. It could've been a mumble but with the baring of teeth. He felt confident he'd hit the nail on the head. Dean's chocolate brown eyes were bloodshot and his skin drawn, his honey blond hair roughly brushed but not styled.

"Good afternoon, sunshine," Nick said, and Dean replied with another low growl.

He was dressed in his usual attire of slacks and a pale sunflower yellow shirt which clashed horribly with his blue tie. Nick couldn't believe Dean still wore the pansy-arsed shirts he'd started wearing to defend his manhood. It had been years since the LAC had made fun of him, but typical to his style, he'd told them to go to hell and had continued to wear the pastel and feminine coloured shirts, daring anyone to say something. Nick had made the mistake of pointing it out once or twice, and was responsible for the constant ribbing in the first place.

"You look like hell, my friend," Nick observed.

Dean sent him a glare. "Yeah, well, I was at a robbery until three o'clock this morning. What's your excuse?" Dean challenged, his hackles up, ready to bite.

Nick held up his hands in surrender, watching his partner remove his weapon holster and place it in his top desk drawer before practically collapsing into his chair. He knew when to back down.

"Forget I said anything, man. Just trying to lighten the mood."

Dean finally appeared to notice the thick tension in the air. He reclined in his seat, stretching his long body out. His thick golden eyebrow quirked up when his gaze landed on Amelia, head down, fingers practically slamming on the keyboard as she typed. She hadn't looked up and by the tight thin line of her lips, they knew from experience it wouldn't be a fun day. Dean sent him an enquiring look. He shrugged in reply before turning his attention towards Kellie.

***

Darryl knew when Dean's foggy mind cleared.

His eyes widened and his mouth parted, his jaw almost resting on his chest as he took in the beautiful woman standing before him. Dean gave her a slow stare that made Darryl clench his hands into fists. What the hell was wrong with him? Would his hackles go up every time a man dared look at Kellie? He'd almost ripped Nick's arms off when he'd pulled her in for a hug. What the hell was going on between those two?

He knew Nick didn't get involved with women he worked with, but obvious affection existed between the two of them. An easy friendship and camaraderie that made him jealous. He rubbed a hand over his face and felt the beginnings of his five o'clock shadow.

He had no reason to be jealous, but apparently he hadn't got the memo yet. Nick was allowed to date whomever he wished, and so was Kellie. He glanced at the woman who stood in the middle of the Pig Pen—the name for the Detective Unit's bullpen—oblivious to the male attention she received as she watched Amelia. He shivered at the memory of her soft, satiny female skin against his much rougher male texture when they'd shaken hands. She was beautiful, completely feminine, and that seemed to call to everything male in him.

She may have worn three inch heels that made her legs look like they went on forever, but she still stood several inches shorter than his six-foot frame. His gaze roamed her body in appreciation. Her breasts were small but pert and demurely covered by her blouse. When she moved, he caught the outline of her lacy bra beneath. Was she wearing a matching pair of underwear—maybe even a thong? Her hair had been styled artfully, and he knew if he ran his fingers through what were sure to be soft tresses, every strand would fall back into place. His body warmed, his blood rushing south and his fingers tingled to do just that.

What was happening to him? He'd never had such a visceral response to a woman before. Especially one who worked for the enemy. He couldn't forget that. What the hell had happened between the two women to bring about the animosity he'd witnessed in Harris's office? Whatever it was, it had been buried deep. It made for a volatile combination.

He hoped she wasn't out for blood. She could easily destroy Donovan. He prayed his instincts about her were correct, and that she planned to do just as she said, that she wasn't out to ruin careers.

"Kellie Munroe, Detective Senior Sergeant Dean Matthews. Sergeant Munroe is IA." Darryl made the introductions, though he didn't feel in the mood to share her.

How ridiculous. He had only met the woman roughly thirty minutes ago. He knew absolutely nothing about her, and what he did know, he wasn't sure he liked. His body desired her, and why not? She was an attractive woman, but he had no designs on her. Certainly no rights.

It had been a while since any woman had taken his interest. It was like an electric shock to his system.

Kellie turned to face Dean and smiled. Dean blinked in surprise as she came closer and held out her hand. He shook it politely before releasing it.

"I'm not all that bad," she told him.

Amelia gave an unladylike snort. "Kellie is here to watch me. Apparently I can't do my job without some paper pusher observing me. Someone who has no idea what real police work is like. When was the last time you held a gun, Kel?"

Kellie's eyes narrowed at Amelia; there must have been something about what she said that hit a nerve. Her easy demeanour disappeared and a hardness washed over her.

"You shouldn't be concerned with my competencies, Mia. I'm not the one dangling over a precipice."

Darryl moved to intercede before it got out of hand. He never thought he'd be juggling two women like they were grenades missing the pins. He placed his hand on Kellie's back to remind her of where they were and glared at his partner.

"How about you two knock it off?" he suggested.

They both nodded, and he dropped his hand, feeling her absence from his touch acutely. He seriously needed to get a handle on himself.

Kellie stared at Amelia. She looked like she wanted to say something, then decided against it as Amelia scooped up her files.

"Let's get this over with."

Chapter 6

Amelia stared across the interview table at Michael Lambert, all while trying to ignore Kellie's constant presence as she stood unobtrusively in the corner beside the door watching the interview unfold. She didn't need this right now, still felt pissed, annoyed that Kellie of all people had been sent to make a judgment call on her actions. The unresolved past caused her to feel the pain she had long ago pushed aside. Her temper had risen to the surface, making her more volatile than usual, and was barely containing the emotions she kept buried.

She swallowed around the lump in her throat and ruthlessly turned her attention to her suspect before she did something unforgivable—like cry. She had known Kellie worked for IA just two floors above her, but she'd always kept her distance and had managed to unintentionally avoid her. But now she was here, her blue gaze unwavering as she seemed to stare straight into Amelia's soul. She felt her judging and condemning gaze, almost buckling beneath the weight of it.

There was nothing she could do about that now, or even in the foreseeable future. Best to focus on the here and now and close the case so Kellie would go away. The less time spent together, the better.

She confirmed for the record that Michael Lambert had denied having a solicitor present and marvelled at his obvious cockiness. He didn't seem the least bit afraid he was under the suspicion of double homicide. This made her wonder why. He wasn't a hardened criminal and should've been at least sweating from nerves. His lack of concern was intriguing. He wouldn't be as easy to crack as she'd first thought.

Michael's face was swollen in several places and after the first aid officer had a cursory glance, he'd been placed in the interview room. That had been hours ago. She would've interviewed him earlier but she and Darryl had been subjected to legal prattle about her altercation before being called to immediately report to the boss's office.

Darryl sat beside her and allowed her to take the lead. He would remain quiet unless he thought he could be of assistance. Until then, he stared with cold brown eyes at Michael in a bid to unnerve him. It worked on most criminals and they played off one another depending on the personality of the suspect they were interviewing.

She glanced down at the file she held in her hands. After apprehending the son-of-a-bitch, she and Darryl had fingerprinted the little prick and ran them through NAFIS—the National Automated Fingerprint Identification System. They had discovered that young Michael Lambert was a career felon, starting small at age nine, stealing chocolate bars from convenience stores. He had since moved on to bigger and better things such as double homicide at the tender age of nineteen.

"Mr. Lambert, can you account for your whereabouts last evening, between eleven and one a.m.?"

He stared mutinously at her.

"I don't believe you're grasping the gravity of your situation, Michael. Your car and therefore *you* have been placed at a double homicide. So do yourself a favour and answer the question."

He smirked but remained stoically silent, crossing his arms over his chest in an attempt to show his defiance. The move was ruined when he winced from the injuries she had given him.

"You think you're going to walk away from this? Two men are dead and someone has to pay for it. If it wasn't you, now is the time to speak up and tell us a name. Otherwise, your bruises will be the least of your troubles."

He narrowed his eyes at the reminder that he'd been bested by a woman. He may have thought of himself as a gangster wannabe, but they both knew the truth. He was a poser and he'd gotten lucky last night.

"Fuck you, bitch."

Amelia nodded. "Ah, he speaks."

"You got nothing on me, and you know it. Nothing more than my car *allegedly* at the crime scene. I say it wasn't. Your witness can argue it until he's blue in the face, but it don't change nothing."

He smiled at her as if he had her beat. The glint of fear in his eyes betrayed him. He wasn't as emotionless as he wanted to be and in way over his head. She almost felt sorry for him. Almost. She would've been more sympathetic if he hadn't have come at her with a knife. His behaviour told her more than his words. There was someone else out there pulling his strings. Lambert felt safe, as if untouchable under the man's protection. She knew only a few men exerted that amount of power.

He might skirt the assault charges, a fact that grated but she would get him on murder. Maybe not today or tomorrow, but he would not go unpunished. She hated the fact that he'd been right about the evidence against him. She would find it hard to push for a conviction.

The only thing that could save him now would be to offer up the man behind the scenes. The coward who made teenagers do his dirty work.

"Doesn't change anything," she corrected him, and his eye twitched in anger.

"Fuck you."

"You really shouldn't have given up school, Michael. You might've had a more extensive vocabulary if you'd have stayed."

Lambert rose to his feet in one swift move and lunged at her. She deftly grabbed his arm, twisting it behind his back hard enough that she heard the tendons strain and slammed him face first into the table. Blood spurted from his nose and he started mewling.

"Detective Donovan," Kellie said sharply. Amelia glanced up and saw her furious expression.

"A moment outside. Now." She turned and opened the door to the interview room, waiting until she and Darryl had stepped through before closing it behind her with a distinct *click*.

"What now, Kellie?" she asked, suddenly exhausted. The little prick had been getting on her nerves.

"He was deliberately pushing you and you played right into his hands. He'll walk because of your actions in that room. He may be a punk but he has rights and you're violating each and every one of them."

Amelia blinked at the red haze clouding her vision, hating how she was right. "You're protecting him? He's a murderer."

She couldn't believe it. It was bad enough to be told his assault on her wouldn't be charged, a lack of witnesses and the fact her injuries were inconsequential in light of his. But now a woman she'd considered a sister was against her. Was it any wonder she was pissed?

"Alleged. But it's not him I'm protecting…it's you. If he had any brains at all, he would press charges against you. Police brutality while in custody. Your career would be over in a second. No wonder you have IA breathing down your neck, if that's the kind of shit you pull on a weekly basis."

"Come on, Sergeant Munroe, you know Donovan upholds the law."

Kellie glared at Darryl. "But who upholds her, Detective? Cops are not above the law. They're to apprehend, not punish. Partner loyalty is great, Detective Hill, but be careful she doesn't bring *you* down."

He returned a cold stare. "I believe in my partner. You should try it."

Kellie snapped her teeth together audibly. "Look, Mia, I'm not the enemy here."

"Yeah? You sure about that?"

Kellie let out a long breath. "Stop fighting me and start thinking. He's a smart kid and he'll outlast you. You've already lost the assault charge. Anything he says in there now, any lawyer would have thrown out citing coercion. Try another avenue. You're a hell of a detective, and I'd hate for you to lose your job. But I'd hate it more if I'm the one taking it from you."

Amelia heard the sincerity in her voice, though it annoyed her that she had dared comment on her treatment. She hadn't been there when the little shit had drawn his knife and if she'd made one wrong move, he would've gutted her. These people had no idea about the situations she dealt with every day, the fear she felt, and the instincts that took over that had her reacting first, sometimes with excessive force but not always.

"The evidence against him is purely circumstantial. We're going to need more. Get his alibi then cut him lose," Darryl suggested. "We'll bide our time and then go at him again fully charged."

She hesitated as she stared at Kellie. She had a better idea, a way to lull Lambert into feeling omnipotent. He would be suspicious of Amelia if she let him go, but if Kellie did it, he might actually believe he'd outsmarted them. He would certainly underestimate her with her blonde hair and blue eyes.

"You do it," she told her, not unkindly.

Kellie gave her a look that said she understood her intention, then nodded and slipped into the interview room, leaving the door open an inch.

"Mr. Lambert, Kellie Munroe. Internal Affairs."

Amelia listened as she apologised profusely for the way he'd been treated, and assured a complaint would be filed. She even went as far as to ask him if he wanted to file charges for assault.

Darryl slanted her a look as they both listened to her compassionate voice. Amelia barely restrained her smile; she was living up to her expectations and more. She heard him consider it through the crack in the door but then graciously declined. Obviously, he figured he was better off making a clean break.

"That bitch is crazy."

"I assume you mean Detective Donovan? She will be dealt with by her superiors, Mr. Lambert, I assure you."

"So I can go then?"

"You'll be free to go once you provide me with an alibi. Until then, I'm afraid I'll need to detain you for twenty-four hours so I can make my own investigations into your whereabouts."

Kellie actually sounded apologetic.

"I was at home," Michael mumbled.

"Is there anyone who can verify that?"

"Sure."

The room went silent and she assumed he was writing down a list of mates who would lie for him. It didn't matter. Once the forensic team had a chance to analyse the evidence, she was sure they'd be able to poke holes in his story. Once they had him by the short hairs, they'd make a deal with him to give up his boss if he wanted freedom again before he died. Until then, he would be followed. She texted Dean on her phone to ensure he was in position and let him know the suspect was due to leave shortly.

"Thank you for your cooperation, Mr. Lambert. I appreciate you coming in to clear up matters," Kellie said warmly.

Amelia's gut churned as Kellie escorted him out of the interview room and into the custody of a uniformed officer who would release him. Lambert gave her a look of triumph. She waited until the elevator door closed on his smirking face before spinning on her heel and stalking off down the corridor.

Chapter 7

Darryl joined Kellie at the elevator, having declined riding down with Lambert and Officer Prescott. She jabbed the call button with her index finger and for the first time he noticed her manicured nails. They weren't long, barely a few millimetres past the quick but they were definitely feminine, polished in the French style. He imagined them digging into his back during the height of her climax and immediately his trousers became too tight. He mentally cursed himself. He'd been semi-hard since she'd first walked into Harris's office and it seemed he was doomed to remain in that state while she was with him.

He gave her another covert sweep just as he'd done in Harris's office. She was beautiful, no doubt about that. Her blouse and skirt hiding a naturally slim yet curvy body, and legs that went on forever that made him think of them wrapped around his waist. He shifted his position to ease the ache in his groin. He breathed in the scent of her floral perfume, feeling the curl of desire in his belly and tried to ignore it. She was off-limits. He didn't plan on getting on Donovan's bad side—if she had a worse one—by sleeping with the enemy. Not that it was any of her business who he slept with, but he didn't want to feel as if he'd betrayed her. He wasn't about to get between two women with obvious issues even if Kellie was susceptible to his advances.

He'd seen the emotion in her eyes earlier and knew despite the coolness she projected that there was hot passion flowing beneath the surface. He would love to see it put to good use. He almost came just thinking about it.

The elevator door opened and he indicated with a gesture for her to precede him. She hit the button for the fourth floor and leaned back against the walls of the carriage, her hands reaching out on either side to hold onto the silver safety railing. The elevator began its ascent. They rode in silence for a moment before she spoke.

"Detective Hill, I would like to ask you a question—off the record. Do you trust Amelia with your life?"

He didn't have to think about the question, and replied truthfully.

"Absolutely. We're a small team, a family. If you can't trust your unit you shouldn't be here. We have enough trouble with everything out there," he said, indicting to the outside, beyond the LAC's walls to the streets of Harbour Bay, "…without fighting each other inside."

Kellie nodded. "Do you believe that she uses excessive force? Are her actions one step too far?

Do you think she could handle these situations differently?"

If Amelia had done something wrong, he wouldn't lie to Internal Affairs about it. She was a great detective and they had to protect their own, to a certain degree. If Amelia were a dirty cop, he'd have no issues hanging her out to dry…but he knew she wasn't.

"No, I don't," he told her, absolute conviction in his voice. "Sure, sometimes she has to rough them up a little, more so than any man would need to. I don't mean to sound sexist here, but even though we don't treat her any differently, the fact of the matter is that Donovan has to prove herself out on the streets. She has to be harder, tougher than anyone else, because they see her as a woman and not a cop. They think they can run roughshod all over her and walk away. I've seen it happen and she can't afford to give them an inch."

Kellie stared at him for a beat and he wondered what she was thinking. She suddenly smiled and he felt like he'd been punched in the stomach.

"Thank you for your honesty, Detective. Believe it or not, I'm not out for blood. If neither of us does our jobs right, then chaos will ensue. Rules will be broken and advantages will be taken. I'm going to see this case through whether Mia likes it or not, but I am on her side and I wanted you to know that."

"Might I ask why you two aren't friends anymore?"

She looked taken aback, as if that was the last question she had expected. She swallowed hard.

"People change, Detective. They grow apart."

"I know, and she's a hard person to love. I can see how she might push someone away."

"You've got it wrong. She didn't push me away. I pushed her. Some things are hard to forget," she told him bitterly, then gave him a look to say she wasn't about to discuss it further with him.

"Maybe you should try. She needs someone in her life, someone outside of these walls. Someone who can put up with her bullshit."

She slid him an amused look. "Thank you, Detective Hill, but why do you think I'm the one who needs to do the forgetting?"

He watched Kellie walk down the hall, just barely holding in a whistle of appreciation, the gentle sway of her hips forever burned into his mind as they moved to the left and right under her navy blue skirt. He sighed loudly. It had been a while since he had spent any time with a woman, and Donovan didn't count. She was one of the boys no matter what chromosomes she had coursing through her body.

He waited until Kellie was out of sight before he pressed the button to return to his floor and had leaned back against the wall in something almost like pain. He had spent the last several years focused completely on his job, with no time to spare for anything else.

He was a goal orientated person, having come from a structured career military household. His days had been mapped and timed, leaving no room for error. His father, a brilliant and strict man had been a little too hell-bent on the rules that governed his family. Although, looking back on it, raising three unruly boys meant his father may have had a point. He and his brothers, Jack and Chase, had not made things easy on the colonel.

His father must've done something right, he reflected, since all three Hill boys served their country. His two brothers followed his father's footsteps and joined the army. Chase, the youngest, was currently serving in Afghanistan. Although Darryl chose law enforcement instead, his father couldn't be more proud. He'd known from a young age that he wanted to be a police detective and his whole life had been planned around it. Though now that his dream had finally come true, maybe it was time to redefine his needs.

Darryl logged into his computer. Donovan glanced up from the folder she'd been reviewing.

"Doyle reported in," she said. "Lambert hasn't shown any signs that he knows they're tailing him."

"He won't, either, if Matthews is driving," he replied. Dean had mastered tailing people, just as he mastered everything he put his mind to. The man was skilled.

He reviewed the recent interview, pissed that they had to let Lambert go. He knew in his gut the man was guilty but that didn't hold up in court. Still, he hated to lose. It was another thing he had in common with Donovan other than a strong work ethic. Neither of them wanted to go home before a case was closed and put to bed. It was probably the reason why they worked so well together.

"I just hope he leads them to his boss," Donovan said.

He nodded, agreeing. He'd noticed Lambert's

fearless attitude, and knew just as she did that he wasn't the one calling the shots. It didn't sit right with him to allow a murderer to go free, but whoever was behind the order needed to be taken out. A man who could lightly sentence two men to death in such a callous way was someone he wanted off the streets.

Harbour Bay has its fair share of crime, but thankfully nowhere near that of Sydney or Melbourne. Their days were usually filled with robberies, car thefts, domestic disputes, or vandalism. There was the occasional hit and run, or suicide, and an increasing number of murders, whether vehicular, accidental, or intentional.

Not that long ago, he had seen more than enough murder victims to last a lifetime when the Butcher had come to town. He had been secondary on the taskforce. A case nobody had wanted simply because the man had been a ghost, a transient with no morals.

He'd almost killed Natalie, Matt's psychologist wife, although they hadn't been married at the time. He remembered the way Matt had looked after taking the Butcher down and how close he'd been to losing Natalie. Darryl knew he never wanted to be put in that position. A relationship proved hard enough for a police officer—the long hours, constantly being on call. He didn't want to add occasionally being a target for homicidal killers to the list.

Donovan stood and stretched, breaking his rapidly declining thoughts.

"I'm going to the gym for a while to clear my

head and work off some of this excess energy," she said. "When I get back, you and me will go over what we have."

He nodded. "I'll bring the pizza. It's going to be a long night."

***

Kellie reviewed each of Amelia's arrest files in hopes of finding a pattern—or rather, a lack of one. She took what Detective Hill had said about Amelia being a woman into consideration. In what could be defined as a man's job, or at least held the monopoly of men over the years, it would be hard for a woman to join the ranks and certainly not without proving she was just as good or even better than some of the men.

He had a valid point and she'd wanted his opinion. As Amelia's partner, he worked with her the most, and had seen her in different circumstances and situations, both threatening and non-threatening. She wanted a proper assessment.

Even Kellie, when she'd first been hired in Internal Affairs, had to work harder than everybody else to show them she wasn't just a pretty face or simply a receptionist to bring them coffee when they so desired. She knew how people saw her and admitted to using that to her advantage once or twice. Like with Michael Lambert earlier. People saw what they wanted and most thought her brainless. Lawyers and cops from other cities were the main culprits, those who did not know her personally. She was always surprised how often they underestimated her. They all left wide-eyed and open-mouthed after deciding how badly she'd screwed them.

She tried to think about the situations Amelia might face on the job, applying Detective Hill's logic. Men saw women as obstacles, nothing more. Even a woman wielding a gun or some such weapon weren't considered a credible threat. They simply believed they could work around her. Turn themselves from prey to predator, stalking her, intimidating her until she backed down.

She scoffed. She could imagine Amelia's response to that. From what she'd learned, her old friend would gladly hand them their balls.

It took a strong woman to control such a situation. Men had more strength. It was just a fact of life. No matter how hard you trained, all it took was one second of distraction and they had you. It would be easy to forget your own strength when fighting for control and compliance. Overcompensating in an effort to subdue a less than cooperative criminal—especially when the adrenaline would be pumping.

She'd been in the same situation once and when you're fighting against an unknown factor, you're not interested in playing fair, only in being victorious. But to be absolutely sure, she would have to see Amelia Donovan in action.

Chapter 8

Michael Lambert strode through the side entrance of Dick Coleani's restaurant, hiding the fear consuming him. That cop scared the crap out of him. He hadn't allowed it to show, knowing Coleani had his back and soon he would join the ranks of the men Coleani trusted most. He made his way past the shelves of supplies. Coleani had made it clear, he was never to enter via the front. He understood. The five star restaurant was his main place of business and his most lucrative although there wasn't a piece of Harbour Bay that Dick Coleani didn't have control over.

A man he aspired to be. Even if he wasn't sure he could stomach how he was getting there.

He found the man in the office behind his mahogany desk. He stood when Michael approached. Coleani was not a young man, closing in on fifty. He'd been running Harbour Bay since his teenage years and the hard work showed on his face and in his ice cold grey eyes. His hair was peppered with grey, and his face held a few days' growth as it always did. His lean body was strong even for a man of his age, though he delegated most of his jobs out to his men.

"Ah, Mike, you're late," Coleani said.

He hastened to apologise as he always did when Coleani used that tone of voice. The tone of a disappointed father, which was the role he played to all his men, having watched them grow up within his organisation.

"Sorry, Mr. Coleani. I had some legal problems."

He nodded. "Yes, so I heard. You're looking a little purple around the edges."

He gingerly touched his swollen face.

"Nothing I can't handle. They have nothing on me. No fingerprints, nothing, only that some neighbour saw my car speeding away from the scene. Sorry, Mr. Coleani, for not anticipating that. If it will help, I can remove the witness."

He prayed for the affirmative. Anything to prove he wasn't a screw-up, that he could do as he was asked.

Coleani shook his head. "No, that would not be wise, not with the police nearby. Tell me, what about the scene?"

"They found just a smidge of cocaine. Nothing to link the killings to you. I policed the brass and did as I was told."

"So everything went as planned, except for the car?"

"Just an oversight, Mr. Coleani. It won't happen again."

"Good. I don't like my boys to fail me."

He flushed with embarrassment at the reprimand.

"Tell me, Mike, what about these detectives, do they pose a threat?"

Michael shook his head adamantly. "No, not at all. They have their own problems at the moment."

Coleani appeared intrigued. "Tell me about them," he said. A demand, not a suggestion.

He swallowed hard. Being in Coleani's presence always made him nervous.

"Well, there was Detective Hill and a Detective Donovan—a chick. There was another chick, too. But she's not a detective. She introduced herself as being Internal Affairs. She was the one who released me."

Coleani raised an eyebrow. "The IA chick, did you happen to catch her name?" he asked.

He tried to remember. He'd mostly been terrified. "Munroe, I think. A hot blonde."

"Donovan and Munroe," he repeated out loud.

"What is that, like *Cagney and Lacey*?" he joked, his smart mouth covering the anxiety twisting his insides. He'd thought nothing of killing. But the reality was different from his imagination. As were the consequences.

Coleani pinned him with a look that said he didn't appreciate his brand of humour.

"No. Donovan and Munroe both lived in my neighbourhood years ago. They were a real nuisance to me. Although...I thought I got rid of that problem. Nevertheless, if they choose to interfere again, I will have to do something permanent."

***

59

Dean watched as Lambert exited the restaurant and moved toward his car. Beside him, Nick hit the oval button on the digital camera and in the silence of the car the *click, click* sounded loudly as a succession of photos were taken. Nick looked briefly at his work before grunting, telling Dean in his own way that they'd gotten what they needed.

Lambert pulled the Saab out of the parking spot and into traffic. After a beat, Dean followed, losing himself in the flow. Should the kid happen to look back in his rear-view, it was doubtful he and Nick would be spotted.

They followed him for another ten minutes until he pulled off the main road and into the tenant's parking of a run-down, low-income housing apartment building. The building itself, the name Houston faded on the side, had seen better years. It had been built back in the seventies and allowed to rot when the owner went bust and the government took over the deed. Several windows were broken, a few taped closed with plastic bags. It was the kind of place where cockroaches the size of Chihuahuas roamed about, mould and rust just another colour scheme.

Four young men approached Lambert as he made his way toward the open front door of the building. Obviously security was not a priority for these kids. Dean heard the camera snapping away photos and knew Nick was hoping to capture the perfect shot. The gangly teenagers surrounded Lambert and from the looks of it were singing him praises, high fiving him and patting the man on the back. Apparently, they believed he'd done something pretty fantastic.

These morons were most likely the alibi he'd supplied. Their type stuck together so long as there was something in it for them.

Dean waited as the light began to fade, the sun sinking behind the building. The kids welcomed Lambert like a conquering hero. And to think, it had only taken two lives. But then life was cheap around these parts. Dean was disgusted. He'd seen enough life snuffed out during his tour overseas.

The son of scholars—both professors at Harbour Bay University, his father in mathematics, his mother in English—it had been assumed he'd follow in his parents' footsteps and teach, or become a doctor or lawyer. But he'd had no intention of sitting down all day and knew he wasn't cut out for a desk job. To say John and Georgia Matthews were surprised when he'd told them he'd enlisted in the army was an understatement. But they'd supported him without question through his entire career and was thankful to have such wonderful parents.

"By the looks of those guys, they're going to be partying all night. I doubt we'll need to stay and keep watch. I'm going to head home. You want me to drop you somewhere?" he asked.

The youths all disappeared into the building and Dean started the engine and pulled away from the kerb. He rubbed a hand over his eyes, feeling as if someone had rubbed sandpaper over his corneas. He needed about eighteen hours sleep, but he would be lucky to squeeze in four or five.

"Yeah, back at the LAC. I'll grab my car and head home. It looks like we caught the shit end of this investigation, huh? Following Lambert."

Dean shrugged. A job was a job and he'd taken on his fair share of shitty assignments; this one didn't even come close. "Someone's got to do it. It may as well be you and me. Besides, I doubt this case is going to be glamorous no matter what your task." He smirked. "But I reckon you just want to be around Munroe, am I right?"

Nick glared at him. "You know I don't screw around with people I work with. Kellie is a friend, nothing more."

Dean gave him a sidelong glance. He was the type who could easily be the playboy with his good looks and no effort charm, but he wasn't and Dean admired him for that. Especially when women did practically everything to get in his pants. Nick was a chameleon, fitting easily into any role. The charmer, the sleaze, the kidder, the stoic—it impressed the hell out Dean, and even though Nick pissed him off half the time with his joker attitude, there was no one else he'd rather be partnered with.

Especially since he was no prize. He knew he was a moody S-O-B. Never the prankster, always the serious one. He'd seen too much to float around life with a *glass half-full* outlook. Pessimistic, not optimistic. That was how his co-workers thought of him, an introvert who liked to keep to himself and never shared his thoughts or bared his soul.

Dean Matthews was damaged. He'd lost a part of himself on his last tour which he could never get back. His colleagues could never understand why he kept his distance, why he had to remain detached. He couldn't care. It caused him too much pain.

Caring only made a man weak and vulnerable and easy to hurt and manipulate. Just look what it had done to Tony, he reminded himself. He steered away from the horrid memories because he knew the nightmare had been a reality. Screams, blood, begging, watching someone he cared about die.

One thing was for certain. Dean would never fall in love, would never care about a woman so much he couldn't live without her.

"How do you think the IA case is going to go down?" Nick asked, breaking the silence.

Dean shrugged. He had no idea. It was a fifty-fifty chance. Although he believed that if Donovan was kicked off the force, it would be a colossal mistake. The sassy, tough-talking, back-chatting woman didn't know the meaning of giving up. He'd worked with her on and off for years and respected the hell out of her. Sure, she was rough around the edges but she was an asset, and he had to pity the person who couldn't see that.

"No idea. I just hope your friend knows what she's doing."

"Kellie's a professional," Nick assured him.

He hoped so.

Ten minutes later, Dean pulled his car into the loading zone at the LAC. "See you tomorrow," he said, and with that, Nick climbed out of the car and shut the door.

Chapter 9

Amelia worked off her suppressed anger in the gym. Her face taut with rage, her lips nothing but thin strips. Her body coiled tight, she pounded the boxing bag hard, causing it to rock precariously back and forth on the chain attached to the roof of the gym. Bottled up emotion fuelled her. She sensed Kellie's approach and felt the familiar burn inside her. She didn't look up or acknowledge her old friend as she hit the bag harder than before. She wasn't mad at her; she was mad at herself, at the past, and at the situation.

Kellie stood to the side, just within her peripheral vision, and Amelia knew it was deliberate. She gave the bag a left jab followed closely by a right hook and another left. Quick puffs of breath exited her mouth as she exerted herself. She darted an annoyed look at Kellie. She stood with her hands resting on her hips, in an unflattering pair of black stretch pants and a tight pink tank top but she managed to work the ensemble, looking elegant with her hair pulled back off her face in a ponytail. Amelia knew it was nothing she tried to accomplish; it was natural and ingrained in her. She had looked that way for as long as she could remember.

Amelia could feel Kellie assessing her, probably determining just how volatile she was at the moment. She was amazed she'd even approached her. Many of the men at the LAC knew when she hit the bag she was not in a good mood and it was best to keep clear of her, but Kellie had never been one to put up with her crap and had fought her all the way. Until she hadn't.

Not the easiest teenager, she hadn't changed much—only gotten worse. Her temper had shortened with age, and her patience wore thin much quicker these days.

She'd had a habit of putting herself down and was easily discouraged. A memory skittered across her mind of Kellie refusing to let her give up. Back then they'd been inseparable, both born in a section of Harbour Bay known as Coleani's territory.

A sadistic man, he oversaw every criminal element in town. Years ago it had only been a twelve block radius of his strip club, the *Satin Thong*. The neighbourhood was a breeding ground of druggies, prostitutes, and a healthy number of homeless. The council liked to pretend it didn't exist and thus Coleani was free to continue ruling over the inhabitants and making their lives more miserable than they already were. Amelia had lived with her grandparents at the caravan park, whereas Kellie and her mother had resided in a tenement a few blocks south.

"I'm sorry it had to be me." Kellie's voice came through her self-reflection.

Amelia shrugged. If it hadn't been her, it would have been some other IA agent with a career to make for themselves. Looking at it objectively, she was better off with Kellie. She wasn't the type to stab someone in the back just to get ahead. She worked hard, and from what she had heard around the office, got to the truth and never made any decision without being absolutely sure.

She was certainly the Kellie she remembered. Even back then, she'd been honest and loyal. The blonde hair and blue eyes often fooled people into thinking she was either brainless or a push-over, but growing up in their neighbourhood, nobody had the luxury of being one or the other.

"Are we going to talk about it?" Kellie asked softly.

"What's to talk about?"

Kellie caught hold of the bag as she took another swing, the impact reverberating along her arm since she was unprepared for the lack of motion in the punching bag.

"You're obviously angry with me."

She narrowed her eyes. "I think I have a right. You're the one who walked away and destroyed ten years of friendship."

Mascara coated eyelashes fluttered at the charge.

"I couldn't do it anymore. I wanted to forget and you wouldn't let me. It was in every word and gesture. I was ashamed and embarrassed and every time I looked into your eyes I saw sympathy."

She swallowed against the lump in her throat.

"What did you expect? It didn't just affect you. It almost killed me too, watching you suffer, knowing I couldn't do a damn thing to help you. That I wasn't there to protect you when you needed me."

She slammed her fist against the bag hard, which moved only slightly with Kellie holding it still. She took a step back to compensate for the force of the blow.

They had been friends since they were children. Back then, Kellie had been the ambitious one and she had simply followed. Or rather had been dragged since Kellie refused to leave her behind. Then their world had changed overnight and Kellie had pushed her away. Not knowing what else to do, she'd allowed it. It was her biggest regret. She didn't make friends easily, and due to her job and the hours she kept, along with her personality, she could count the number of friends she had on one hand.

She smacked the bag harder. "You just left. No explanation. Nothing. I was left wondering what the hell I did wrong, thinking you blamed me for being hurt."

"Mia, I'm so sorry. I had no idea you felt that way."

"It doesn't matter now."

"Of course it does," Kellie said as she tapped her fingers against the thick plastic coating underneath her hand. "We're going to be working together. We need to resolve our issues."

"Just like that, huh?" Her mouth twitched into a smile.

"It's only you, Mia, who makes it difficult, you

know."

She shrugged and didn't deny it. Denying it would be futile since it was the truth, but it wasn't something she could easily get over. Hell, it had been twelve years but that night still haunted her. Kellie wasn't the only one who had lost something. She had also lost a good friend.

"I accept my actions have caused irreparable damage but I want to make it right. Or at least near enough to. Come on, Mia, let's go hash this out Donovan Style. Don't look so surprised. I read your file. Plus I know you. If there was anything that you couldn't fix, you'd fester until an opportunity came along to cut loose and let it all out."

She moved to the boxing ring in the centre of the room before turning around. She raised an eyebrow and motioned with her hand towards the ring. Amelia frowned before following her.

"Cut the crap, Kel, you know I'll wipe the floor with you in a matter of minutes."

Kellie climbed through the ropes into the ring and turned back to face her.

"That confident, are we? My, you have an ego. I bet you've been dreaming of kicking my arse for years," she teased. "Well here am I. Come on, take your anger out on me. Let me take away your demons."

"Don't push me. I might take you up on that offer," Amelia warned, noticing they'd caught the attention of some of the officers working out. Some were even inching closer in hopes of overhearing. There was nothing more interesting than Amelia Donovan being challenged by a perky blonde. She didn't plan on being anyone's entertainment.

Kellie shook her head, donning on a pair of gloves.

"Are you afraid you'll hurt me? You can't, no one can...not anymore. You need this. Hell, I need this. Relax, it'll be a fair fight. I've been practicing. What have you got to lose except maybe their respect?" She motioned to the flock of men moving towards them, eagerly exchanging bets. "Let's work off some of that aggression of yours. It's not healthy to keep it bottled up. Believe me, you'll feel better once we're done."

"She wouldn't be Donovan if she wasn't aggressive, that's what we love about her," someone said from the crowd. It was followed by male laughter.

"You're just pissed she wouldn't sleep with you, Kurt," another said.

Amelia rolled her eyes and climbed into the ring. "You always knew how to make a spectacle of yourself," she said. "Well, there's no backing down now. Not if you want to save face."

Kellie appeared unconcerned. "I was never planning on backing down."

"I've got twenty on Donovan," Officer Kovak shouted to no one in particular.

"I wouldn't be so quick to make that assessment, Kovak," a familiar voice called out. Nick Doyle appeared ringside. "The blonde packs a punch."

Amelia huffed out a deep breath. Could this get any worse? She was never going to hear the end of this.

"Don't cry to me, Kel, if you break a nail."

"So long as you don't cry to me if you break something else."

They faced off, the sounds of the men surrounding them dying off as she centred herself. As far as she was concerned, they were alone.

Kellie parted her stance, making it wider as she moved at an angle to improve her chances of staying on her feet. Amelia mimicked her action, having spent time in the ring and out of one herself. She knew how to fight—fairly and unfairly—and knew all the dirty tricks to use against her opponent should it come down to that. Which it usually did when she was up against a street criminal.

Amelia waited, her vision narrowed, her mind moving into survival mode. She was no longer fighting a game with an old friend; she was fighting a threat. She patiently waited for Kellie to make the first move, hoping to manoeuvre her into doing what she wanted. She didn't have to wait long.

Kellie's first hit was direct and hard, even blocking her attack and pushing her back a few steps. Amelia took a deep breath before going on the attack, sparring with her across the ring, back and forth. Each jab and punch was a direct hit, designed to hurt and demobilise. This was not a friendly match; the competitors fought for a championship, and they both treated it as such.

Hit, block, hit, block. Left, right, left, right. Each hit jarred her to the bone. They were both breathing heavily, their clothes damp with perspiration, clinging to their bodies. Amelia didn't hear the encouraging shouts and cheers coming from outside the ring; she was completely absorbed with anticipating the next hit.

Kellie went low, then high, trying to knock her off balance, but she remained steady on her feet. Years of dealing with persistent crooks gave her an advantage. She could outlast and outwait her, knowing sooner or later she would make a mistake or get sloppy and that would be Amelia's time to strike.

She had to admit, Kellie was good; she hadn't been lying when she said she'd been practicing. Her moves were professional, quick, simple and effective. The force behind each blow was staggering and Amelia could feel her body burning, this being one of the best workouts she'd had in a while. The anger simmering just below the surface came alight, fuelling her body when she should've been exhausted.

She blocked another of Kellie's blows, moving to the side simultaneously as she pushed her arm wide, landing an unguarded gloved fist into her stomach. Her body instantly bowed down as she tried to protect itself, and Amelia took the opportunity to go at her again as she immediately righted herself. She landed an indirect blow as Kellie moved at the last second, the punch hitting her in the arm rather than the chest, spinning her around.

Amelia took the advantage and jumped on her back, hooking her arm around Kellie's neck and adding pressure. She didn't have time to adjust to the new position as Kellie recovered, flipping Amelia easily over her shoulder and onto the mat beneath their feet.

"You hit like a girl, Donovan," she taunted as she drew closer. She heard the gasps coming from the crowd. No one dared tell Amelia Donovan she was a girl at anything. "You're being soft on me. Stop protecting me Mia. I can take whatever you've got."

"Are you kidding, Kel? You're barely standing."

Kellie jabbed at her forcefully then ducked, barely missing her return fist. She went down into a squat then pushed up from her feet, her head ramming into Amelia's unprotected stomach, knocking her off her feet and onto her back. Kellie's head jerked left and right as she dodged the fists flying at her head, struggling to pin Amelia's arms. She straddled her using her knees to push her arms down into the mat.

"Okay, who has Jello?" a male voice added to the chortle of excited viewers.

Amelia turned her head slightly and saw that everyone in the gym had stopped to watch. It could've been the fight of the year, the way they were treating it.

"Hey, keep that shit up and we'll go a round after. Have some respect, O'Malley," Nick told the over-enthusiastic officer. From the look O'Malley gave him, he understood completely that Nick wasn't joking.

"Is that all you've got? You're going to let me win?" Kellie asked as she pushed at her, shoving her into the mat. "Where's all that anger and fury now?"

"You're pushing me."

"I always had to. I know you may never forgive

me. Hell I'm not even sure I forgive myself. But know I've never blamed you. Never wished it was you. Walking away was the hardest decision of my life."

Amelia jerked away from Kellie, her emotions raw. She knew Kellie was painting herself as a target and taking on her anger, urging her to put the past behind her.

Could she? Her closest friend turned her back on her, during a time she'd needed her the most. She'd been sixteen and her best friend had been hurt. She'd had no idea how to help her through it.

"You did nothing wrong. It was too much. I was in a dark place. The darkest," Kellie explained, her eyes imploring her to listen, to understand. "I wanted to reach out but I was afraid you'd tip me over the edge. I almost ended it, downed my mother's pills and booze. I didn't want to drag you into that. I called Ed and he got me the help I needed. I asked him not to tell you because I didn't want you to think less of me."

Ed had been the detective on her case. A man she respected. Her mentor. It hurt to know he'd kept Kellie's secret from her. Guilt consumed her. She had been there the entire time, through each of the police interviews, had watched as Kellie became more withdrawn. By the end, she'd become a shadow of her former self. Her friend had been so desolate to the point of taking her own life and she'd not known. Not one inkling. Of all the reasons she'd thought over the years for Kellie's sudden departure, she'd never once considered it had been her actions that drove her away.

Kellie certainly knew where to slide the blade for maximum damage. Amelia wanted to dissociate from the memories and emotions her words brought, not wanting to feel but she couldn't, powerless to stop them from having an effect on her, sharp and painful. The fight went out of her.

Amelia raised her hips, bringing her body off the floor and twisted like a pretzel, unhorsing Kellie from her perch. She tumbled to the side, losing her grip on Amelia's arms. They each sat up, breathing heavily.

A collective groan came from outside the ring as money exchanged hands once more. Slowly the crowd dissipated as it became apparent the show was over. They made no attempt to move, and Amelia wasn't entirely sure if she could. Her muscles felt like wet spaghetti.

"So, you ladies work out your differences?" Nick asked good-naturedly as he joined them in the ring.

Amelia glared at him. "Don't you dare say a word," she warned.

Nick sent a smile her way, unfazed at the warning. He reached down and lifted Kellie to her feet before giving her some instructions on how to improve her technique.

Amelia stood, slightly incensed. "Hey, you work with me, remember? You may want to rethink where your loyalty is."

"What?" Nick asked innocently. "I was just trying to help...unless of course you'd like me to instruct you?"

"Quit while you're ahead, Nick," Kellie told him.

"While you still *have* a head," Amelia muttered.

"I'll leave you to it, then. Quite a show, ladies. I fear for any man who dares cross you."

He left them, moving over to the weights he'd probably been using before Amelia and Kellie had starred centre stage. Kellie waited until he was out of earshot before she spoke. "So, are we good?"

Amelia took off her gloves and placed them on the bench nearby.

"Yeah, we're good."

"There's something to be said about Donovan Style. No bullshit, just anger and fists...works every time."

***

Fifteen minutes later, Amelia startled when Kellie placed two glasses and a bottle of Scotch down hard on her desk. She had been so engrossed in the lives of the two dead men, she'd not heard her approach.

Kellie wheeled over a chair from Dean's empty desk. The Pig Pen had been deserted as was most of the floor, their fellow officers either out on call or catching up on missed sleep. She sat down and poured two fingers of Scotch into each glass.

Outside, darkness had fallen over the city, casting shadows throughout the streets, offering places for the thieves to hide, ready to pounce on the first unsuspecting person.

There had once been a time when Harbour Bay had been a thoughtful and caring community striving to better itself. Now, only the tourists believed that. The city had become overrun like all large cities had been by the disrespectful and cruel, preying on the weak, and it took the police everything they had and more to crack down on crime.

She and Kellie had both showered and changed back into their work clothes. The desire to fight had dissipated, leaving only exhaustion and a need to mend their friendship. They had been through too much together to let it all go.

She hadn't thought her protective hovering had made matters worse. Guilt twisted in her gut. All these years she'd been angry with Kellie for walking away but she'd practically been pushing her.

Why the hell had she not said anything?

"I've done a lot of things I'm not proud of, but I can't change any of that," Amelia said. "I can only move forward and hope the crap doesn't follow me. I never thanked you for getting me out of there. I know I owe you for everything, and one day I'll find a way to make it up to you."

Amelia raised her glass, making her declaration a toast as well as a promise.

Kellie shook her head, her blonde strands falling over her shoulder.

"You owe me nothing. What you did, you did on your own. You never thought yourself good enough for anything…but I knew better. I knew the real you, and you're worth more than anything in this world. Don't forget that. You're here because you wanted to be here, not because of what I did."

Amelia shifted uncomfortably. She'd never been good at accepting or examining her feelings, especially not feelings that continued to grow, whether it became a friendship or a sexual relationship. But she knew Kellie was right. She had been put down so much in her younger years, told how worthless she was so many times she'd begun to believe it. Kellie made her realise long ago that she had so much to offer, that she wasn't as useless as she'd thought.

If it hadn't of been for Kellie's attack, she'd never have found her true calling. She couldn't imagine being anything other than a cop.

Amelia bit down on her bottom lip. She never wanted to admit just how much she wanted and needed Kellie in her life. She'd changed, hardened over the years since Kellie's abrupt departure. She'd never wanted to allow anyone else power to hurt her like the person she'd trusted the most. She thought she could live without her, that she could just close the door on that part of her life, but the two women were connected, closer than she'd ever thought. She could forgive Kellie, knowing now all that her friend had battled, though she wished Kellie had confided in her.

"I love you, Kel. I didn't want to after…but I do and you know I don't say that to anyone easily. I'm not the touchy feeling type of person, but I missed you, missed what we were…and if you ever mention this night to anyone, I will kill you."

"Your secret is safe with me. I'll never betray the fact that deep down under all that thick skin, you're just a girl with a compassionate heart."

Amelia frowned. "Don't push it or I'll wipe the floor with you again."

"Not tonight, I'm too tired. Maybe we can go back to the old times?"

Amelia laughed. "God, I hope not. I don't think the LAC could handle it."

They broke off as Darryl sauntered up to them carrying a pizza.

"I see no furniture broken, so I assume you've decided to play nice?" he asked. She glared at him before noticing Kellie doing the same. He put his hands up in surrender. "Not going to say another word."

Wise decision.

"Hey, Hill, where have you been?" A rookie named Cade Watson shuffled past. "You missed the sweetest fight. These two were all teeth and claws, best fight I've ever seen..." He hurried off when she and Kellie turned to him. The poor ginger haired newbie had not yet learned the fine art of dealing with women. Especially armed women.

Wide-eyed, Darryl glanced back at them and Amelia tried for an innocent expression. She knew she failed when his eyebrow rose.

"So a fight, huh? Is a hospital visit required?" he asked, his gaze drifting slowly over Kellie. So, that's how it was. She shouldn't be surprised; the woman was gorgeous inside and out.

"You might need one if you don't let it drop. We've worked it out," she said bluntly.

Darryl grunted as if disbelieving, then settled back into his chair. "Already forgotten."

"So, what are you doing? Maybe I can help," Kellie said, putting them back on track. "I'm part of this case too, and I want to see it closed. I may not be a detective but I have two eyes and a brain."

Amelia studied her for a moment. "These are the records for our two dead guys," she said, tapping a couple of manila folders.

Kellie opened the first file. "Geez...large enough? Reminds me of your file," she said to Amelia wryly. "Wow, was there anything these boys weren't into? Quite the alphabet of offending charges."

"You ever heard of a man named Dick Coleani?" Darryl asked Kellie.

Her head jerked up. "Sleazy Coleani?" She turned to Amelia. "Yeah, he used to run our neighbourhood as kids. What about him?"

"Well, it appears that's where Lambert headed after we released him. Butler and Benedict also used to work for him," Darryl said.

"The boys apparently decided to go it on their own."

Kellie made a *tsk tsk* sound. "Coleani would not appreciate that."

Amelia agreed. If anything could be said about him, he demanded loyalty from his employees and wasn't kind to those who betrayed him. She had been unfortunate enough to see his handiwork once—her first lesson in anatomy, and she'd never forgotten.

Darryl opened up the box and grabbed a slice of pizza. He took a bite and chewed thoughtfully. "Both Benedict and Butler have been part of his crew since puberty. They were both from foster homes and were regulars at his youth centre."

"You mean his tax deductible recruitment

centre," Kellie corrected.

Amelia grinned. Kellie wasn't one for mincing words no matter her stance on rights for criminals. Coleani always brought the devil out in her. Had since they were teenagers.

She leaned back in her chair. "We had our tech boys take apart their hard drives and found they were running a website out of their home."

"What type of website?"

"An all stop shop for your pharmaceutical needs, catering to the illegal side of course."

"How enterprising of them," Kellie commented.

"It seems the boys had a five-year plan, and hoped to become big real estate moguls. They already bought up six houses on Hamilton," Darryl added.

"Moving in on Coleani's territory…never a good plan if you want to see your next birthday," Amelia said.

Kellie frowned. "Hamilton isn't Coleani's territory."

"He's moved up in the world."

Chapter 10

Kellie rolled fitfully in her sleep, the blanket twisting around her waist. In her mind she was back in the gutter, wishing, praying to die. Warm, sticky liquid rolled down her cheek from her forehead, which burned, the pain slightly below unbearable. Her whole body felt bruised and battered, used and discarded, and a sickening disgust threatened to drown her. The worst thing was knowing she would live to remember and relive the night over and over again.

She couldn't move, no matter how hard she tried, her limbs refusing the orders her brain sent. She listened to the thud of running footsteps, the small splash of stagnant water as those feet hit a filled pothole. The shouts of frightened people beside her filled her head, telling her to hold on. The sharp siren shrieked in her ears as the ambulance approached and the pungent scent of urine and the garbage in the alley filled her nostrils, making her want to gag.

Her body was jostled as someone lifted her into a vehicle, the blue and red flashing lights aggravating her eyes. She moaned as needles were shoved into her skin. Instantly she felt better, her mind and body weightlessly soaring through the sky. She let the sensation take over her body. Soon her pain dissipated, leaving only sweet pleasure as the morphine kicked in.

She felt serene until hands touched her body and head and she started struggling groggily. When the hands restrained her, she screamed. The words tumbled out of her mouth but as she heard them sounding far in the distance, they made no sense to her, just a bunch of gibberish. She dug her fingernails into the nearest hand and was rewarded with a sharp intake of breath.

"Calm down, miss. We're here to help you. You've been hurt and we can't heal you if you don't stop moving," a voice said, a moment before her hands were bound to the stretcher.

"Stop, please, no more," she screamed as she bucked wildly.

"Shhh, miss…"

Kellie felt a soothing hand on her face and hair. She bit down on her lower lip as a sharp stab of another syringe penetrated her skin. Tears rolled down her cheeks as her body relaxed without her permission. Her eyelids grew heavy and drifted shut as her racing heartbeat slowed.

"She's lucky to be alive, poor girl," she heard someone say.

"I don't think she'll see it that way when she regains consciousness," another voice, filled with

sympathy and compassion, replied.

Kellie rolled over in her bed, unable to stop the flood of memories.

She awoke when someone drew near while she lay vulnerable in the hospital bed.

Her eyes opened wide in terror and she almost screamed at the intruder, feeling vulnerable as she lay in the hospital bed, her mind and body broken.

"Don't touch me!"

Surprise etched into Mia's mocha tanned face.

"I'm sorry," she said hastily, her gaze wandering up and down Kellie's prone figure lying beneath the light muslin hospital sheet.

Deep down, she knew she should apologise. Her friend had done nothing wrong, had in fact only tried to comfort and support her. But she couldn't find the words or the energy to take the bite away from her actions, and didn't care to do so.

Her body felt tender all over, her head pounding, and she could feel something wrapped around her crown. She moved her hand towards her head and the needle in her hand pinched as it tugged against her IV. She winced at the new pain as she touched the white gauze bandage protecting her head.

Kellie turned away from the now blurry face, her hands clenched into fists as sobs welled in her throat and her heart constricted in her chest.

"Kellie," Amelia said softly.

Another voice spoke her name, too. It was familiar yet she couldn't place it. The deep voice belonged to a man and her brain screamed at her not to open her eyes, but she couldn't help herself. As if she no longer had control over them, they opened and she stared into the cruel face of her attacker.

She opened her mouth to scream, but nothing came out as he approached her with a deadly calm demeanour, reaching out towards her as he prepared to finish the job. She struggled to stand, her body weighing her down so she couldn't move.

She bucked wildly on the bed, willing herself to wake up as in her mind she felt him touch her.

"No, no, no, no," she whimpered.

Please, Kellie, wake up…wake up now, she told herself, knowing she was in the midst of a nightmare.

She coughed as huge hands caught hold of her throat and squeezed. She reached up to hold onto his hands as she fought him with everything she had. Her nails dug deep into his skin and blood dripped out from the small half-moons she left there.

The world spun around her and she could smell smoke and body odour. Not the normal odour from a man, but something worse, something dark and wrong. Kellie stared into brutal dark brown eyes just before everything went black.

She jerked up in bed, a scream tearing through the dark room. Her blanket fell to the floor in a heap as her fitful movements pushed it off the bed. She could hear her own screams inside her head and outside, filling the otherwise silent bedroom, her shriek piercing her eardrums. She collapsed back, her head falling on the pillow as perspiration coated her forehead and her clothes stuck to her overheated, damp skin.

She fought to catch her breath, her hand resting over her heart as she willed it slow. It had been years since she'd dreamed about that night and the events after. The case involving Coleani was bringing about old memories she preferred to keep hidden, never to see the light of day again.

On shaky feet, she made her way to the bathroom that adjoined her bedroom and turned on the tap to the shower. She stripped out of her sweat soaked pyjamas as she waited for the water to heat up, and when it did she stepped into the glass cubicle and washed the remnants of her nightmare away.

Forty-five minutes later, she was dressed to kill in her red A-line skirt and black V-neck blouse. She had put her hair in a loose chignon and had slipped into her favourite pair of black heels. She couldn't sleep and had no desire to try in case her past returned to haunt her. Since it was too early in the morning to do anything around her house, she grabbed her purse and climbed into her white Ford Laser. A moment later she was driving off down the street.

***

Kellie stepped through the doors of the LAC carrying a bright pink box and a travel coffee mug.

She pressed the button for the second floor on the elevator, and waited in silence as it took her there.

She entered the Pig Pen and stopped short. Darryl sat at his desk, his gaze moving from his computer monitor to a sheet of paper. She glanced around at the other empty desks and let out a deep breath before moving slowly to join him.

She hadn't expected him to be there and wasn't sure how to deal with it. There was something about him that set her on edge. It wasn't anything he said or did. It was just... him.

She was hyper aware of him, the attraction bone deep. He set her body ablaze, made her grow warm every time he was near. She'd never experienced the sensation before and wasn't sure if she liked it or not. Her body belonged to her. She didn't want anyone else to have control over it, but when butterflies fluttered in her stomach every time she caught him looking at her with heat in his eyes, she knew that it belonged to him, if only for the small time they were together.

She'd felt the small spark between them the moment they met. It wasn't anything spectacular but it was disconcerting. It made all rational thoughts leave her head and left her floundering.

Not that she'd ever act on those desires. She couldn't share more than her body with carefully selected bed buddies. Some were fine with that. Others wanted more. For them, it was like trying to draw blood from a stone.

She knew her shortcomings which was why she never looked in her place of work for night time entertainment. Not that she had many other choices since she was always working, anyway.

Sensing someone else in the room, he turned his head in her direction. His face showed surprise as his gaze found her. She stopped short of his desk and smiled brightly. As infectious as it was, he smiled as well.

He was too damn sexy.

"Surely it's not morning already?" he asked, stretching.

"Kind of, but very early morning."

"So what are you doing here?"

"I couldn't sleep or rather preferred not to," she replied, hoping he wouldn't ask why. The last thing she wanted to do was discuss her very real nightmares with him.

Darryl interlocked his fingers and cupped the back of his head, leaning back in his chair to eye her. "So you came in early," he concluded. "How did you know I was still here?"

Heat suffused her cheeks. "Um…awkward. I didn't know you'd be here. I actually came looking for Nick. I thought it was his turn to be on night shift."

Darryl nodded. "We swapped. But he should be arriving soon, so feel free to wait for him."

Kellie waved him off with her hand. "Nah, his loss is our gain. I have freshly baked donuts and they're best eaten hot," she told him, not exactly displeased by Nick's absence. Maybe the time spent with Darryl would give her answers as to why her body seemed to sing in his presence. "Besides, maybe I get to actually have some. Nick usually gobbles them up before I have a chance to pig out.

You in?"

He nodded as he stood and brought a vacant chair toward his own. He sat back down as Kellie took her seat, placing the box of donuts before him. She crossed her legs and she caught him looking at her naked thighs where the fabric of the skirt had ridden up. Liquid heat pooled low in her belly and her mouth dried. He clenched his hands into fists as if forcing himself not to reach for her, making her imagination soar. Suddenly she pictured him tossing her down on his desk and running his hands up and down her body. She willed herself back to reality and pushed away those decadent thoughts, deciding to save them for when she was home alone.

Darryl took a donut and stuffed it into his mouth. She smiled at the obvious pleasure on his face and was thankful Nick hadn't been there when she'd arrived. Nick may be good looking, but he'd never turned her on with a single glance like Darryl seemed to do.

"Tell me, what do you think about the case?" she asked him, her gaze probing his brown eyes.

"It was sloppy. At first glance, it looks professional. But I'd say it was a first time killer by the amount of evidence he left behind," he said.

"That makes sense. An initiation or graduation. Do you believe it could be retribution? It's a powerful motivator."

He shrugged and once more leaned back in his chair, dripping the raspberry centre from the donut onto his shirt. He cursed under his breath and swiped the blob with his finger, slipping it into his mouth. When she handed him a serviette, Darryl coloured as if suddenly remembering she was there. That didn't do much for her ego, she thought, then reached up and swiped the small dollop of raspberry from the corner of his mouth.

His eyes darkened and she pulled away. She was pretty sure they were both skirting close to a sexual harassment suit. He poured some water from his drink bottle on the desk and wiped his shirt clean— or near enough before tossing the soiled serviette in the small trash can beside his desk.

He cleared his throat. "I believe it's a possibility, and we'll know more when we investigate further. I don't like to base my opinions on conjecture. I like hard facts and evidence."

Kellie leaned forward and scooped up a cinnamon donut before taking a small bite. She chewed thoughtfully.

"Okay, fact...Benedict and Butler were poaching on Coleani's territory. He isn't known for his restraint."

"Coleani didn't pull the trigger," Darryl pointed out, playing devil's advocate. "Lambert did."

"But you can't argue that Coleani is up to his ears in this. He may not have made the shot. That would be beneath him, but he was definitely involved and had prior knowledge."

"I'm not arguing, but what we know and what we can prove are two entirely different things. Coleani has been pulling the strings on his boys for years and everyone knows he doesn't do his own dirty work anymore. Which is why he's been so hard to catch. We can't pin anything on him and have it stick. He's as slippery as an eel."

A loud banging sounded behind them, and both she and Darryl glanced over as Amelia—dressed in jeans, boots, a Broncos shirt and a leather jacket— strode towards them, her long gait eating up the distance while the scowl on her face warned them, *approach at your own risk.*

Kellie stood and placed the travel mug down on Amelia's desk. She gave Amelia her bright jubilant smile and said, "Here you go, sunshine."

Amelia glared up at her, her mouth disfigured into a snarl.

"Fuck off, Kellie," she growled.

"And a good morning to you too," Kellie replied, her smile never wavering. She knew what got on Amelia's nerves; bouncy and energetic was at the top of the list. "Still not a morning person I see."

Amelia shook her head. "Jesus, Kellie, what the hell are you wearing? We're not on parade here."

Kellie looked down at her clothes, then over at Amelia's casual look. "What's wrong with what I'm wearing?"

She turned to Darryl, who shrugged and said, "I'm not getting involved in this."

Kellie fingered the hem of her blouse self-consciously. She liked her clothes, which screamed professional, and gave her a slightly cool, *keep away* sign that saved her time knocking back unwanted advances. She was always the aggressor, never allowing another control. It was the only way she could be intimate without panicking.

Amelia took a sip of the coffee from Kellie's travel mug and her eyes bulged as the caffeine entered her blood stream. She felt some satisfaction when Mia looked down at the cup in surprise. She liked her coffee strong, especially on days like this when she'd had little sleep the night before and knew it would be a long and tiring day.

"No offence, but your outfit is a little stiff," Amelia said. "You know, rigid. The kind that says you don't know how to have fun, that you have no idea what spontaneity is."

"They're work clothes. They're supposed to be bland and practical."

"All I'm saying is, how are you supposed to run down a criminal in three-inch heels? I don't see that as being practical."

"I sit behind a desk five days out of seven. I'm not chasing anybody down any streets. I don't need a lot of movement or comfort in my clothes."

"Yeah, well, you're not in the office anymore, sweetheart. While you're a part of our team, you might have to do that, and I'd rather you not break an ankle."

"I'll keep that in mind."

"Good, because we're going to make a little visit to Coleani and ask some questions and if we're lucky, ruffle some feathers."

Kellie's body temperature dropped at the thought of casting her eyes on the man she'd hated for so long. She had never met him in person, never wanted to, and had managed to avoid it. Now it seemed her luck had run out.

"I'm sure we can manage that."

Amelia smiled at her, the look in her eyes telling her that she'd thought of the times they'd interfered with Coleani's business in the past. It was about to happen again.

"I'm sure we can."

They'd been threatened by Coleani's runners more than once in her youth, but she'd never been scared. No one did anything without Coleani's authority and she wasn't afraid of him. He'd already taken everything he could from her, and she'd doubted he even knew she existed—or cared, for that matter. She was nothing but a spit in the ocean to him. It had been a bold move to go up against Coleani, but that hadn't stopped her from speaking out against the obvious corruption. Her voice had been lost in a crowd of people. Nothing she ever did made any dent in the world, and she figured if she pissed him off, she would hear about it. He'd almost been a stepfather to her. Even now, she practically gagged at the thought.

She steeled her backbone, glad she'd dressed in her business attire, not casual like Amelia. She would need every bit of protection she could get, and as they said, the clothes made the woman. She felt confident and powerful in her heels and suit.

And she would need every ounce of that confidence to get through the day.

Chapter 11

"Boss, there are some police officers who wish to speak to you," the burly bodyguard said as he led Kellie, Amelia, and Darryl through the restaurant to the table where Dick Coleani was having lunch.

"Well, by all means. What can I do for the police this fine day?"

Coleani didn't appear how Kellie expected him to. Although she did recognise his Hugo Boss suit that retailed in the thousands. He hardly looked the type to run the biggest crime organisation outside of Sydney.

A chill raced down her back when her gaze met his. Did he know who she was? Did he see the resemblance? No, she doubted he would even remember the name Jules Munroe.

"Mr. Coleani?" Amelia made the introductions for herself, Darryl, and Kellie. She seemed just as sceptical.

Coleani nodded. "What can I do for you, officers?"

His voice revealed only mild curiosity, that or

humour at having the cops inside his restaurant. She felt his cold gaze once more and met his stare, resisting the deep urge to turn away. She thought she saw one side of his mouth minutely lift in amusement or admiration, but in the end she decided she'd imagined it.

Kellie glanced about the restaurant. It wasn't the health code violation it had been years ago. Now it had a new location, five stars to its name and charged fifty dollars a plate. The walls were done in merle, framed photos decorating their surroundings. Each showed a group of young boys in their early teens. Coleani's merry band of drug dealers and murderers, she guessed.

It's nice he's so proud of them, she thought scathingly.

The tables were covered in sunflower yellow damask tablecloths. Both the seat area and the backs of the chairs were padded with black cloth, creating a comfortable setting for long sit-down dinners and conversation. Kellie lifted her gaze from a restaurant Gordon Ramsey could be proud of to take in the occupants of the room.

Besides Coleani and his bleached blonde companion, the room only held three more people or at least three more she could see. The first was the man who'd brought them to Coleani, his gym-toned body bulging. What interested her the most was the forty-five beneath his black work shirt. His shirt sported the word *Coleani's* over his right breast pocket. A quick glance at the other two men standing by the exit told her they were all packing and that the situation could turn from bad to worse in a split second.

A light hand on her elbow shocked her into tearing her gaze away from the weapons, and she faced Darryl. His expression told her he had seen the armoury as well.

She cleared her throat. "Looks like you've come a long way, Mr. Coleani."

"I always said I was destined for greatness," he replied smugly.

"Interesting décor. I remember you didn't use to go for all that," Amelia commented, "when you were too busy running your other businesses."

Coleani smiled. "Things are changing. You have to move with the times or go under."

"Like starting up *dot-com* companies?" Kellie asked, and was rewarded with Coleani's narrowed eyes as he glared at her.

His gaze roamed her body slowly as if searching for weak points. "Is that what you're here to talk about? The murders of Carl and Kevin?"

"You've heard about it? That's rather interesting, considering it only happened yesterday."

"What happens in my neighbourhood is always reported to me," Coleani told them piously.

"Funny, I always thought of the neighbourhood as belonging to the city of Harbour Bay," Darryl said.

"Semantics, Detective. So, do you have any further questions for me or are you just wasting my time?"

Amelia appeared unconcerned. "I'm sorry, Mr. Coleani, that the murders of boys you were once close to is an inconvenience. But we should be out of your hair soon since you should have some knowledge as to who the perpetrator might be. After all, everything that happens in *your* neighbourhood is reported to you."

Darryl moved in front of Amelia to draw attention away from the combustible vibes he seemed to sense. Tension, thick and ripe suffocated Kellie. She forced herself to calm down. The history between them was almost palpable and she had to remind herself they were here about the double homicide.

"Can you tell us something about them?"

"They were good boys," Coleani replied noncommittally.

"You mean malleable and eager to please," she said, earning her a glare from Amelia, who had returned to bad-ass detective mode.

"I get the feeling you don't like me very much, Officer."

"I suppose you must get that often enough. Surely that doesn't bother you, Mr. Coleani. You look like you have thick skin."

He chuckled as if he found her funny, but she knew he didn't like being challenged. The irritation was clear in his eyes. "That is quite true. I've had a lifetime of making enemies. Now I only make friends."

"But your price is rather high, isn't it?" she asked, not able to remain quiet. "In exchange for your friendship, you want blind ignorance. Tell me, how did you deal with their betrayal? I doubt they got a slap on the wrist and a stern lecture."

"The only punishment I hand out, young lady, is

my disappointment. I let Kevin and Carl go, without any references, without any protection. There are people out there who would take advantage of young, defenceless men like them. Alone in the world, unable to look after themselves. I was afraid they would come to a bad end but I can only do so much. My people must know and understand that betrayal of any kind will not be tolerated."

"Your boys are resourceful, Mr. Coleani. They would've landed on their feet had they not been murdered. They were smart and quite savvy, to tell you the truth. I saw their plans. They were meticulously thought out and had they continued, their business would have rivalled yours," Amelia said.

"Then it was a good thing for all involved that they were taken out of the picture. Imagine what destruction their business could've done to the city had they lived. It certainly would've been more work for all. I believe the man who took care of our problem deserves to be commended, does he not?" Coleani said with a cruel smile.

Kellie bit down on her tongue. She was tempted to say something but knew she was already on wafer-thin ice. She was only a visiting member of the team and had no real standing in the investigation. As it had been pointed out before, she wasn't a detective.

She watched the men surrounding them. She'd seen both Amelia and Darryl spare the occasional glance towards them, as well. Their sharp eyes seemed to determine if they were a threat, or if they'd moved in the slightest from their initial positions.

They were outnumbered and outgunned, making her nervous. She knew Coleani well enough to know how he really dealt with those in his way.

Kellie steeled herself, not wanting to show fear or any other emotion that might please him.

Darryl stepped forward, drawing complete attention. "Do you know a man named Michael Lambert, Mr. Coleani?"

He frowned. Years of dealing with the police had made him quite the actor. "I don't believe so. Should I?"

Kellie shrugged nonchalantly. "He lives in your neighbourhood, attended your youth centre, and was even employed at one of your businesses. Surely you've met him?"

"I employ many boys and unless they stand out from the crowd, I never meet them in person and I don't visit the youth centre anymore."

Amelia rolled her eyes. "No, now you just have your lackeys do the grunt work for you."

"The pleasures of being a boss. I can delegate all those jobs that I find tedious to someone else. That's why we strive so hard to climb the career ladder, is it not?"

Darryl crossed his arms over his chest and leaned against a supporting wall. "We believe him to be the perpetrator. We're in the process of getting a warrant. All we're waiting on is some results from forensics. He will be arrested and charged for his crimes and anyone connected with him will go down with him."

"And you should know him," Kellie said. "After

all, he did kill for you didn't he? Do you always have other people fix your problems for you?"

Coleani lit a cigarette and inhaled deeply before slowly exhaling, allowing the smoke to fill the room and tickle Kellie's nostrils.

"I'm just a businessman, Detectives. I pay my taxes, provide jobs for my people, and safe places for their children to play and learn. I am a pillar of the community. I don't go round killing my people."

His people. Christ, he really believed himself to be some kind of king who looked down on his serfs, working them until they were no longer useful. She doubted Coleani would be very tolerable to the mistakes of others. When Butler and Benedict had betrayed him, he'd immediately cast them aside. No room for apologies and forgiveness—once lost, it could never be recovered.

"Just because you colour outside the lines and use laws to cover your illegal activities doesn't mean that one day you won't get caught," Kellie warned him, having made his life hell twelve years prior when she refused to bow down to his dictatorship. Back then, she'd felt invincible, foiling more than one of his drug deals. If she could put him behind bars, she'd find a way.

"But until then I will have to stay goodbye, Detectives," he replied, unfazed. "I'm done being accommodating."

Darryl gave him a sharp nod. "Thank you for your cooperation, Mr. Coleani. I hope we haven't taken up too much of your time."

He turned and laid a hard hand on her waist as he

faced her. The unbreakable hold he had on her forced her to turn with him as he moved past when she would've preferred to stay and continue their little chat. Had she not yielded, she would've been forcibly dragged out. Amelia followed.

Darryl didn't release her until they were outside. She jerked away from him, flustered and oddly turned on from being in such close proximity to him and his alpha behaviour.

She let out a deep breath and rearranged her clothes, ironing away invisible creases with her hands in order to waste time while she reorganised her thoughts and calmed down.

She took several deep breaths and inhaled the salty air from the nearby harbour. Coleani's restaurant was in a prime position down on the promenade. Around them, tourists shopped and walked along the wharf. An old couple sat on a metal bench and fed the seagulls. It was a perfect day, warm with a light breeze and many of the city's residents and visitors were taking complete advantage of it. The harbour was filled with sailboats setting forth to an island destination for fishing or just a lazy day on the beach.

Kellie couldn't enjoy it, not with an open double homicide to tend to. She glared back at the restaurant, not yet open for business. Wait-staff were setting up the outside tables with their frilly white umbrellas on the dock that extended over the water. Coleani would've spent a fortune for that luxury, and as always, when his name passed through her mind, anger reared its ugly head.

She fumed at his gall. Men like him infuriated

her because they believed they could do whatever they wanted, and damn the consequences. Her hands curled into small fists with impotent rage. It was always the innocents who got hurt in the end. Those who had done nothing to deserve the cruel hand fate dealt.

"What was all that about?" she demanded as they walked to the car.

"Funny, that's what I was going to ask you," Darryl retorted. "What was with all the attacking in there? We're lucky if he doesn't call the boss to lodge a complaint."

"IA investigating IA, that would be something," Amelia joked.

Kellie glared at her, in no mood for her brand of humour. "Coleani is a scum bag."

"What happened to the woman who said even scum have rights?" Darryl asked.

She glared at him for throwing her words back in her face, then gritted her teeth as she opened the car door. Coleani was a sore subject. Her mother's face flashed before her. She ruthlessly pushed the image away.

"It's just seeing him there on his lofty perch after all he put us through as kids. We had to grow up way too fast."

Amelia's light brown eyes were filled with understanding and equal frustration. "I know, Kel. Believe me, I'm right there with you. But he didn't give us one thing we could use against him. That man is as cool as a cucumber. I guess you need a certain set of balls to get you to the top rung. It makes me think of all the things he did to get there."

"But the question is…" Darryl began as he climbed into the driver's seat of his police issued Commodore, "Did we learn anything at all? We pretty much already knew he was guilty."

"He's narcissistic enough to believe himself to be a king, and like any king, when his kingdom is being threatened he will do everything in his power to do something about it."

Kellie leaned against the back seat. "I only hope Michael Lambert comes to his senses quick enough to see Dick's true nature. He is not his saviour but will be his executioner. I guarantee it."

Chapter 12

Michael's heart raced when he caught sight of the green Commodore following him. He'd seen it on and off all morning as he drove around completing transactions for Coleani. Was Coleani checking up on him? He doubted it. Coleani would be less subtle. It had to be the police. Neither option was reassuring. Were they trying to trap him?

Of course they are, he screamed at himself. *They know you killed Benedict and Butler...two men you called your friends until the chance to be one of Coleani's treasured lieutenants came knocking at your door.*

He tried to act brave and distant, liked to think their deaths meant nothing to him, but he couldn't. He had lived a hard life but nothing had prepared him for squeezing that trigger and ending two lives.

He no longer believed Coleani would protect him. He'd screwed up. He knew what happened to those that did. He'd killed them. Men he'd considered friends. Now he didn't think Coleani ever had his back.

He ran a hand through his already dishevelled hair. How long had they been following him, and what had they seen? Did they know about the deliveries he'd been making? They must, which meant it was only a matter of time before they arrested him.

Coleani must never know.

But how could he continue with the police after him? He couldn't go to prison. That's where his father was, serving twenty years after a drunken brawl led to manslaughter.

His mother was no better, having packed up and moved to greener pastures with the first bloke who'd so much as paid an ounce of attention to her. No, he knew he would never survive inside. He was weak, easy prey but he couldn't betray Coleani, not after all the man had done for him. Clothed him, fed him, given him a place to live and a job. He'd been set for life after proving he had the right stuff.

But what if he asks you to kill again? Can you do it? An inner voice taunted him.

"Oh, God," he whispered.

If they interrogated him again, it would only a matter of time before he gave in and started spilling the truth about Coleani's drug operation. Then he'd be a dead man. Coleani's power spread wide. He doubted he'd ever live to see his testifying day.

He had to get away, away from Coleani and away from Harbour Bay—hell, away from New South Wales. He'd never been anywhere else but he had always thought he'd like to see Queensland one day. He had been mesmerised by the pictures he'd seen of the Great Barrier Reef.

Now was the time to do it. He'd been tucking away money for years. Every penny he earned, he'd kept, even skimming a little off Coleani's clients. While the rest of Coleani's *sons* were drinking, snorting, or fucking away their hard-earned cash, he'd been expecting a rainy day. The only good thing his whore of a mother had taught him before she left was how to save money, and her advice had stuck over the years, even after the memory of her face had disappeared.

He spared another glance in the rear-view mirror. Shit, the Commodore was still there. He couldn't exactly skip town with the cops on his arse. How would he lose them? A horn blasted beside him and he realised he'd been too busy looking back at the cop car to watch the road. He jerked the wheel, bringing his car back into his lane.

Whatever you plan to do, Mikey, you'd better do it quick.

Up ahead, the amber light turned red and like a man going to his slaughter he prayed for forgiveness should his next stop be meeting his maker. He stamped down hard on the accelerator and shot through the intersection unscathed, then heard the sound of two cars colliding and glanced back to see his shadow stuck behind the crash.

Michael deliberately slowed, not wanting to call attention to himself. He was a nervous wreck by the time he turned off the ignition outside his apartment building.

He knew he didn't have much time, only a small window of opportunity to get lost. He ran up the inner staircase two at a time, the lift having been broken for years, then opened the door to his small one-bedroom apartment and pried up a floorboard where he kept his money. He grabbed his old backpack and stuffed the loose notes into the large section, zipping it up once he cleared out every last fiver.

He didn't bother packing clothes. All that shit could be easily replaced. Looking around, he didn't believe he'd ever miss this place. When Coleani had first offered it to him, he'd thought it a palace—a place of his own. But now he saw it for the dump that it was.

He chastised himself for wasting time and made his feet move. He reached the door and yanked it open, his heart pounding as all rational thought exited his head. He forced himself to smile as he looked over at seventeen-year-old Toby McLinden, another of Coleani's boys, a fellow ex-foster home child.

"Hey, Toby, I was just heading out. Got to make some drops for Coleani," he told the boy.

It wasn't a lie; he had decided to run halfway through his regular drops and still had a shitload of product sitting in his Saab. Hell, he could easily sell that later when he was out of danger, and he would probably need the money.

He stepped out of his apartment, shut the door behind him, and started down the stairs. He hoped Toby wouldn't comment on the backpack. He wasn't sure what he'd tell the teen, and right now his brain wasn't functioning properly enough to come up with a lie.

He heard Toby behind him as he descended the

stairs.

Relax, he's probably just going out. Don't freak out or you'll tell him you're hiding something.

Toby was the kind to report on his own mother, if he had one.

The kid was on his heels as he walked over to his car, dropping the backpack on the passenger seat. He'd rounded the hood and opened the driver's side door when Toby suddenly touched his arm, startling him.

Michael glared at him. "You want something?"

"Not me. Coleani. He wants to see you right now."

Oh, shit. I'm a dead man.

"Can't it wait? I don't want to disappoint Coleani's customers." That was the last thing he cared about, but it amazed him how scared he could be. Hours ago, being stuck in an interrogation room at the LAC had seemed like the worst thing imaginable. The prospect of confronting Coleani was much worse.

Toby shook his head. "Boss wants to see you *now*."

Michael let out a deep breath, appearing outwardly calm but shitting bricks on the inside. "All right. I'm on my way."

"I'll drive with you."

Michael clenched his hands into fists. He knew what Toby was doing—making sure he did what was requested of him.

Think, damn it, think. Maybe Coleani has no idea. Maybe he wants to commend you or even throw you an initiation party. That was feasible, right? After all, technically he *had* passed the test.

He started up the car and drove out onto the street in the direction of Coleani's restaurant.

"So, do you know why Coleani is so anxious to see me?" he asked, hoping for something to calm his frayed nerves.

"Nope. Just that he expects your arse to be in his office pronto."

Oh, fuck. This could very well be his last day alive.

Chapter 13

Nick jumped out of the car as Dean radioed the accident in. The scene around him was a chaotic mess that reminded him of a war-zone. The intersection of Howard and Evans wasn't usually a high accident zone. Named after the founding father of the town, George Howard and the once infamous convict escapee John Evans the two streets created a T-junction dead centre of town.

Two crumpled cars lay slightly off to the side, having spun around after the initial collision. The traffic light embedded in the side of one vehicle seemed like a permanent feature, the car curved around the thick steel pole. The other car's hood had been crumpled like an accordion. It was hard to determine who'd been going in what direction.

The shrill whine of a siren told Dean the first responder was on his way. He and Doyle would certainly need all the help they could get. Traffic continued to pile up, and it was only three-thirty in the afternoon. It would be a nightmare come rush hour, since the Howard-Evans intersection was the most frequented in town. Over seventy percent of Harbour Bay citizens used it on a regular basis.

Nick rushed over to a late model Ford and took a quick inventory while Dean moved towards the other car, which resembled something out of a *Bathurst 1000* crash and quickly assessed any possible danger as he approached.

He glanced through the tinted window at the driver and knew without opening the door and feeling for a pulse that the driver was dead. He shouted at a few bystanders to stay the hell back as they inched forward, and prayed the uniforms would get here soon to control the masses. For now, his authoritarian voice would have to do.

He pushed back his suit jacket to expose his gun holster and badge, informing the crowd that he was in charge before checking the other windows for other possible passengers. As far as he could see, the driver was alone and therefore the only casualty. He eased open the passenger door with a great amount of difficulty, the interior of the car resembling a sardine can as both sides compressed internally, crushing the life out of the driver as the external walls pushed into each other, fighting for dominance.

Dean prepared to lean over the centre console to remove the driver's wallet and hopefully his ID, which would make informing the next of kin easier, hopefully before they learned about the accident from the media and saw their loved one's car on the news.

With one knee on the passenger seat, he reached across and stopped dead.

Shit! In the centre of the back seat, he discovered a child's car seat, placed so the child could look out the front window. It sat on an angle, the sides cracked as it couldn't hold off the excessive force. He hadn't seen the child from the window since the tint was so dark.

He navigated through the small confines and checked the small body for a pulse. He let out a relieved breath, feeling the light throb beneath his fingertips.

He wasn't sure how he would get the kid out. The little boy was unconscious, for which he was thankful. No child should see his father dead, and Dean had no idea how much pain the child might be in. The safety seat had taken the brunt of the accident, protecting him like it was designed to, but had also tightened around the child so that it was possible the kid had a broken rib or something just as worrying.

Dean retreated from the car as he saw a marked police vehicle pull up. Two uniformed officers exited, one already heralding the spectators away. The other uniform began running towards him, recognising him instantly. Relief showed on his face.

"Doyle and I are witnesses. We were following a suspect who must have panicked when he saw us and sped right through the intersection, causing the crash," he told the cop, whose name was Huxley. "I've got one casualty and a minor trapped in the back who is currently unconscious. Stay with him in case he wakes up and inform dispatch we'll need a rescue team. The kid's in there tight."

Huxley swore to himself, and Dean jogged over to the other car where Nick had been helping a woman in her thirties out of the driver's seat, her body visibly shaking. Tears ran down her face and she was in a state of shock, her eyes much too wide to be taking anything in.

"Back-up just arrived. One survivor," he told Nick, who nodded, understanding what had been said and what hadn't. One survivor. Which implied one or more casualties.

Nick eased the woman over to the kerb away from her car and out of danger when the rescue teams, ambulance and traffic diverters, arrived. Loud sobs escaped the woman's mouth and Nick pulled her into his arms, allowing her to cry all over his linen shirt. He rubbed her back, giving comfort to her as he looked up at Dean as if to say, *what else could I do?*

Dean wasn't good with women. Crying or not. When they were emotional, it made things worse. After being partners with Nick for over three years, they had come to an understanding, each playing off one another's strengths, each knowing his limits. This was Dean's. He didn't have use for someone who allowed their emotions to rule over common sense.

Horns tooted in the distance as motorists became impatient. The heat of the day made him sweat, and he knew it would be more than just a little uncomfortable in the cars without air conditioning. People exited their vehicles, and Dean listened to the officer as he barked orders for people to return to their cars, his tone making it clear that if they didn't do it willingly, he'd be more than happy to oblige in escorting them back.

He left Nick with the overwrought female and moved towards the uniformed officer who'd arrived with Huxley. He spoke briefly with the officer, getting an estimation on when they would be joined by more members of Harbour Bay Police.

He ran stiff fingers through his blond hair and cursed the day's events. He hadn't expected Lambert to spook. The man had been overly confident when he'd walked out the doors of the LAC.

The teen wasn't in as much control as he'd like to think. Was he getting concerned over his part in the murders as Coleani's lapdog? Maybe the youth had a conscience after all and felt guilty. Now would be the time to swing down and usher the kid away, before Coleani got his hands on him.

Within minutes more police vehicles arrived, a swarm of navy uniformed cops descending on the scene, taking over witness detail and directing all the traffic away from the scene while an ambulance struggled to get through the heavy traffic.

A bright red and white Harbour Bay fire engine stopped just outside the perimeter Huxley's partner had cordoned off, and a bevy of well-trained firemen added to the rapidly growing response team.

The woman continued to sob hysterically in Nick's arms, not allowing him to leave her as she was escorted to the ambulance for a check-up.

Had he been in charge of her well-being, Dean would've shaken her off long ago and told her to get a grip, which was why Nick handled the fairer sex. Dean watched as his partner leaned over and conversed with the paramedic who immediately nodded and retrieved a needle which he promptly tested for air bubbles and then injected the woman who—thankfully—started to calm down.

Dean worked tirelessly under the harsh UV rays as he liaised with the firemen who continuously attempted to free the little boy. The mother had been notified and waited impatiently for news on her only child and last living piece of her husband.

Goddamn Michael Lambert. He had caused all this. One man was dead, another life hung in the balance. A woman was overwrought—two when he considered the mother—and for what? *Because of a murdering son-of-a-bitch.*

He made a fist, badly needing to hit something. Being a cop wasn't as glamorous as they made it out to be in movies. It was rare to save the damsel in distress from the bad man. Instead, the day was filled with handing out speeding tickets, arriving at domestic disputes, and acting as mediator. Not exactly the finer life, but Dean couldn't imagine doing anything else. He had lived a life full of violence and there was no turning back from that, no pretending it hadn't happened or that it didn't exist. He wondered how others, like Nick, handled the situation, having no background in the dark depravity he'd become accustomed to.

He moved away from the noise created by the rescue teams, yanked his phone off his belt, and dialled a number.

"Donovan." Amelia's voice came through loud

and clear.

"Hey, it's Matthews."

"Where are you? I expected a report an hour ago."

"I don't work for you *yet,* Donovan." He knew he would one day soon, but not now. "Doyle and I are at the accident on Howard-Evans."

"I heard about that. Bad one, right? So why are you calling?"

He leaned against his car. "Just wanted to give you an update. For one, Lambert caused the accident. He's spooked and is probably about to run."

"I'll let the others know. Anything else?"

"Yeah, Nick took some surveillance photos of Lambert coming out of Coleani's and a couple more today at his various drops. We recorded their addresses so if Lambert won't talk maybe one of them will. But I doubt they'll be able to tell you anything other than Lambert's name."

"Coleani always covered his arse well. Can either of you get away to collect Lambert?"

"Nick's got his hands full with a woman and I'm co-ordinating a rescue at the moment." He took a deep breath. "It's not looking good for a kid, Donovan."

She swore.

"Tell me about," he said. "Some days it doesn't pay to get out of bed."

He hung up and immediately shoved a pair of sunglasses on to shade his eyes from the harsh glare. Dean hoped they got to Lambert before Coleani did, because he wanted to be face to face with the kid who'd caused so much damage.

If Lambert believed Donovan was the daughter of the devil, just wait until he met Dean Matthews.

Chapter 14

Amelia sat on the edge of her desk, facing Darryl and Kellie, whose diamond stud earrings winked in the sunlight that streamed through the large embankment of windows directly behind them, the long cream roller blinds drawn half way, giving off just enough daylight without blinding.

Coleani had surprised her. He'd not at all been what she'd expected but there'd been no mistaking the coldness of his eyes or the arrogance of his position, which he'd achieved by killing his former mentor and gaining control of his organisation. Coleani had built on the small following until he had an empire, with young guppies ready to do his bidding.

"Doyle said that when they followed Lambert home last night he was greeted as a conquering hero at his complex. Both he and Matthews agree that they're more of Coleani's men."

Kellie frowned. "They won't talk," she stated unnecessarily, one hand on her hip.

Amelia wanted to clobber her old friend. Ever

117

since they had returned from Coleani's restaurant she had been a woman on a crusade—a dangerous one, at that. Amelia didn't like whatever was going through Kellie's mind and she'd have to keep a close eye on her if she had any plans on keeping her safe. Right now, she was her own worst enemy and messing around in Coleani's business was a sure way of getting shot.

"Yes, we know that, Kellie, but our main objective here is to bring Butler and Benedict's killer to justice. That's what we're paid to do," she said, trying to reason with a woman who didn't want to be placated. "I understand that by bringing in Lambert we're really not helping anyone. But at the moment, arresting Coleani is out of the question."

Kellie gave her a stormy glare that chilled her.

She wanted to scream. What did she want her to do? *If I could get away with it, I'd walk down to Coleani's this very second and put a bullet through his head.*

Anger flushed her face and zinged through her blood. Her already short temper frayed to the point of snapping. Agitated, she clenched her jaw in an effort to avoid saying something she'd regret. Kellie always brought out the protective side of her. She could understand her frustration, as they had shared the same childhoods. Together, they had seen the worst humankind could offer. But, then again, her mother had never worked for Coleani, so maybe Kellie's hatred ran a little deeper.

Darryl glanced from one woman to the other, clearly sensing the raw emotions pulsating between them. "Lambert is green," he added. "Way over his head. That night was no doubt his initiation into the inner circle. Coleani probably demands all his high ranking lieutenants take a life. That way, they're in as deep as he is should anything go south. They're just as liable."

Kellie snorted. "And this is a man free to walk the streets of Harbour Bay? All while we chase our tails and charge his lackeys for completing their tasks as ordered."

"The LAC has been trying to nail Coleani's arse for over twenty years. The man is like Teflon—nothing sticks," Amelia said, exasperated. She was really beginning to lose what little patience she had. "Our only hope would be to turn one of his men."

"You know full well his little cult members are hardened criminals. All of them would lay down and die for him. Not even a Donovan interrogation would yield results."

"Don't let Coleani cloud your judgement," she advised.

Her phone rang. She reached over and answered it, her voice crisp. "Donovan." She paused. "Where are you? I expected a report an hour ago."

Both Kellie and Darryl perked up, waiting for news.

"I heard about that. Bad one, right? So why are you calling?"

***

Kellie began to pace back and forth, her body stiff with tension, as a feeling of uselessness settled

119

uncomfortably over her. Darryl rubbed the back of his neck as he watched her, his brown gaze caressing her body with interest as if trying to understand what made her tick. His avid attention knotted her stomach in a way she couldn't understand. She mentally pushed Darryl aside, though that was a chore in itself and focused on the one-sided conversation.

"I'll let the others know. Anything else?" She paused again. "Coleani always did cover his arse well. Can either of you get away to collect Lambert?"

Darryl straightened, and Kellie stopped and stared.

Amelia swore and caught her gaze, then hung up the phone.

"Matthews?" Darryl asked.

"Yeah, apparently Lambert caught sight of his tail and sped through an intersection causing an accident and heavy traffic jam. Good news is we have enough evidence to take him down."

A barrage of rapid gunfire put a stop to Kellie's reply. Amelia dropped to the floor beside her desk, using the heavy duty object as cover while Darryl pushed Kellie to the ground, covering her body with his and pressing her into the hard carpet. She didn't fight him, going willingly, too terrified to argue. She wanted to squeeze her eyes shut, to block out her surroundings as her body began quivering beneath Darryl's in fear, but she couldn't, not when other people were depending on her observations to keep them alive.

She looked left, then right, expecting to see

furniture combust into a thousand pieces. The sound of breaking glass and surprised screams and shouts swam around her head until she had no idea where they were coming from. The next room? The floor below? The floor above?

The building's internal security system started blaring, sounding much like the old World War Two air-raid warnings, and the shrill noise hurt her ears, threatening to burst the delicate drum. She was on the verge of losing it and for a second she imagined herself in the middle of a war zone, taking fire. That's certainly what it felt like, only Darryl's weight and heat seeping through her clothes and warming her chilled body kept her sanity.

The world went silent momentarily before a loud squeal she presumed was a rubber tyre connecting with the asphalt reached her ears. They remained on the floor for several minutes after the gunfire stopped, until it was decided they were safe.

Amelia lithely got to her feet and surveyed her surroundings, her take-charge personality a real blessing in situations like this. "Is everyone all right?" she asked.

Several affirmatives were given as their cop instincts took over, immediately seeking intruders or injured parties.

"Someone shut that damn alarm off," Amelia shouted.

Darryl rose in one swift motion, pulling Kellie up with him and instantly wrapped his arms around her trembling body. "Shhh," he whispered in her ear, rubbing his hand gently up and down her back in a comforting gesture. "It's all right. It's all over."

Amelia returned, placing her hand on Kellie's shoulder, concern evident on her face as she took in her condition. "Are you okay?" Her voice sounded strangely soft and nurturing.

Kellie nodded and pulled away, her hands shaking. Darryl reached over and wiped his thumb across her cheek and it was then she realised she'd been crying silently. Long ago memories had bombarded her, flashes of a gun appearing in her vision, along with the sound of a bullet exiting a chamber and finding its target.

"I'm fine," she managed to say, her voice calm and steady even though she wasn't. She scanned the room, noting that it had been untouched.

"The damage has been confined to the ground floor," a uniformed officer reported to the room at large.

Kellie stepped away, her legs unsteady at first. With each step, she grew stronger.

As if having no will of her own, she found herself opening the door to the fire exit and descending the staircase, Darryl and Amelia on her heels. When they reached the ground floor and entered the general reception area, glass crunched beneath her shoes, along with the occasional piece of broken wood. The back wall where the ***Harbour Bay Local Area Command*** sign hung bore a resemblance to Swiss cheese.

Kellie took in the devastation. Uniformed and plainclothes officers moved about the room purposefully. She recognised a few members of the forensic team who were quickly snapping pictures and sorting through the debris.

Doctor Stone attended to the few injured, thankfully finding nothing more than a few cuts and bruises.

The lobby was a large open space where to the right of the entrance stood the sign-in desk, and to the left were two navy blue couches. Each sported tears in the fabric where the bullets had entered. A glass coffee table with magazines and pamphlets somehow stood untouched between the destroyed couches.

Past the waiting area was the cafeteria and its multitude of tables and chairs. Glass littered the floors and a slight breeze filled the lobby through the broken windows. The buffet station had also been shot up but the kitchen where the staff had been working at the time was behind a thick protective wall and remained intact.

An older uniformed officer trudged over to them. "I caught sight of the shooters and recognised a couple of them as Coleani's boys. Not one over the age of eighteen by my estimation."

"How many were there?" Amelia asked.

"Three shooters and one driver as far as I could tell," the veteran officer, Bryce Prescott, said. "Didn't catch a plate number but it was a dark Honda CRV."

"Any casualties?" Darryl enquired.

Bryce shook his head. "I don't think so. I've sent some men around to the offices beyond the wall to check things out."

They all turned to the wall where high calibre bullets had ripped straight through the plaster and insulation into the office beyond, and out the other side. Streaks of daylight peeked through the hundred or so holes. Thankfully, the only thing in that area beyond the building was water.

"Good, then the only damage was structural."

"Which is going to cost the taxpayers hundreds of thousands," a deep baritone voice stated angrily. They all turned to face Superintendent Harris as he barrelled down on them, his face red while a vein throbbed visibly in his temple.

"Just send the bill to Coleani, Boss," Amelia quipped.

Harris sent her a withering glare. "It appears Coleani didn't take kindly to your visit earlier."

Kellie didn't doubt it. "Apparently. But I'd say he knows nothing about this. He's more for the subtle approach. This was the work of his younger *associates* who probably think they're protecting their boss. Mark my words, when he does learn of this, heads will roll...literally."

"I've already posted a couple officers outside and they're vetting everyone who pulls in. I don't want another repeat of this afternoon," Harris told them.

"They won't be back," Amelia said. "They did what they came to do."

Harris scowled and Kellie knew she didn't want to be in his shoes right now. It was a public relations nightmare. If the police weren't safe from the likes of Coleani and his cohorts, what chance did the general public have?

"I've already called Hoskins down in facilities and told him to bring something to cover the windows until replacements can be ordered and fitted," Harris said. Several maintenance men were already sweeping up the broken glass. He turned to Amelia. "I don't want a war to break out in retaliation but he is to know that this thing won't be tolerated, understand?"

Amelia nodded.

Prescott moved to the reception desk where he talked quietly to Mandy, the forty-something woman who had the misfortune of being at the desk today. Her eyes were wide but she appeared calm, a great woman to have in the midst of a crisis. She had already rounded people up and delegated tasks. Mandy had probably been a drill sergeant in a previous life; she certainly fit the bill and barking orders seemed to be second nature.

"Let's go find Lambert," Amelia said. "Matthews seems to think the quicker, the better. For all we know, this was a delaying tactic so they could dispose of him before we could get our hands on him."

Chapter 15

Amelia chewed on the end of her pencil. The adrenaline that had been coursing through her bloodstream earlier during the bullet spray had dissipated, leaving her exhausted and emotionally drained. Usually, she lived for this stuff, but today she was finding it hard to summon up much needed energy.

She tried not to let it show. She couldn't afford to appear weak or emotional. No woman of power could because the moment they did they were torn asunder by the competition. Never mind that some of the best leaders in the world had been women. No, a woman was far too emotional. She was going to prove everyone wrong.

Years ago, she had joked about becoming one of Coleani's girls. God, how long ago was that? It seemed like another lifetime. She hadn't been serious, of course. Even back then, she had standards and self-respect. Most people in their neighbourhood never managed to scramble out from beneath the garbage, but both Amelia and Kellie had. She hadn't always liked the way Kellie pushed her, though she understood why and was grateful. In those days, her friend had been determined to claw her way out of the tenements she'd lived in.

Amelia's memories of the neighbourhood weren't as bad, though she could smell the strong scent of urine and dope that always permeated the air. During the day it was bad enough, but at night it was the stuff nightmares were made of and the weak were preyed upon. While her mother hadn't been a peach, at least she hadn't prostituted herself out like Jules Munroe and she hadn't lost a father she had loved deeply. Her childhood had been uneventful if not boring, but she had been surrounded by her grandparents' love, care, and support.

Kellie had no one but her.

She'd been more than her best friend. They were sisters—at least the closest to sisters either of them would get since neither of them had siblings.

Amelia threw down her pencil with disgust. This case could very well be the death of her. It constantly brought up memories better left forgotten.

Amelia struggled to keep her eyes open. She had been running on empty for hours now. As she glanced around the Pig Pen, she considered her career. She loved this place. It was overrun by males but they were for the better part supportive and the kind she could trust to have her back.

From the moment she had stepped through the reception doors downstairs almost seven years ago, she had been on a rampage to be the best, not just to prove it to herself but to the people around her. She had never before had such responsibility and power and the knowledge she was doing something worthwhile in her life boiled her blood.

She had climbed the ranks faster than most of her fellow officers and she knew that they resented the hell out of her, but she worked hard for her achievements. She felt a moment of worry as she wondered if it had all been for nought. If Kellie chose to, she could end her career. Her old friend didn't know how much she treasured this job, how much she needed it.

It was all she had in life. Something she was good at.

"What the hell happened? It looks like World War Three broke out downstairs," Nick said, interrupting her thoughts as he entered the Pig Pen. His shirt wrinkled and damp at the armpits. Dean, looking very much the same, followed.

"Just about," Amelia replied with a yawn.

Dean gave her a once over. "If possible, you look worse than we do."

"Combined," Nick agreed.

She glared at them both. "Gee, thanks, make a girl feel special. No wonder you two are single. Did you get everything cleared?"

Nick nodded. "Yeah, the fire brigade were washing the streets as we left. Man, that was a bad smash. One of the worst I've seen. Thankfully the kid was okay."

She agreed. She hated when innocents were hurt, worst still when they were kids.

"We tried to locate Lambert but he's disappeared

and right now he's a low priority to the LAC," she told them, clearly not agreeing. "Boss wants us to find the little shits who opened fire downstairs. Prescott got a description of the shooters and a make and model of the vehicle."

"We'll certainly keep an eye out when we're on the streets," Dean said. "I'm going to grab and shower and a change of clothes and get back out there. Maybe if I'm lucky I'll find Lambert but I doubt it. He'll turn up though, someday."

"Yeah, but I'd rather question him and not leave it to Stone," she quipped. "Dead men don't give up their secrets. I'm heading home. I'm beat and have a ton of shit to do tomorrow. I'll see you ladies later."

A moment later she was walking across the parking lot of the LAC towards her Toyota Kluger. She loved the bulky car; it had a sense of imperviousness about it. She climbed behind the steering wheel and a few seconds later she was joining other late night drivers on the somewhat quiet streets.

She stopped in at Tanner's Steak and Grill, the local dive haunted by Harbour Bay's police force and other emergency services employees, and quickly ordered a hamburger with the lot to go. She was too tired to cook but her stomach had begun to growl and was reminiscent of a lioness's roar so she had wisely chosen to feed it.

Amelia devoured the hamburger the moment she got home and now lay on her cool sheets looking up at the dark ceiling, her stomach satisfied. She wondered at the future. Her dreams were so close to being fulfilled—close, but still precariously fragile. She could practically taste her promotion in her mouth.

Kellie had promised to be fair, to judge her by what she saw in the here and now. There had been a time when Kellie knew everything about Amelia. The good, the bad, her wants and needs, her dreams and wishes, her fears and desires, but she didn't know who she'd become. Just as Amelia didn't know who Kellie had become after that fateful night. They had both changed, both grew up, both strong, independent women who were more acquaintances than friends. Something she hoped to change.

She didn't believe she'd done anything wrong; she'd had no other choice. She was a cop, not a kindergarten teacher, so a certain amount of violence was to be expected. She didn't like playing the female card, but she felt like she was being unfairly judged. Men like Matthews and Hill could use their superior strength to disable a target but for her it took a little brute force to get compliance. It was part and parcel of her chosen profession, something she would have to get used to.

Not unless you're kicked out, an inner voice taunted.

Amelia took a deep breath and sat up in her queen size bed. She liked her apartment; it wasn't flashy or decorated with expensive furniture that would take years to pay off but it was home and suited her needs. The external walls showed the red brick of the building, the internal plasterboard painted a sunny yellow—not her choice but the previous tenant's. She had moved in the same time she'd been hired at the LAC and had been there ever since.

She wrapped the afghan blanket she'd snatched from the end of her bed over her shoulders, immediately feeling the warmth it trapped between her body and the fabric. Having Kellie walk back into her life shook her more than she'd like to admit and not just because she'd always fallen short beside her friend. It stirred up feelings she'd thought long ago dead. Kellie was not only her friend but a constant reminder of a past she could not change.

Amelia liked to believe she was untouchable, but if there was ever a weakness, Kellie was her Achilles heel. Even after twelve years, the friendship they shared was still there, buried deep within two women who fought to get past one event in their lives—the event that changed them forever in more ways than one. Amelia marvelled at how strong Kellie had always been. Even in her darkest hours, Kellie struggled and sought help, not allowing her rocky emotions get the better of her.

While she had been sarcastic and still was, Kellie had more guts than a whole platoon of soldiers. She never backed down from a fight, never gave up, her tenaciousness giving her a solid reputation.

When a lesser person would've bowed down and slunk off into the shadows, Kellie had grown stronger, more stubborn, and had the force of a cyclone crashing against the shore.

She admired her more than she would ever know. Could they somehow become close again?

She stood and walked over to her closet. She flicked on the bare bulb, then rummaged through a shoe box. She found what she was looking for and pulled it out, bringing the object with her as she sat back on the bed.

In the photo, Kellie stood beside her. It was the only item she'd kept from her past. The only thing she wanted to be reminded of. A friendship that had never died, if only put on hold. A moment when life had been ahead of her, the world a vast and exciting place.

A lot had changed in twelve years. Lives had been destroyed, careers created from the remains. She wasn't sure she would ever forgive herself. The past seemed to haunt her no matter what she did or where she went. Kellie had told her to forget, that she should not feel guilty, but Amelia did. Survivor's guilt, the psychologists called it, and they were right. It haunted her more than anything because it could have easily been her.

Amelia doubted she would've had half the strength it took Kellie to get back on her feet and keep moving. She'd always surprised her. When other women would given up, she had worked even harder to keep going. Even when she'd believed all had been lost she'd still called out for help, fighting the hopelessness she'd been drowning in. Determination. Courage. Words she associated with Kellie. Life had often knocked her down yet she'd continued to get back up.

Tears burned in her eyes as she stared down at the photo. Her grandparents had taken the picture, shortly after Kellie's sixteenth birthday. Her present to her best friend shone brightly from around her neck. The gold locket had been taken along with the Kellie she'd once known.

Amelia placed the frame on her bedside table, no longer wanting to keep it locked away unseen and forgotten.

Chapter 16

Kellie kicked off her shoes and leaned back in her office chair, a sigh of pure pleasure escaping her lips. It had been a long day and she was frustrated at the lack of progress they'd made. There had been no sign of Michael Lambert at his apartment and no one could tell them when he'd last been seen or where he might be right now.

If Michael had any brains, he'd be halfway to China by now. The two detectives hadn't disagreed with her assessment of the situation. She frowned. She was a detective too, in a way, even if she and her oldest friend didn't view it the same way.

But determining whether an officer was guilty of misconduct was a hard choice to make and an IA officer had to see the evidence, read the reports, and know whether to kick the officer to the kerb or not.

She had been a cop for almost seven years now, but had never felt the desire to go for her detective's exam or a higher rank. She liked her job and did it to the best of her ability, with many short-comings that would've hindered her in any other position.

She was a desk jockey and it suited her temperament well. She wasn't one for confrontations, despite being able to spar with the best of them, her sharp tongue cutting even the most arrogant and self-assured officer.

She'd never planned to go into law enforcement. Her only goal as a kid had been to leave the neighbourhood, and she had dabbled with the idea of being a doctor or a lawyer, but in reality anything was better than the future waiting for her under Coleani's thumb.

It wasn't until she turned sixteen that she met Detective Sergeant Ed Graham. She couldn't recall what he said or did that inspired her, but when she enrolled at Harbour Bay University at eighteen, she found herself thinking about him and what he stood for, what he'd wanted out of his career.

He'd told her it wasn't glamorous, that some days it downright sucked, but when it came to picking her courses she'd selected justice administration and criminology. When she received her diploma and had gone through basic training at the Police College in Goulburn, Kellie returned to Harbour Bay and worked her way through a variety of desk jobs until she found her true calling.

It amazed her how her short association with the detective had such an impact on her life. Had Amelia experienced something similar?

But unlike Kellie, she'd had no failings hampering her choice of vocation. That time of her life had been extremely educational and had changed her astronomically. She couldn't see herself doing anything else even with the bad hours and horrible pay—which was exactly what Ed Graham had told her it was like.

A cop's job wasn't easy, knowing what happened in the world and being powerless to stop it without the proper evidence. Knowing who the bad guys were and watching them walk out of the LAC with smirks on their faces, always getting the better of the police, since they were bound by law to follow certain rules.

Twelve years ago, Coleani commanded only a twelve block radius. His base of operations, his restaurant along with his strip club and so called pharmacy, all dominated one street—Lowell Avenue.

Kellie shuddered to think how much more he had gained over the years. He was a determined man, a man who started at the bottom. Thirty or forty years ago, no one had heard of Dick Coleani, a snotnosed kid who worked from sun up to sun down, a man whose violent and sadistic nature put him on the radar of Charles Wright, the Al Capone of Harbour Bay who trained Coleani from a child and turned an already rotten kid into an even worse teenager and a cruel, brutal adult whose only goal in life was to extend his empire.

Kellie remembered walking past the drug dealers trying to make a sale, the occasional overdose victim lying in the doorway of the local convenience store. By six, she'd overheard many of her neighbours' marital disputes and the screams of pain that followed. She'd shopped for groceries at the most infamous store in the neighbourhood which acquired the title of most robbed.

She had always admired the poor teenage boys who were either courageous enough or stupid enough to work there and it always seemed to surprise her when nobody noticed the filth they lived in.

She logged onto her computer and retrieved the double homicide file. The crime scene photos immediately appeared on her screen and she clicked through each slide.

Her stomach rebelled. She could never understand how someone could do something so horrible to another person and often wondered where people's hearts were.

The answer was simple. Some people didn't have a heart.

"What are you still doing here?" Darryl said from behind her, causing her to jump. "Sorry, didn't mean to startle you," he added. "I should've hummed or something. I know what it's like to get absorbed in a case. Even Donovan's gone home for the night."

Kellie raised an eyebrow at him as he parked his gorgeous bottom on the side of her desk. "Really? That is amazing. I didn't think she ever went home."

He smiled. "Some days it seems like it. So, what are you still doing here, sticking your nose in my case?"

She crossed her legs and leaned back in her chair. "It's my case, too, Detective Hill, and if I choose to review it, that's my prerogative."

"Wow, you have a bite, don't you? Donovan didn't warn me."

"I'm sorry. I'm a little tense at the moment. Meeting Coleani brought back a lot of memories I'd rather forget and this afternoon's adventure is still fresh in my mind."

"It must've been hard for you, growing up as you did, in that neighbourhood under his thumb."

She nodded slowly. "It was. Everyone says life is unfair, but you never want to believe that. The naive and young like to think that good always triumphs and the bad guys get locked up. It's a nice dream, but it doesn't exist and that's extremely frustrating." She rubbed her hand over her forehead, trying to erase a headache that had snuck up on her. "No matter how many of Coleani's boys you get off the street, there's still more and it won't ever stop. Not until we get Coleani himself, and he's such a slippery bastard."

Darryl rested his hands on either side of his thighs as he took in her fierce expression. "I take it this is about more than just the case?"

"You must be a detective," she said sarcastically before smiling. "Mia and I were lucky. We got out of a place no one ever leaves unless they're dead. My parents tried. They wanted something better for themselves, and it was clear it wouldn't happen there. My father worked himself to death for no benefits, nothing to pass on to his wife and child except a mountain of bills my mother couldn't handle.

"I was ten when I caught her coming out of Coleani's strip club smelling of smoke and sex. She wasn't a bad mum. She just wasn't good at taking care of herself, let alone anyone else. Once my father died, she went downhill fast. She tried her best but couldn't break even. It was then I decided I wouldn't live and die in that neighbourhood. I would get out and nothing would stop me."

Kellie still remembered that day like it was yesterday. She had never been so disappointed with her life. While her father had been alive, things were good—not great, but not bad either. After he died, her mother existed in a drug induced coma, and Kellie had to take over the responsibilities of paying bills and making sure there was food in the house. Her mother had been weak, wanted the easy way out, and in the end had sold her body for a pittance.

"Looks like you made good on that," he told her, admiration in his voice.

"But to what end? Men like Coleani are still out there. The scourge of mankind, to put it dramatically. He sets out to ruin people's lives to make money. He uses little boys and makes them into monsters, bottom-feeders like himself. I hate that man."

"Maybe you should recuse yourself from the case. Especially if you're going to make this personal."

She scoffed. "Don't kid yourself, Hill. They're all personal. Every last one of them. I bet you can remember every victim you ever had, am I right? You can probably remember the circumstances of each case and could recite how each one of them died. So don't tell me it isn't personal for you."

"No, but the difference is when I'm on a case, I don't think about the people involved. I think about the evidence. That's all I see. That's all I can afford to care about. Any wrong move and a lawyer can have a case dismissed," he told her coolly, his disdain for lawyers coming through loud and clear. "Sure, when it's all over I think about the injustice, but the law is there for a reason and I have to believe the right thing will eventually be done. Coleani will have his comeuppance. I guarantee it."

"Before how many more lives will be ruined? One day, Detective Hill, you will get involved in a case where it will be personal and you won't be able to make that distinction. You'll think with your heart first and your head later, but that won't make you any less of a good cop." She stood. "Passion is what drives us. If you don't care about the people, how are you doing the right thing by them?"

She slipped her feet back into her shoes and grabbed her purse. Darryl also stood, causing them to stand mere inches apart. Kellie stepped back, removing herself from the intimate circle. She could feel his body heat even after she stepped away and her heartbeat raced.

"You may be right, Kellie, but I hope that day is far away. I've seen what cases like that can do to a cop. It makes them take chances, even take the law into their own hands and I'd rather not join them. When you start to feel nothing…or too much…it's time to move on."

"I'm not about to step away, Detective, but I will try to be objective about this. It'll be a trial, I know that. I don't hate easily, but when I do, I have good reason. We have a case to close and justice to be had. Will you walk me out?"

Darryl nodded. "Sure. Come on."

Chapter 17

Kellie followed Darryl across the deserted car park of the LAC. The moon, bright and full reflected on car windows, overshadowing the small insignificant stars around it. The ground was damp from a quick shower earlier in the evening and the clouds bringing rain had caught the humidity in the air.

She moved cautiously across the pavement towards her car. Silently, Darryl slowed, matching his usually long stride to her skirt-hindered smaller ones. She was always edgy at night, alert for any danger. She held her keys in her hand, having removed them from her purse earlier while waiting for the elevator to open so she could escape the male dominated carriage.

She was acutely aware of him, his presence overwhelming her. Every breath she took filled her lungs with the decadent scent of him—spicy and woodsy and completely male, sending her stomach fluttering. Her hormones were in chaos and her body craved him. She'd never had such a potent response to a man before. She felt off-balance, her world turned upside down. God, she wanted him.

Nick could be considered hot, but Darryl blew him out of the water with his sexy liquid brown eyes and short hair. He was just so—*wow*. It was the only word she could think of that described him. Six feet of healthy male. Wide shoulders. Thick, strong chest. Hard, defined pecs.

There wasn't a soft part anywhere on him. She'd felt that and more when he'd been on top of her during the attack. At the time, she hadn't fully appreciated her position. But in the aftermath, disappointment filled her that she hadn't been able to enjoy that delicious weight bearing down on her, his chest crushing her breasts, his warm breath on her face as he stared deep into her eyes. She imagined him slowly lowering his head to take her lips with a rough, passionate kiss full of promise.

Her blood heated with arousal and an ache began, gaining momentum with insistence she do something about it. And fast.

Kellie tried to move quicker but a combination of her heels and tight skirt made it impossible. She silently cursed her outfit and Amelia, who had been right. She would've killed for a pair of jeans and sneakers right about now. If only to get away from the delicious male beside her. The man was in serious danger of being attacked by a blonde with carnal thoughts. Her overactive imagination painted vivid pictures of what she could do to him.

She bit back a moan and a curse. How dare he have such control over her? She could barely think with him around and she was perilously close to losing her sanity. Was he even aware of what he did to her? Of what she'd like him to do to her?

Candles. Silk sheets. Darryl's impressive naked chest. Her cries of pleasure.

"Do you see your mother often?"

The sound of his voice almost had her tripping over her feet as she startled once again. Darryl reached out and caught her arm before she landed face first. She murmured her thanks even as her face flamed. Thankfully it was dark enough that he wouldn't be able to see.

Seriously, what the hell had happened to her?

She should be thinking about the case, Coleani, Mia, and a thousand other things instead of fantasising about Darryl. It was hardly professional and she was pretty sure it fell under sexual harassment. She tried to push thoughts of him aside and focused on his question.

"No," she replied, coolly. Thoughts of her mother always had that effect on her and this time she felt thankful for it. Anything to cool off the desire she had for Darryl. "She OD'd a couple of years ago. I guess she figured I no longer needed her here, so she just ended her pain."

Darryl sent her a sideways glance. "I'm sorry."

She shrugged. Her mother had been gone long before she'd died.

"Don't be. She was never a very strong person. Even before my father died. She was a follower, happy to go along with someone else's plans. What about you? How did you end up in Harbour Bay?"

She felt the topic of conversation was safe enough as she led him towards her car. She had to admit she was interested in knowing more about him. Even if it would simply add more fuel to the ever growing fire inside her. She wanted to know him. She wanted to connect with him and not just in the most basic of ways.

"You don't know? I thought you would've read it in my file," he stated, obviously fishing for information.

"You know that would be an invasion of privacy. Besides, I rather like asking questions. It helps me fine-tune my people reading skills. I like to know when someone is lying to me."

Darryl smiled almost indulgently, and touched her arm, stopping her. The touch burned and he quickly released her. Had he felt it too?

"Okay. I moved around a lot as a kid. My father was in the army, so when I finished my Detective's exam I looked for a permanent position which led to Harbour Bay. Satisfied?"

Hardly.

"So do you think you'll stay here? I mean after all those years of moving around, I'd think you'd want some semblance of stability, am I right?"

He took his time answering. "You're right. I want a place to hang my hat, so to speak, and I really think Harbour Bay may be that place. I just don't know yet. Time will tell."

"Harbour Bay's not so bad. Discounting the serial killer and Dick Coleani, of course, but of all the places in the world, it's home, and I'd never want it any other way."

Darryl gave her a onceover that warmed her from the inside out, the heat in his gaze enough to enflame her. "I can certainly see the appeal."

She blushed and turned away. The harbour's salty breeze washed over her, the bright beam from the nearby lighthouse glowed through the darkness. She glanced back, uncertainty creeping up her spine.

She hated being out in the open, vulnerable to attack. There were so many shadows where a person could hide in the parking lot. She felt herself slip into panic mode. She gripped her keys harder, the serrated edges of the metal digging into her palm as she watched the distance grow between her and the building housing Harbour Bay's LAC. Bright yellow lights shined through the windows where the night shift were hard at work.

The elongated L-shaped light mud brown, four-storey building was a hideous piece of architecture. Once a convict barrack, it had been renovated in the seventies to accommodate the growing police presence in Harbour Bay, and today it was the second largest Local Area Command in NSW.

A stone memorial, a tribute to Harbour Bay's officers who'd fallen in the line of duty stood in the courtyard of the L which housed the entrance to the building. The grounds surrounding the LAC were lush and well maintained. During the day, many admired the vibrant coloured pansies planted in the garden beds that drew attention away from the building behind them.

She was relieved by Darryl's presence. It was nice to know she wasn't alone in the dark. That he would protect her, just as he'd done earlier under the rapid gunfire. She shivered at the memory and knew she hadn't come to grips with the fear she'd felt at that moment. Hours later, she still rode the adrenaline high although it slowly ebbing and she knew she would crash soon enough. Hopefully, no one would be around to witness her meltdown.

Kellie stopped at her white 2010 Ford Focus sedan. Small droplets of water remained on the roof and windshield. Kellie pressed the button on her key fob. Her indicator lights flashed as she unlocked her car. She opened the car door and threw her purse onto the passenger seat before turning to face Darryl.

"Thank you for walking me. I appreciate it…and the company."

Darryl nodded, his dark gaze watching her. "After a day like today it's smart to be vigilant."

Gunfire. Cries. Glass shattering.

Kellie shivered at the memory. Her gaze drifted to his lips. A lifeline as she felt herself begin to spin out of control, the past threatening to swamp her. His lips were long and thin. Sensual. What would it be like to taste him? Would once be enough to sate her? Or would she become so addicted to him that she wouldn't be able to think straight? She mentally shook her head. Her mind was already scattered.

Standing so close to him, she could feel the heat from his body. His reassuring presence empowered her, making her stronger even when her knees wanted to buckle. Or was that *because* of him? Darryl Hill was hazardous to her mental health. And probably her heart, too, if she let him. He had the ability to shatter her if she wasn't careful, if she allowed the walls around her to fall. But it was tempting, and she wasn't sure she could ignore it.

"Can I ask you something?"

Darryl rested his hip on the side of her car as he crossed his arms over his broad chest. "Sure. Fire away."

She glanced away as she gathered the courage to ask the question that had been tormenting her. "You and Mia—you're just partners?"

Darryl frowned. "Yeah, what else would we be?"

"Amelia's an attractive woman and you're a good looking guy. You spend your days together," she said slowly. "Something could have formed and spilled over into the night."

Darryl unfolded himself from his lazy position and stood to his full height. She tilted her head so that she could keep looking him in the eye.

"I spend all day with Doyle and Matthews too. Are you going to suggest we also get it on?"

Kellie backpedalled. "Don't get me wrong. It's fine if you two had or have a personal relationship."

However, the very idea of Mia—or any woman—sharing this man's bed caused jealousy to rear its ugly head. She'd never been the possessive type, but Darryl proved she didn't know everything about her own identity.

He searched her face and she wondered what he saw there. Hopefully not the raw desire she felt.

"Donovan's a great woman. Feisty, loyal, a good cop and an even better partner…but there's no way in hell I would sleep with her. For one, she doesn't appeal to me that way, and I'm not about to ruin a good friendship just for a roll in the sack. Secondly, I doubt I'd survive the night without getting handed my balls in the morning."

Relief flooded her. "What about other women? Are you currently involved with anyone?"

Darryl stepped closer, invading her personal space. Her heart hammered painfully in her chest, and her breath caught in her throat. He was a scant inch away from touching her and her body quivered. She swallowed hard and suddenly her breath returned in quick, short puffs.

She held his gaze. His eyes glittered in the dark as he noted her reaction. She wet her dry lips and his expression turned hungry—no, *starving*. She had never seen that look on a man's face before. She felt lightheaded.

His brown eyes held her captive. "Why do you want to know?" he said, his voice feather light, his breath tickling her bangs.

"Because I don't get involved with men who belong to someone else."

Was that her voice? She hardly recognised the husky timber that was more Kathleen Turner than Kellie Munroe. It wasn't the first time she'd propositioned a man, always the aggressor, needing to control the situation but this was something more. She refused to analyse it though most would say what she feeling was a direct result of her earlier fear or her unbalanced equilibrium due to her adrenaline high. She was happy just going with shared attraction. Something she was sure he felt though wanted to fight.

She stepped forward until their bodies touched and laid a hand on his well-defined chest, just above his heart. It galloped beneath her touch. She smiled.

He wasn't as unaffected by her as he seemed. His nostrils flared and his pupils dilated as she lifted her head, her lips tantalisingly close. It wouldn't take much for either of them to cross the small distance and press their lips together.

He shuddered. "This isn't a good idea."

She slid her hand up the row of buttons on his shirt and deftly popped them open revealing the wide expanse of his chest. She slipped her hand inside to stroke him, feeling the wiry hair beneath her soft palm.

She held his gaze. "Answer the question, Detective."

She knew the game she played was extremely seductive, and Darryl had been right when he said it wasn't a good idea. But nothing had ever felt this right.

"I'm all yours," he replied, the words sounding like they'd been torn from him.

She liked the sound of that. "Then…come home with me tonight."

Chapter 18

The front door to Kellie's house banged loudly against the wall as they pushed it open. Darryl shoved her none too gently backwards, his lips pressed against hers, his tongue stroking the fire burning in his gut. Kellie clung to him, her arms around his neck, pulling him closer.

He held her hips tight, crushing her body against his, and she felt so good. Soft and womanly. She tasted of peppermint and he'd never liked the flavour more. The front door slammed shut as Darryl kicked it closed with his foot. His body was hard and aching, screaming for release. It had been a while for him and never had it been so hot; the mere touch of her had him close to coming in his pants.

He'd never wanted a woman as much as he did right now. Kellie had slipped past all his defences and he couldn't care less. She'd surprised him with her seduction tonight. It had been the last thing he'd expected as he'd walked her to her car. He was still reeling. She seemed so sweet and innocent but there was a fiery temptress beneath her wholesome good looks. He'd gone hard in a rush as he heard her husky voice announcing her desire for him.

It had taken everything in him to keep his hands off her. Then she'd upped the game, moving against him, her hands slipping inside his shirt to touch his heated, naked skin and all he could think of was returning the favour.

He'd almost taken her up against her car in the damn parking lot, he'd been so ready for her. But common sense had prevailed for a time and he'd followed her home, the ache in his groin so damning he'd almost driven off the road twice. Only the knowledge of what was waiting for him had him keeping his hands off himself. He wanted Kellie to touch him, to bring him pleasure.

She was so damn beautiful, her lips swollen from his kisses, her face red from whisker burn where he'd rubbed his cheek against hers. And she was his—for tonight, anyway. Damn, he didn't want to think about tomorrow. Not now.

He kissed a trail down her slender throat and nipped at her with his teeth. He couldn't stop the groan that escaped his lips. His hands slid down her back and cupped her bottom, pulling her against his straining erection. If he didn't slow down, he would embarrass himself.

Her fingers crept into his hair and he could feel her breasts press against his chest as she drew him closer for another mind-blowing kiss. She sucked on his tongue and his dick jerked. Was she purposely trying to get him to lose control? Hadn't she already driven him to madness? Must she continue to taunt him?

Her leg slid up his side, reaching his waist, the motion bringing her that much closer to him. She yanked his shirt from his pants with impatience and his stomach muscles bunched beneath her exploring hands as she traced his abs. She murmured her approval of his body.

"Kellie," he gasped as her small nails grazed his sensitive skin.

She made an animal sound and suddenly his shirt fell open, the sound of loose buttons hitting her hardwood floors reaching his ears as she pushed his shirt from his shoulders and stared down at his chest.

The look in her eyes was almost his undoing. Had any woman ever looked at him as if he was ice cream topped with warm chocolate sauce, minus the calories? He knew he wasn't bad to look at and spent hours in the gym to accomplish it, but she made him feel like an Adonis. Her gaze, darkened by desire, caressed him. He shuddered when her mouth touched him, her wet tongue swirling around his nipple. His hands tightened on her and more blood rushed south.

What was he doing? Her mouth continued its slow torture as she focused on his other nipple. His back arched beneath her ministrations. She was hell on his self-control and now he was about to do something he couldn't regret, but knew nonetheless that it was a mistake. A problem they could do without. He and Kellie were working together, and would see each other every day. This had to be the stupidest thing he'd ever considered doing. And the most pleasurable.

Dammit.

What a time for cold reality to hit him in the face. His chest heaved with the effort it took to breathe.

Her hands moved to his belt and started tugging. Darryl grabbed her wrists, stilling her movement. He was an idiot to try to stop this, but he in good conscience couldn't go through with it. Not only were they colleagues but she was his partner's old friend, and Amelia would probably kick his arse should she discover his attempts to seduce Kellie, though she seemed to be doing most of the seducing. He merely went along with her.

Why the hell was he stopping?

His entire body screamed at him to keep going. To drop Kellie to the floor and thrust himself deep inside her, to possess her in the most intimate way. But with the little self-control he had left, he stepped painfully away from her.

He was rock hard, and *uncomfortable* wasn't the word to describe his agony.

Kellie gazed up at him with a frown on her flushed face. Her blonde hair spilled over her shoulders and her blouse was in disarray. He didn't even remember scrunching it in his hands. He'd never seen anyone so utterly sexy and once again fought for self-control.

"This isn't a good idea," he said.

Her harsh breathing filled the otherwise silent room. She stepped away from him and collapsed on the nearby sofa as if her legs could no longer hold her up.

"I thought we'd already established that."

"I figured it needed to be said again."

Kellie crossed her legs. She hadn't done it in a provocative way but the simple action almost brought him to his knees.

"It's more than that, isn't it?" she asked, her head cocked to the side.

Darryl ran a stiff hand over his head, his hair so short the strands barely reached the tops of his fingers.

"Besides us working together, or the fact that your best friend is my partner?" He stared at her. "I'm not into one-nighters."

Not this time. Not with her. Once would never be enough.

A shattered expression fell across her face. Had he been right in figuring that tonight was about more than shared desire? Did Kellie simply want to reaffirm the fact she was still alive after the assault on the LAC earlier? He understood her need and the resulting adrenaline rush. He just didn't want to be a convenient lay for her.

From the moment they'd met, he'd fought his attraction, and if what he'd seen that night was any indication, Kellie had been fighting it too. The desire between them had been simmering for a while. They'd ignited too quickly and dangerously.

But his reasons were more than enough to make him back away. He didn't want to sleep with her only to have her kick him to the kerb the next day. As much as it killed him, he'd rather walk away than have her only to lose her once the sun came up. There was something about Kellie he couldn't touch, beneath the walls she'd built, and he wanted her to let him in. He wanted all of her.

You dumb shit, Darryl. You should be thankful that a beautiful woman like her is willing to sleep with you at all.

Most guys would've been cheering at the idea of *no strings attached* sex. Instead, he wanted all or nothing.

"Then we have a problem, don't we?" she said.

"Would you consider it?"

Her eyes widened as she stared at him. She swallowed hard.

"A relationship?" she asked.

"You tie me in knots, Kellie. I want you. Not just for tonight or even a couple nights. I want you." He searched for the right word. "Always."

She stood and paced the room with agitated movements. "You don't know me."

"No, I don't. But I want that to change. From the moment you walked into Harris's office, you turned me upside down. For years I thought I didn't want to be tied down. Then I met you. You're unlike any woman I've ever met."

"Why can't you just be happy with one night? I'm not made to last and go the distance. I have issues. It's not fair of me to lay them at your feet."

He stepped forward. "I don't care. Let me in. Dammit, Kellie, I'm falling for you hard and I'm not ashamed to say it."

She turned away but not before he saw the light sheen of tears in her over-bright eyes. "Darryl." Her voice was soft and full of agony. He strode to her and pulled her against him, wrapping his arms around her.

She trembled, her skin ice cold. He kissed her lightly on the forehead. "Trust me."

She pulled away from him with a jerky movement, staring at the nearby wall. "When I was sixteen, I was raped. I couldn't stop it. He was just too strong." She hugged herself tightly. "The bastard shot me and left me for dead."

Darryl recoiled as his gut twisted painfully and a burning rage ignited inside him. He forced it away. Now was not the time.

She slid her fingers into the silky tendrils of her hair and flipped a section across her head to flop down the other side. He moved closer and caught the scar at the side of her head where the bullet had grazed her. She'd been damn lucky, and that meant he was too. A few inches to the right and he'd never have met this wonderful woman. He traced the line of her scar. She tensed at his touch. He couldn't help himself as his lips followed the path of his finger. It would've hurt like hell. He was amazed at her strength. He didn't admire many people—only his father, his brothers, his colleagues, and now Kellie.

"I don't like guns," she said. "Every time I'm close to one, I turn to jelly."

Which explained that afternoon and how shell-shocked she'd been after the last gunshot. He once more swept her into his arms just so that he could feel that she was alive. It had happened long ago but for him, it had only just occurred and his hand shook with emotion as he ran his fingers over her hair.

"Did they ever find the arsehole who did this to you?"

He hoped not, because he would love to meet the man who'd hurt Kellie and rip him limb from limb. His level of hatred and rage toward the man surprised him.

She shook her head. "Unfortunately, no. I'm just another of Harbour Bay's unsolved crimes. Believe it or not, there's quite a few, and it wasn't from lack of trying on the part of the detective. In fact, I was surprised at his level of determination." She glanced up at him and pinned him with a look. "Don't feel sorry for me, Detective," she warned.

"I don't." He saw that his words shocked her. Had she been expecting pity or sympathy? Was that what she'd received from everyone who knew the truth about her—even Amelia? His response had her studying him closely for signs of lying. He stroked her cheek and marvelled at the softness beneath his fingertips. "I believe what happens to you in the past makes you what you are today. And I happen to like the woman before me very much. You have strength very few people have and a heart of gold. I don't know many people who would put up with Donovan this long."

She smiled and his heart expanded at the sight. He'd been ruined for all other women. But that was okay because he had his heart set on this one. He wouldn't give up on her no matter how hard she fought him.

"Kellie," he said softly, as he leaned down and placed his lips on hers. They were soft and malleable beneath his own. The passion within him ignited once more as she began kissing him back. His tongue slipped inside her mouth and stroked hers. Her skirt slid over her hips to puddle on the floor as he lifted her easily. Her arms stole around his neck even as her legs wrapped around his waist. Her back hit the wall as he pressed himself against her. It was like they'd never stopped, picking back up from the moment he'd broken the sensual haze. He caught the hem of her blouse and raised it up, tossing it across the room as his gaze moved to breasts.

She had lovely breasts, small and pert beneath the lace bra. He growled and quickly removed the offending article of clothing. His gaze feasted on her hungrily before he leaned forward and took one pink nipple into his mouth and delicately sucked on it, causing her to arch her back and moan.

He took his time teasing the bud until it hardened, then moved onto the other. Kellie dug her nails into his shoulders as his hands freely roamed her body. When he reached the junction of her legs, he slipped beneath the edge of her panties and into the warmth of her body.

She rode his hand as he moved his finger within her, his thumb finding the pleasure nub hidden beneath her folds and applied pressure.

Her head thrashed back and forward on the wall as little mewling sounds escaped her mouth. Her desire-filled gaze caught his as she climaxed, and he swallowed her shout of pleasure as he pressed his lips to hers. Kellie went limp in his arms, her softness nestled against his straining zipper. Small beads of perspiration dotted his forehead with the effort it took not to follow her into sweet release. He held her close and made his way down the hallway to her bedroom, placing her gently on the mattress.

Kellie reached out and pulled him to her. He stood between her open legs as she worked on his zipper, gently sliding it down, allowing him to jump free into her waiting palm. She stoked the head with her thumb before sliding to the sensitive underside until he thought he would burst. When he felt her warm breath, he knew he would die soon if he didn't have her. She pulled his pants and boxers down together, pooling around his feet as he removed the rest of her clothing.

He pulled the condom from his wallet. He ripped open the foil packet and rolled it over his hard length.

She giggled at the fierce look he knew to be on his face as he leaned down and kissed her once more, positioning himself at her opening. She stopped when she felt him nudging against her and her face turned serious.

"No promises," she told him.

Darryl stroked a finger down her cheek. "One day at a time," he compromised before thrusting deep inside. She gasped and tightened around him and everything felt right with the world. He moved within her, setting a fast pace. She lifted her hips to meet his thrusts and soon they were both soaring through the sky.

Chapter 19

Under Toby's watchful eye, Michael knocked on the outer door to Coleani's office and waited for the answer. His hands betrayed his fear and he stuffed them in his pocket, praying he wouldn't embarrass himself by soiling his pants.

Please God, I beg you, get me out of this alive.

He prayed for a better life than the one he had. If only he'd had a better start, seen Coleani for the trouble he was, and made a deal with the cops. Dammit, he'd been so stupid and now he'd pay the price.

"Come in," Coleani's throaty voice called out.

He stepped into the office and walked over to the desk where the man himself waited. He didn't notice the plastic floor lining coating the concrete under his feet as he walked, his entire focus on the man who was either his savour or his executioner.

Michael swallowed, trying to dislodge the large lump in his throat that threatened to choke him, his mouth suddenly as dry as a cotton ball. Liquid fear ran cold through him, chilling him from the inside out.

"You wanted to see me, Mr. Coleani?"

He hoped the old man wouldn't hear the quiver in his voice. He ruthlessly pushed his nerves aside and held his head high to meet his eyes. His heart almost gave out at the unforgiving stare he received.

Coleani sat back in his chair and regarded him while he fidgeted under the scrutiny. "You messed up, Mikey," the older man told him, disappointment in his voice. "Now I have the cops coming to the restaurant asking me questions."

A shiver raced down his spine as if someone had just walked over his grave. He fought the second shiver the image evoked.

"I'm sorry, Mr. Coleani, I am. I didn't expect them—"

Coleani held up a hand, signalling silence. "You must now answer for your mistakes, Mikey. I will not bail you out of this. You must pay."

He let out a deep breath. He would gladly go to the cops and tell them his part in Kevin and Carl's murders, just so long as they protected him from Coleani.

"I'll do anything you want. I'll surrender to the cops. I'll confess and accept my punishment. I swear I won't utter one word about you," he promised. Twenty years in prison would surely be better than certain death. Maybe Coleani would be lenient, but he reminded himself if there was one thing that couldn't be associated with him, it was leniency.

Coleani regarded him coldly, a look that could turn grown men to stone. Michael lost control of his bladder, feeling the warm liquid running down his leg and smelled the ammonia wafting up to his nose. Tears burned in his eyes and for once he knew true heart-stopping fear.

He barely had time to react when caught movement out the corner of his eye. He half turned towards the man who'd just entered the office when the trigger was squeezed and nothing but darkness followed.

***

The body fell to the floor, dead weight. A neat round hole in the forehead. Blood and brain matter had splashed across the plastic sheet in a macabre pattern. Wayne Burton stood staring down at the body with distaste as he holstered his weapon.

"Well done, Wayne," Coleani praised him. "Now get that disappointment out of my sight."

Wayne nodded, surveying the damage he'd just caused before bending over and wrapping the plastic sheet around the body. He had done this before, so many times that he barely had to think about it, the actions merely second nature.

He had work to do tonight, and there was plenty of darkness left before the sun came up. Plenty of time to get rid of the body. He lifted it over his shoulder like a sack of flour, stopping only when he reached his car. He opened the trunk and placed the trash inside before driving to the local lookout. He dropped the body into the harbour without a second thought or a twinge of guilt.

The kid had failed Coleani, and that was

unacceptable. He was lucky to have gotten off easy, and the kid never saw it coming.

As Wayne waited for the body to get swallowed up by the water, he thought about what Coleani had told him before the kid had shown up. Kellie Munroe was alive and stirring up trouble. Years ago, he hadn't bothered to check the newspapers for details on the teen's death. There had been no need to because she should've died. It was certainly not for lack of trying on his part.

But she was nothing if not resilient. He had watched her from afar all those years ago. Nothing brought her down. No matter what life threw at her, she'd just soldiered on and persevered. Wayne remembered how hard she'd fought.

What kind of woman was she today? Full of fire and self-importance, he assumed, just like twelve years ago. A slow one-sided smile crossed his face. He would enjoy seeing her again. Like a fine wine, she would only improve with age.

A slow burn of anticipation spread throughout his body at the possibilities and he hardened in a painful rush. She'd always had that power over him, even as a teenager. He had often lain awake at night, wondering what it would be like to have her. His dreams had been nothing like reality.

He remembered every detail of that night. How she'd fought him until he'd finally overpowered her. She had no idea how the fight had his blood burning hotly in his veins, making him want her all the more. He still couldn't believe he'd missed. She should be dead. But he wasn't concerned. His freedom was proof he'd defeated her. Anticipation ignited a blaze inside him. He would see her again, and he looked forward to it. He'd never been able to recreate that fire, and knew she was the ingredient that made it so fine.

As a young man, he'd crushed on the blonde angel, fantasised about being with her, for her to look at him and *see* him. But that was all it would ever be—pure fantasy. She couldn't appreciate his kind. When Coleani had ordered her to be put down, he'd been overjoyed.

To taste her again would be bittersweet.

This time, he would finish the job he'd started twelve years ago.

He would make sure she died this time.

Satisfaction filled him, knowing he had a second chance, and he would take the memory of her to his grave. He reminisced over her futile struggles beneath him and grinned savagely. She would fight him harder this time, and the warrior in him revelled at the idea of taming her.

Soon, my dear, I will be with you again. But first I'll let you wonder when and where I might show myself.

Anticipation coursed through him as he planned to savour her fear.

You'll be frightened, won't you? I'd like to see you frightened. There is nothing more intoxicating…

He turned back to his waiting car, deciding to rectify the problem and make Coleani happy. Otherwise, he'd be the next body to go over the cliff and into the harbour.

He didn't plan on letting that happen. He'd

worked too hard to gain the man's trust and dependability. He was loyal to his master and owed him everything he was today. He wanted Coleani to announce him as heir to the old man's empire.

One day, he'd be running Coleani's enterprise.

But first...he would play a game with his angel. And then...he would kill her.

Chapter 20

Dick Coleani sat in the dark, a glass of two hundred dollar whisky in his hand. He took a sip, savouring it before swallowing, letting the honey-coloured liquid warm his stomach. If he drank enough, it would send him to a blissful place.

He frowned as he thought of all the time and money wasted on Michael Lambert. He had been one of the smarter boys, the one with the highest possibility of return on his investment, and now it was all for nothing. Michael had failed him, just as so many others had, just as Carl Benedict and Kevin Butler had. It was such a waste.

He couldn't find good help anymore.

He was getting old, but not so old that he could ignore such stupidity and greed. After all, he was the man who wrote the book on it. He couldn't believe the gall Benedict and Butler had. He couldn't comprehend how they'd believed they could get away with it.

Surely, they didn't think he'd simply allow them to poach on his territory. He didn't get where he was by being soft and forgivable.

He had worked hard, every day kissing the arse of every man higher than him, which in those days was just about everyone. He'd bided his time, taking notes and watching. Waiting for his time to shine.

Kids today—no one respected their elders anymore. Coleani had, though. He'd taken what his mentor had given him and been happy with it—right up until the day he had killed him and taken over the business. It was a move no one had tried with him.

Youngsters today didn't have the balls to confront him. They didn't have the courtesy to attempt to knock him off before they tried putting him out of business.

He showed them. No one crossed Dick Coleani and lived to tell the tale.

His thoughts shifted from his boys to an annoying blonde. She should have been taken care of a long time ago. He remembered the days when she had been a thorn in his side.

How she'd walked around his neighbourhood with her nose in the air thinking she was better than everybody else, better than him. He had been petty, though, and had taken his rage out on her mother. Jules Munroe had been so easy to break and use. She had practically begged him to do it. All alone in the world with a daughter to raise. She'd fucked him the first chance she got for a steady pay cheque.

It hadn't taken long for the novelty to wear off and the need to punish the teenager again rose within him. Added to her constant interference, he decided it was time to penalise her.

He had sent his best man to do the job. At the time, Wayne had been in his mid-twenties, Coleani's right hand man since he'd reached adulthood. He'd recognised the man's inner brutality from his youth, knowing he'd found an heir. A man he could trust. He hadn't been disappointed, not once in the years since.

Not until now.

But he couldn't blame Wayne entirely. The situation had been out of his control and it wasn't as if he hadn't accomplished the task Coleani had given him. Kellie had been sufficiently taken out of the picture. For the past twelve years, he had been free of her. Until Michael Lambert had inadvertently put Coleani back on her radar.

And if he knew her at all, she wouldn't be leaving him alone anytime soon. Kellie would be a pain in his arse until he could be rid of her. He knew she'd been investigating him, and practically declared war against him. He was prepared to meet her on the field of battle, but only one of them would walk away.

He tightened his hands into fists. Things were quickly getting out of hand. He was losing control over everything he held dear. All his hard work was being flushed down the drain because of stupidity. It was time to rein in his boys.

They were already making too many decisions on their own, taking stupid risks. Only today a group of his boys took it on themselves to lay siege on the LAC. Morons. Didn't they have a fucking brain between them? That was the last thing he needed—Harbour Bay Police parking outside his businesses.

He needed to clean house. He couldn't allow such free thinking among his people. They all needed to know who was boss and why. He wasn't about to tolerate insubordination.

He had worked too long and too hard to let everything fall apart now because his boys assumed they could do better than what he was offering.

Years ago, no one would've dared defy him. Now he found he was constantly being tested. That fact did not sit well with him.

He picked up the file Wayne had brought him earlier and studied the photos within.

What a waste, he thought as he stared down at the pictures of the boys he'd taken a chance on, given opportunities to.

He wasn't a man who abided failure or disloyalty and very few got second chances. First they had to prove themselves.

He took another swallow of the fine liquor as he waited for Wayne to return so that he could assign him another task.

Chapter 21

Alec Harris finished his glass of Scotch as he sat in the dark, his eyes narrowed as he stared at the front door, waiting for his daughter to come home. He ground his teeth in frustration. Sophie was already three hours past her curfew.

He knew she did it purposely to piss him off. But he wasn't in the mood for it, not tonight—not any night. He was already on edge after the assault on the LAC. The last thing he wanted was a battle of wills against his own daughter.

Sophie was headstrong, stubborn, and wilful and knew how to push him to the limit in a matter of seconds. She had also inherited more than her fair share of sass from her mother. The things he loved about his wife he hated in his daughter and it was just his luck to have passed on his shortcomings to Sophie.

He glanced at the small illuminated clock on the DVD player nearby and his blood boiled. If she had been a few years younger he would've tanned her hide for such insolence. She knew he wouldn't tolerate her being late home. The cop in him only enforced the insecurities of the father.

He knew full well what went on after dark and had no desire to see Sophie caught up in it. Why couldn't she just see that he was doing his best to protect her by asking her to follow such simple rules as being home at ten o'clock?

He'd sent Caitlyn to bed an hour and a half ago and his heart ached at the worried look on her face. She was always concerned when he and Sophie argued and knew without a doubt they would argue tonight. Neither of them were able to give an inch and both of them always stood toe to toe. He had a temper and Sophie was a match to his fuel.

If only he could assure Caitlyn he wouldn't lose his cool, but the honest man in him knew it was more than likely he would be lying. Just one more year and she'd be eighteen. She'd already told him she couldn't wait to escape his rules, and that she wouldn't heed them anymore.

Alec knew she planned on leaving home the moment she became an adult. It was his fault. It irked him that even when he tried to meet her half-way she pushed him into grounding her for weeks—hell, even months.

He would always worry about his daughter, no matter how old she got, no matter how capable she was. She was his little girl. Nothing could change that.

The lock clicked nearby and he instantly became alert. His stomach twisted in knowledge of the confrontation about to take place.

Sophie, the spitting image of her mother at the

same age—all blue eyes and blonde hair—came through the front door, her hair cut severely at the shoulders on a jagged angle. She held her shoes in her hands and was trying not to make any noise.

"A bit late, isn't it?" Alec asked from the shadows.

Sophie jumped. "I thought it was early, actually," she countered and his restraint slipped.

She always seemed to have a quip at the ready and always had to have the last word.

"Don't push me, girl," he warned. "One of these days I'm going to bug your phone with my own GPS and show up wherever the hell you are and drag you home kicking and screaming."

She squared her shoulders, preparing herself for battle, and Alec inwardly sighed.

"I'm not a child," she declared defiantly.

"You're my child. You think I like waiting up for you? Do you think I love our little wars each night? Because I don't, Sophie. I'm damn well tired of them."

"Well then, go to bed," she said, as if that was the ultimate answer.

"I wish I could. But as a parent I wouldn't be able to relax until I knew you were home safe. Don't you have any regard for me at all? Do you like knowing I'm worried about you?"

"Of course not!" Sophie yelled and crossed her arms under her breasts in a defensive gesture. "But I can take care of myself. I'm not stupid and I'm always careful. I never accepts drinks or lifts from strangers. I never go out alone but God, Dad, you smother me with your rules."

"You've been drinking?"

Sophie rolled her eyes. "Of course that's all you heard. Not alcohol, Dad, just soft drinks."

"You don't know what it's like for me, Soph. I'm a cop. I know what goes on out there. I've seen too many little girls never return home from a night out, too many parents broken hearted at having to identify their child's remains at the morgue. Hell, even Harbour Bay isn't safe anymore."

Why couldn't he have had a nice, non-troublesome daughter like his goddaughter? The daughter of Caitlyn's childhood friend, Bethany Bennett, was a few years older than Sophie and never gave her father grey hairs or mini heart-attacks. Not that her father would notice if she did. Bethany was very low on Dirk Bennett's list of priorities.

Poor kid. Alec had been surprised she had grown up in to the wonderful well-adjusted woman she was and not into some raging lunatic, or one of those girls who pierced everything in sight and had multi-coloured punk hair. While some might see her life as gifted, he knew it hadn't always been pleasant.

But Bethany was not his problem. Sophie was.

"Many people go through life untouched," she told him.

"And many don't."

"I wasn't alone, okay? Colin was with me. I was perfectly safe."

"Colin? You're still hanging around that lowlife, Soph? I thought you were smarter than that. That guy spells nothing but trouble and he's far too old for you," he lectured, knowing it would do no good and more than likely add to the damage.

"He's not too old for me. He's only twenty-four."

"That's too old," Alec thundered and moved towards her with intent. "He hasn't touched you has he? If he has—"

"You'll what? Put him up on statutory rape charges?"

"Don't test me, girl," he snarled. Where she'd gotten her two-pronged tongue, he didn't know. Not from him and certainly not from her mother.

Tears burned in her eyes and Alec wanted nothing more than to pull her into his arms and hug her like he had when she was a little girl. They had been so happy then. But she wasn't a little girl anymore and that was the problem.

"God, I hate you. You're such a—"

"A bastard, I know, but I'm a bastard who loves you," he said simply, and watched as the fight went out of her, leaving her limp.

It was hard to fight someone who told you that they loved you. Tears leaked over onto her cheeks and she refused to look at him.

"I love him, Daddy, and nothing you say will stop me. You can't control me forever."

Alec shook his head, suddenly very weary. Discussions with Sophie always sapped his strength. "I don't want to control you, sweetie, I just want to protect you."

She gave him a glare. "Well, I can't tell the difference with you. I'm not a little girl. I'm almost an adult and you should trust me."

"You're my daughter. I can't help but worry about you. It's part of my job, and I'm sorry, but I just don't like Colin. There's a quality about him that tells me he's no good."

"You've only met him once."

"Once was enough, believe me. I have a sixth sense about men like that. He's going to break your heart, sweetie, I just know it. What's wrong with the guys I've introduced you to?"

"What, those *boys*?" Sophie sneered. "The ones like Cade Watson who are too afraid to anger you by doing something you might not approve of? I don't want boys, Daddy, I want a man who isn't afraid of showing me a good time."

"They're good kids. Kids I can trust my daughter with."

"Kids you can intimidate." She sighed heavily. "I'm sorry for worrying you, Daddy, but I'm not sorry for staying out so late. I hate your restrictions and some days I really hate you. Some days I wish you weren't my father." She stormed up the stairs of their old Victorian home, leaving the knife twisting in his heart. A moment later, he heard her bedroom door slam shut.

Alec sank down into his chair, feeling the fine trembling of his hands. It wasn't anger that had elicited this response but a dead sense of grief. He had lost his daughter, had pushed her over the edge one too many times.

"Alec?" Caitlyn's sweet voice came to him in the darkness. He watched as her silhouette approached and he held out his hand. Caitlyn took it and allowed him to pull her into his lap.

Alec hugged his wife tightly, pressing his face into her soft hair.

"Is everything all right?" she asked softly, as she gently stroked his face.

"No," he replied, swallowing at the large lump in his throat. "I've messed up, Cait. She's really lost to us. I tried to keep her safe but all I did was push her away."

Caitlyn's arm wound around his neck and she planted a kiss on his forehead. "You did what you had to, Alec. No parent has this easy, and one day Sophie will realise we did what was best for her. We're all too aware of what goes on after dark."

"I miss our little girl, Cait. The one who met me at the door with a smile on her face and her newest artwork creation. Now she can barely look at me and when she does it's full of resentment and hate."

"She doesn't hate you," Caitlyn told him soothingly.

"Yes, she does. She told me so tonight."

"She didn't mean it. You remember when I was a teenager, I said all kinds of things."

He suddenly smiled at the memory. "You were a handful. But at least your sassiness was cute," he agreed, falling silent for a minute. "How is it that we gave her the worst of both of us?"

"I don't really see my sassiness as being bad. It's served me well from time to time."

He gave her an incredulous look. "It got you into trouble more often than not, if I remember correctly."

"Yes, but it was also the very trait that made you look at me—really look at me. I can't imagine my life without you and Sophie in it. I'm glad you were hard on me in the beginning. I can tell you I didn't appreciate it at the time but I do now." She stared him in the eye. "And mark my words, one day Sophie will too."

Alec didn't dare to hope. His daughter was more like him than her mother, and he knew exactly how he'd feel if someone tried to rule his life, make his decisions for him. There was no way in hell he would ever forgive them.

Maybe Sophie would be different. He sent up a silent prayer. It couldn't hurt. He would need all the help he could get. He loved his daughter more than life itself, and wanted nothing more than for her to be happy.

"I hope you're right, honey. I really do."

Chapter 22

Kellie stretched her body out beside Darryl. The early morning sunlight peeked through the slit in the curtains. She blinked at the brightness and tried to push the sleep from her mind. This was the first time she had ever let a man stay the night.

It was a turning point in her life. One she could get used to, she reflected. She ran her hand down his chest until she found her prize just below his naval. His morning erection was just beginning to show, and by the time she had explored him, it was fully awake and demanding satisfaction.

She hadn't told many people about her past, only a few within the LAC knew, which was why they had worked around her handicap. Then there was her rape, which even fewer people knew about. Amelia knew, of course. Those who knew included the detective who worked the case, the rapist himself, the psychologist she'd been assigned to, and her boss, Lewis Carlisle.

Now Darryl knew. What had possessed her to tell him the truth?

She had no answer. Temporary brain dysfunction due to sexual arousal, she assumed. He was certainly detrimental to her mental health. She'd thought one or even a handful of nights with Darryl would suffice. Now she wasn't so sure.

She rolled onto her side and placed a kiss on his chest as her hand began exploring his body. Her lips moved against his skin as she descended, taking pleasure in the soft sounds he made as her fingernails scraped lightly across his abs. She wrapped her fist around his arousal and pumped lightly, feeling him harden further from her ministrations. His hips rose and a guttural moan escaped his lips. Kellie leaned down and placed a kiss on the tip before taking him into his mouth. She relaxed her throat to take him deep, her tongue sliding along the sensitive underside of his cock.

Darryl held her head in place as she lathered attention on him. He tensed beneath her hand and knew he was close. She reached between his legs and cupped him, squeezing him lightly. He caught hold of her shoulders and pulled her up his body. She let out a frustrated breath and fought against him, annoyed that he was denying her.

Her nipples tingled as they rubbed against the hairs on his chest and she groaned, her excitement heightened.

"Next time, I promise," Darryl said, his voice husky. "Right now, I need to be inside you."

She practically purred at the admission and forgave him, then reached into the drawer of her bedside table and extracted a condom. Straddling him, she took her time to roll the latex sheath over

180

his length, feeling the pulse throb beneath her fingertips before impaling herself on him, feeling him deep inside, stretching her. She moved slowly at first, making sure she felt him every bit of the way up and down before moving faster and faster as her own body demanded release. She moaned his name as she climaxed, her body going into spasms as she collapsed on top of him.

Darryl kissed her sweaty forehead and mumbled *good morning* in her ear. She smiled and kissed his chest, catching her breath before lifting herself off him, almost orgasming a second time as her sensitised nerves reacted with the friction.

She flopped without grace back onto the mattress, her body sated. Darryl reached over and pulled her into his body and his heat had her snuggling in close to him. The blissful world of sleep enveloped her again as her heavy eyelids closed.

***

Kellie awoke an hour later to Darryl watching her sleeping, and she grumbled. Hopefully, she hadn't snored or drooled. It had been a long time since she'd slept—actually slept—with another person. She blinked to clear the cobwebs from her mind. Maybe when she was more awake she would appreciate the gorgeously naked man beside her.

"You're staring," she complained, around an unladylike yawn. She glanced over at him. The ivory sheet was pooled around his waist, highlighting the golden glow of his skin. She swallowed hard as desire flowed through her and pooled between her legs. She shifted to ease the throb.

His liquid chocolate gaze washed over her and her nipples tightened into hard buds. Darryl noticed and his attention zeroed in on them, burning her with the heat of his gaze. The sheet covering him tented in the most delicious fashion that had her unconsciously wetting her lips. After last night—and this morning—she thought she'd finally been sated.

"You're so beautiful."

Kellie snorted. She knew the truth of how she looked in the morning, complete with bed hair and morning breath. "I doubt it."

"You'll always be beautiful to me," he said, stroking her hair gently. His eyes told her more than his words. He believed what he was saying.

"You know the right thing to say."

She shifted closer to him and kissed him softly, tasting him. The fire built slowly and she moaned. Darryl pulled back and dropped a kiss on her nose.

"A good morning to you too."

She smiled and stroked her hand down his chest. She couldn't seem to stop herself from touching him. He was all hard where she was soft and the differences between their bodies fuelled her arousal.

"I like the way you feel," she told him huskily.

Darryl chuckled. "I can tell."

Kellie slid closer so that their bodies were touching and pressed against him. Darryl held her close and she snuggled against him, feeling cherished and safe. She settled her head in the crook of his arm and took a deep breath, enjoying his unique scent. She closed her eyes and savoured the moment. Too soon, they would need to get up and go to work.

Darryl stroked her back with his hand and kissed her forehead. Despite their many couplings over the past few hours, to Kellie this moment was far more intimate. They lay, their bodies entwined on the bed and listened to each other's breathing. She could get used to this.

Kellie suddenly stiffened. Could she even dare to hope that there would be a repeat? She knew she wasn't the best in bed. There was always a level of control she needed to exert at all times which made letting go out of the question. Her previous partners had given her pleasure but they'd had to work hard for her to achieve it. She figured she wasn't cut out for pleasure so intense she almost blacked out. Last night had proved her wrong.

Could she allow Darryl to slip past her barriers and into her heart? Could she permit herself to love and need him, to rely on him? He was one of the best men she'd ever met and her fear was debilitating. Trust had never come easy for her and she was afraid to give him any power over her.

Intimacy was a new thing for her. She liked her space. Which was why no one ever stayed the night. Not to mention she was prone to nightmares. The last thing she ever wanted to do was to scare the crap out of some unsuspecting guy or attack him in her sleep. She was afraid it would only be a matter of time before he thought her too high maintenance, and she couldn't blame him if he chose to take back the words uttered during passion last night.

"Where did you go in your mind just now?" he asked, seeming to notice her distraction.

"Nowhere."

"Liar." He took her hand and linked his fingers with hers. "Do you still see a therapist?"

His perceptiveness amazed her. "Sometimes when the nightmares become debilitating. Not so often nowadays, but they sneak up on me."

"When was the last time?"

"Yesterday morning."

He nodded. He must have figured that was why she'd been at the LAC so early.

"The doctor says it's due to the lack of closure in my case. That they'd probably go away once he's caught."

Even to this day, she could still smell him. Sometimes feel him on top of her, inside her. She could see his face when she closed her eyes and often had nightmares about that night. He'd been so strong she hadn't been able to fight him.

"I try not to dwell on it. It only gives him more power."

Darryl pulled her tighter against him and she kissed his chest, feeling the small hairs tickle her lips and chin.

"Tell me. How did Donovan react all those years ago?"

She smiled. "In typical Donovan Style. She huffed and puffed and harassed the detective. He pulled her aside one day and said, 'it's not as easy as it looks kid. If you think you have what it takes, why don't you give it a go?'"

"I guess I know how that ended."

Tears gathered. She blinked them away. At least something good came out of that horrible night. Amelia had fallen in love with the work just like Kellie had with Internal Affairs.

"How did you two drift apart?" he asked, breaking the silence that had fallen.

Kellie stared up at her ceiling. If she looked into his eyes, she would have refused to speak. She didn't want to see whatever he might be thinking or feeling.

"I wanted to forget. But every time I looked at Mia I saw how much she thought about it. She blamed herself for not being able to save me. As hard as I tried, it was always between us. She would never forget."

Back then, talking about it hadn't been an option. Her friend may have known all that had happened but not how deeply they'd affected her and she'd been unable to voice them. Until the end.

She hadn't meant to toss a friendship that meant so much to her aside, but by the time she'd come good it's been too late.

She'd not fought and that was her worst mistake. It was something she'd agonised over and until the other night hadn't thought she'd get the chance to explain and perhaps move on and start fresh. She was hopeful she can repair what she'd destroyed.

"In the end I left. I never meant to hurt her. I was selfish."

He rolled them to the side until she lay beneath him. He leaned down and brushed his lips lightly over hers at first, then applied more pressure. His lips moved seductively and a moan caught in her throat. Kellie clung to him as wave after wave of pleasure threatened to pull her overboard into the swirling abyss. Her toes curled and she arched into him.

"You are the bravest, strongest woman I have ever met. I am in awe of you," Darryl said when he finally broke the kiss, his voice ragged.

She blushed at his words and at the sincerity in his voice, then lifted her head and kissed him again. Her alarm sounded, startling them both. They chuckled at the reaction. He groaned and thwacked a hand over the incessant shrilling, effectively shutting it off. He stared back at her with eyes filled equally with promise and regret.

He ran a hand over his whiskered face. "I'd better go home and change."

She didn't want that morning to end. She didn't want the day to intrude on this magic, and she had a suspicion she might never experience it again. Her bottom lip protruded as she sulked and he took advantage of it and nipped on her soft flesh. Heat infused her, but he rolled out of bed before she could retaliate.

She watched with pleasure as he strode about the bedroom collecting his clothes before winking at her. He slipped inside the bathroom and closed the door, leaving her alone in bed.

Kellie collapsed against the mattress, aware of her pounding heart and the huge smile on her face.

Chapter 23

Amelia slammed the stack of papers, held together with an alligator clip, down hard on the café table. The cool salty breeze blew in from the nearby sea and the sides of the oversized fabric umbrella shading them from the harsh morning sunshine flapped loudly. Megan Bailey jerked up from the magazine she was reading to stare at her.

"Sorry," Amelia said.

"Rough night?" Megan inquired, concern in her voice.

Amelia fought back her irritation. It was not Megan's fault she'd been up all night, thoughts of Kellie, Coleani and their case rolling around her head. She took a deep breath and calmed herself. The case would come together and as for Kellie, it was all in the past, and should be kept there. Now she just had to figure out where they went from here. Now that she knew why Kel had left, she should be able move on. Unfortunately her emotions were rarely rational.

She didn't know Megan all that well, but it

187

wasn't for lack of trying on Meg's part. The tenacious woman didn't give up easily and continuously invited Amelia for coffee catch-ups every month and expected her at every birthday and annual holiday get-together she hosted. Amelia felt she simply ignored any attempt on her part to keep some distance between them.

Amelia liked her, as far as females went. She didn't whine to Amelia about broken relationships or half of the other bullshit most women seemed to complain about to their friends. She had known from the start that she was very sensible, which Amelia respected.

Megan always wanted the bottom line and wanted it from the start. She often reminded Amelia of herself, which explained why she allowed herself to accept Megan's invitations, although lately they were becoming demands rather than offers. Just another facet of her personality. If she wanted something, she generally got it, and for some reason she had decided she wanted Amelia's friendship and wasn't the least put off by her prickly thorns.

Amelia wasn't even sure what she had to offer in a friendship or any kind of personal relationship. Her social skills had always been lacking and she definitely didn't have anything remotely resembling tact. Most people took offence to her no-nonsense personality, except for Kellie and Megan. It was almost they were like magnets, all gravitating towards each other as they recognised something in the other that they appreciated.

She'd met Meg when the other woman had called the LAC for research on her first novel.

Through a twist of fate, her phone call had come to Amelia and she'd been intrigued with the storyline and the writer's enthusiasm. She agreed to take a look at the manuscript and comment on the police procedures in her fictional world.

The book had become a bestseller, and Amelia had just finished proofreading the second novel in the series, which was even better than the first. She wasn't one for giving praise unless it was well deserved, but she had to admit Megan's stories captivated her until the very end.

Amelia flopped down into the nearest chair. The promenade was busy as always, even early in the day, and seagulls squawked above as they circled looking for leftovers. She rolled her shoulders. "Terrible night."

"I'm sorry. Want to talk about it?"

"No. Thanks," she added, hearing the harshness of her answer. "Here's your manuscript. I've marked down some suggestions in the margins."

Megan nodded and took a sip from the straw sticking out of her iced tea, making no effort to reach for the stack of papers.

"Well, I'm here if you change your mind. Sometimes talking about the problem can help."

"What good would that do except piss me off more? There's no point."

Megan shrugged her delicate shoulders, her mahogany hair flowing around her head in soft waves as it fell over her shoulders. She was a gorgeous woman at five-foot-six, with a figure most women would kill for. Her small pert nose held a light sprinkle of freckles that was often covered up with a dusting of foundation.

"You have the world on your shoulders, Don," she said, using the nickname she had bestowed upon her. "Maybe it's time to spread the load a little. You can't fix everything that's wrong. You're just one person and it would be suicide to try."

Amelia let out a deep breath, feeling the tension inside her and knowing she needed to get laid. However, she had no viable candidate, so she would have to make do with the gym and something with a lot of sugar and calories in it.

"Yeah, well, someone's got to do it." She couldn't explain her issues surrounding her best friend's rape and how her actions had led a hurting Kellie to walk away. Shame filled her at how angry she'd been at Kellie all these years now knowing the things she hadn't been able to say at the time.

"You're good at what you do." Meg knew enough about her to be able to make the distinction, and often scolded her for working too hard.

"Enough about me." Amelia's thoughts were growing bleak and the last thing she wanted right now was a bout of depression. "How are things going with your cousin?"

Simply sitting and chatting was something she'd once done with Kellie, but after the *event* she had felt less inclined to do so. She missed it.

"Good. Stacey and I are getting along fine," Megan replied, and took another sip of tea. "I know what you're doing, you know. Remember, I write detective stories. Deflecting isn't it called?"

Amelia frowned. "I guess I could benefit from a few of those classes about dealing with people.

What are they called? How to make friends and influence people?"

Megan scrunched up her nose. "I hate those and I doubt you'd be able to survive one. You'd probably end up shooting the instructor." She smiled, obviously finding the imagery amusing. "Besides, I think you're pretty good on your own. So what if you're short? Some people like that. I like that about you, Don. Short and to the point. Your abilities lie elsewhere and they're even more valuable than social pleasantries. It's not as if you'll be charming the criminals you deal with to confess."

Amelia knew she meant every word; she never said anything just to soothe a bruised ego, and she had to admit the words were definitely a balm against her wound. It was nice to be appreciated for one's own worth.

"Thank you," she said stiffly, unaccustomed to such compliments and feeling slightly self-conscious. "Things are tense at the moment. I'm having a few things thrown at me and my new case isn't going the way I'd like it to." Amelia blinked, surprised she had spilled so many personal details.

"If I know anything, it's that you always get your man. I'm sure this time won't be any different. I only wish I could help you. You've done so much for me and it's not as if I have a lot of friends. I'm just as much a social pariah as you are, Don. All I have is you, Riley, and Stacey."

Riley O'Neill was a red-headed spitfire, Megan's editor at the publishing house that printed her books.

"If there is anything I can do for you, anything at all, let me know."

"I appreciate that, Meg."

"I mean it. After all, you did help make Cole Lilac into the detective he is," she reminded her, speaking of the character in her books. "So what are you having for breakfast? I'm in the mood for pancakes with maple syrup."

Amelia left Megan not long after, having indulged in an equally unhealthy breakfast. She was amazed at Meg's confidence in her. It was unsettling. When someone believed you could do just about anything, it only made the fall that much harder.

***

Darryl stepped into the Pig Pen and headed towards his desk.

"Hill, there you are. You're late," Amelia said.

He'd dressed in black slacks and a crisp white linen shirt, and hadn't bothered shaving, thinking how wonderful it would be to rub against Kellie's soft skin and leave his mark.

"Sorry," he muttered, avoiding her stare as he sat down in his chair. He removed his weapon holster and placed it inside the drawer of his desk under the watchful scrutiny of his partner.

A beam of sunlight streaked across the grey carpet from the large windows nearby and he wanted nothing more than to be back in Kellie's bed making love to her until they were both exhausted. Then, after that, he envisioned taking her down to the promenade for dinner or a walk on the beach. He didn't care which, so long as he was with her. Near enough to continue touching her.

"What's with you?" Amelia demanded, getting up from her desk and towering over him. Her dark gaze regarded him.

His brow furrowed. "What do you mean?"

"You've never been late. Not once. You're always here hours before your shift starts, sometimes even beating me here. Today you seem different." She looked him up and down, scrutinising him. Her eyes narrowed. Then she gasped. "You slept with her, didn't you?"

He launched from his seat and took her by the arm, pulling her a few steps away from their desks. "Keep your voice down."

Her face turned to stone, making her look even more formidable. She jerked her arm away. "You did, didn't you?" she accused, her voice softer this time.

"That's none of your business."

"Actually, it is my business because she's my friend. I won't have you using her to scratch an itch. Kellie is vulnerable." She checked the room, ensuring no one could overhear before continuing. "There are things about her that you don't know."

Darryl turned away from her. He had no plans to talk about what happened between him and Kellie. That was for them only as he continued reeling from the experience. They may have only just met but everything between them felt so natural, and he'd be damned if he'd share that with his partner. Besides, he wasn't interested in her warning.

"Relax, Donovan, she told me and that's the end of this conversation. I don't want to hear about this again," he said, a thread of steel in his tone.

"I'll make that decision, Hill. Told you what?"

Darryl stared into her eyes, his own gaze hard and unrelenting. "That she was raped."

For once Amelia was speechless, and Darryl savoured the moment. The look on her face was priceless. She placed her hands on her hips and glared at him.

"What else did she tell you?"

The air surrounding them turned cold and he sought to diffuse the situation. He knew sleeping with Kellie would open something they weren't ready to get into. But he didn't want to cause a rift between his partner and himself. They depended on each other in the field and trust was very important. The moment they decided to write each other off was the day they had to be reassigned.

And as much as Donovan was a moody, hard-hearted, temperamental, sometime rule-breaking bitch, she was also one hell of a cop who he respected the hell out of. There were few people he trusted enough to put his life in their hands, and she was one of them.

He held up his hands in surrender. "That's all. Look, I know she's your friend and I promise you I'm not out to hurt her."

Hell, he could be the one that got hurt. Kellie had her demons and if he wasn't careful she might slip through his fingers. He had no intention of allowing that to happen. Barely an hour since he'd last seen her and he already missed her like crazy. He ran a hand over his whiskered face. It was sad when a man couldn't stop thinking about a woman for five minutes. His bachelor days were over and he couldn't even muster up an ounce of regret.

Kellie had better get used to him being around because there was not a damn thing she could do to keep him away. Whatever issues she had, they'd work them out together. He would be there for her through the good and the bad because that's what people do when they love each other.

He was in love.

Crazy. Stupid. Love.

And he couldn't say he was sorry.

He'd always known that it would be a special woman to catch and hold his attention and Kellie was everything he wanted and more. He only had to convince her to give them a chance. Despite what he'd said last night, he knew she didn't believe him. She had baggage but it wouldn't scare him away. He liked a challenge and getting Kellie to trust in him without constantly having one foot out the door would certainly be that and more.

"Good," Amelia said. "Because she has been through enough to last three life times. If you hurt her, I swear I will hunt you down and make you pay in pain. Is that understood?"

He raised his eyebrow. "It's clear."

They glared at each other for a long while until two sets of footsteps sounded out, moving toward them. They turned in unison as Nick escorted Kellie into the Pig Pen. Darryl's eyes narrowed as he watched her, dressed in a pair of tight-fitting jeans and a white blouse, laugh at something Nick said.

His body tensed. Jealously hit him hard in the chest as he took in Kellie's expression and Nick's close proximity to her. The other man's shoulder brushed hers as they walked and he could see—feel—the easy friendship there. Darryl may have loved her body all night long, but he and Kellie didn't share a history like she and Nick did. Darryl's heart squeezed painfully in his chest as he remembered the morning the day before. Kellie had come looking for Nick and had found him instead. Had his colleague and Kellie slept together? It was common knowledge that Nick didn't screw around with women he worked with but he wasn't impervious. Had one of their heated training sessions spilled over into bed? Images of Nick and Kellie naked, their bodies entwined, danced through his head.

As much as he wanted a future with Kellie, he couldn't force her to feel something. She'd made it clear last night that she wanted nothing more than one night of passion. It was he who'd pushed the issue. Maybe he was a convenient lay. Could he simply step aside and allow her to walk away from him—even if it meant towards Nick?

He liked to think so but he wasn't sure. Despite his feelings, he wouldn't fantasise over a future only he wanted. He had his dignity. He had no issues fighting for what he wanted but he wasn't about to fight for someone who didn't want him.

Amelia roughly cleared her throat, bringing him back to the present. He frowned at her before his gaze drifted once more to Kellie and Nick. They all stared at him strangely and he wondered what they'd been talking about while he'd been busy contemplating.

"What?"

Nick grinned. "Did you seriously just growl at me?"

Kellie blushed and dropped her head to study her fingernail.

Fuck. Had he?

He ran his fingers through his short hair. There was no coming back from where he was headed. If the possessive growl at Nick for being too close to *his* woman slipped out without him being aware, how would he be able to let her go if she chose to walk?

Kellie glanced up from beneath her lashes and her gaze caught his. He felt the air in the room get sucked out. His stomach dropped at the sensual heat he saw there. His body reacted instantly.

"No," he croaked.

Nick appeared unconvinced but let the matter drop.

He seriously had to get a grip on himself. He sank down into his chair and pretended to be busy while he gathered his thoughts.

Amelia's desk phone rang and she reached over and plucked the handset from its cradle and answered with a perfunctory, "Donovan."

Darryl's gaze drifted to Kellie again but she was completely focused on his partner. She was so beautiful it hurt to look at her. Kellie could've easily been a model or a movie star. Her blonde hair was pulled off her face and secured in a tight chignon. She wore little makeup. No foundation, just blush and mascara. He would be more than happy to wake up next to her every morning for the rest of his life. She must've sensed his stare as her head turned towards him and an elegant eyebrow rose. He winked at her and she smiled, memories of what they'd done together clear on her face.

He was so screwed.

"Dispatch just got a call. A DB was found in the harbour this morning," Donovan said, interrupting his thoughts. "The floater's Michael Lambert."

Chapter 24

The body of Michael Lambert was fished out of the water and carried over to the tarp lying on the ground away from the water. First glance told her that he'd been in the water for hours, making any evidence he might have had on him unusable if not completely destroyed.

Doctor Eric Stone, Harbour Bay's Coroner, stood in gumboots down by the water's edge as he examined the decedent. The doctor was in his late fifties to early sixties and was almost a twin to Colonel Sanders of the KFC franchise.

Kellie had often heard him being referred to the white haired man behind his back, but he was well respected. He had worked for the city as coroner for over thirty years. His expertise in the medical field and as coroner had helped solve many cases, and he often went above and beyond his job description, taking the initiative to dig deep when nothing made sense. Nothing seemed to shock him, even in the small city of Harbour Bay.

"What the hell do you think you're doing?"

Amelia demanded as Kellie slipped on a pair of baby blue shoe protectors which looked like upturned shower caps over her boots. She had dressed casually today since there was a possibility they would be out of the office and she hadn't wanted to endanger Amelia or Darryl by dressing inappropriately. She was glad she had. There was no way she would've made it this far down the jagged rocks of the shoreline in a tight skirt.

Although she hadn't exactly been anticipating a dead body when she had chosen her outfit today, jeans were always a solid choice. Unable to bear losing the height she had grown accustomed to, had fished around the back of her closet for a pair of heeled black boots in order to have the best of both worlds.

Appropriately protected, Kellie straightened and followed her friend as she began walking toward Doctor Stone. She studied Amelia.

"Care to give me a hint as to why you're so pissed?" she countered. She hadn't been expecting such anger. She'd thought they were getting past that.

She concentrated on the uneven ground beneath her feet. The last thing she wanted was to fall on her arse or twist an ankle. As usual, Amelia steamrolled ahead, never mindful of the hazards. As far as she was concerned, the world could move for her rather than the other way around. If anyone else tried the Donovan way, they'd be screwed.

"You slept with Darryl."

Kellie lost purchase for a moment at the charge. Her heart raced at the near fall and she glared at her friend's back before moving quickly to catch up to her. Above her the sun shined hotly, her blouse sticking to her skin from the heat. A pelican circled overhead, unperturbed by the human remains.

"So what if I did? Unless you—"

"He's my partner. When I want sex, I look outside the LAC for it."

"Well, I won't apologise for it."

Her back was ramrod straight. Last night had been perfect. She'd *felt*.

For years she'd gone through the motions, working harder at trying to experience what came naturally for others than actually enjoying the carnal act. Darryl was a special guy. One who saw through her flaws and still wanted her. A man who could make her smile with just one look, and turn her on so completely that she became more than ready for him.

What was it about him that made her cautious attitude go out the window?

She wasn't a loose woman by any means, but the idea of lying beneath him had been too much. She certainly never slept with anyone she worked with. Until now. She didn't regret it—couldn't. It had been too wonderful. Too perfect. And she'd opened up to him. She'd never done that with any of her previous partners.

Not that she'd had many.

Only a handful and they had never lasted long. They fooled around a bit, then she'd walked away. Sex but no entanglements. Just the way she liked it. Until Darryl. It both scared and excited her.

Amelia glared at her. "You're being reckless."

"This…from you?"

"You work with him. Office romances never work out. I don't want to see you hurt again."

Tears burned in her eyes at the inflection in Amelia's voice. Deep, unresolved pain sat beneath her cool façade. Would Amelia ever forgive herself for the past she couldn't control? She'd thought explaining her actions would help but maybe she'd only made matters worse.

"He makes me happy."

"You barely know him."

Kellie shrugged. "I'm falling for him," she confided softly, the sound of her voice almost getting swallowed by the sound of the harbour washing against the rocks.

Amelia swore. "You make it really hard for me to protect you."

"I don't need protecting. Not by you, not by Darryl. One event does not define me. I'm stronger than ever, physically and mentally. It may fail. But nothing ventured, nothing gained, and he's worth the effort."

"Even if it gets you hurt?"

"If it wasn't for pain how would we know we're living? I haven't in a long time, Mia. I've existed and the world tasted like ash. Now there're vibrant colours surrounding me and flavours bursting on my tongue. Darryl awakened a part of me that's been dormant. I'll ride the wave wherever it takes me."

She broke away from Amelia, knowing her friend didn't understand. She hadn't been lying when she'd said she hadn't lived and merely existed. Kellie couldn't remember the last time she'd felt anything, even when it came to training with Nick. At first, she'd fought as if her attacker was before her. Passion and anger had ridden her hard. Then, it had all died away leaving her hollow.

In one night, Darryl had pushed past her defences and looked into her soul. She was frightened of what she felt for him, but feeling too much—enough to shatter her—was better than feeling nothing at all. She trusted Darryl. It hadn't been anything he'd done. It was instinctual and since that night twelve years ago she'd learned to trust herself.

Kellie turned her mind away from thoughts of him. There would be plenty of time for reliving those sweet memories when there wasn't a dead body demanding her attention. She knelt down beside Michael Lambert.

She allowed a moment of grief before pushing it aside.

If only he'd been smart enough and turned himself in. He could've been sitting in jail right now, not on his way to the morgue.

Kellie studied the still form and suppressed a shiver. It was the first dead body she'd seen in person. All the others had been photographs inside a case file. It felt different in real life, not as she had suspected. He was pale and lifeless, but he looked normal—other than the hole in his forehead.

Even her non-medical training had provided her with the cause of death. A gunshot wound to the head, blowing his brains onto the plastic he'd been wrapped in.

Had the murderer understood the rudimentary basics of how tide flow worked, he would've known dumping a body into the water at the end of high tide was not the best time to relieve yourself of evidence without weighing it down first. But his mistake was in their favour. When tide had gone out, the body had remained, easily spotted by an early morning fisherman who'd caught sight of something other than a fish.

Kellie watched as Doctor Stone did a preliminary examination of the body, checking his pockets for possible evidence. The plastic wrap was removed and placed into an evidence bag.

"Tell me, Doctor Stone, is there any evidence of torture or bruises of any kind that would suggest he suffered prior to death?"

Stone shook his head. "No, the boy was lucky. I doubt he even saw it coming."

Kellie let out a deep breath. He may have been a double murderer, but the thought of anyone being tortured sickened her.

"His killer was a good shot. Quick, efficient," she said, remembering how inadequate her would-be killer had been.

In comparison, Michael Lambert had truly been lucky. He had been saved from the fears and psychological issues she'd dealt with. To be so close to death, to relive the fear, the helplessness, whenever she let down her guard.

Doctor Stone raised an eyebrow at her somewhat callous statement.

"I just mean it could've been worse," she explained. "More painful if he hadn't died. Efficient is more humane."

She caught Amelia's gaze, knowing her friend understood where her mind had been. She turned away from her perceptive stare, still stinging from their previous conversation, and watched as Doctor Stone zipped the black body bag shut and prepared to have it lifted onto the stretcher nearby.

***

Twenty minutes later, they were back at the LAC. Kellie was fuming. Once again Coleani would get away with murder. She had a horrible taste in her mouth she couldn't get rid of. She was sick of being unable to get him off the streets. He was a parasite feeding off the unfortunates, roaming the city free. Anger made her stomach clench painfully.

She paced in front of Darryl and Amelia's desks, agitated. The ten desks were divided into two rows that faced each other with a small aisle between them. At the desks on either side of them, Nick and Dean had their heads down, engrossed in their individual tasks.

"I can't take this any longer," she said, turning to Amelia. "I want you to crawl so far up Coleani's arse it makes the Taxation Office look good." Amelia raised an eyebrow and glanced over at Darryl as Kellie continued. "One of his lieutenants would have made the kill shot, and we need to find that man and put pressure on him."

"What makes you think we can get him to open up when we couldn't with Lambert? And he was nothing compared to Coleani's inner circle," Amelia stated.

Kellie wrapped her arms about her stomach in an effort to ease the pain. "I'm not thinking about getting them to roll over but about connecting his crimes to Coleani. We may not be able to get him on murder, but an accessory is just as good. At least for the first part."

Amelia smiled. "You mean we get Coleani here on any charge we can find and we'll be able to obtain warrants to go through his properties. It could work if we find something. He isn't as smart as he thinks he is. Only manipulative. It's a sound plan."

She nodded. "You almost sound surprised. Let's access the records from the youth centre and cross reference the names with those working for a Coleani establishment, and see who also checks out with the Department of Corrective Services."

Her blood sang inside her body. For the first time since she'd been handed the case, elation filled her, the possibility of finally nailing Coleani's arse to the wall giving her a high. "He always found the ones with a shitty home life, which makes what he's offering look like nirvana. The Department of Community Services will no doubt have a record of these kids. Domestic disputes and neglect are high on the list. At some point an officer would've been appointed and the child placed in a foster home."

Darryl spoke up. "Well, Coleani's enterprises are spread right around his territory and that's quite the large area to cover. Anything south of Broad and north of Colander is his. That's about…what? A twenty, twenty-five block radius? How many business deeds are in his name?"

Amelia went to her computer and typed his name into a database. Within a minute, the many results appeared on her monitor. Kellie peered over her shoulder.

"Okay, he has fifteen businesses, including the youth centre, strip club, and restaurant. The rest are low yielders, probably nothing more than a way to launder his money," Amelia informed them.

Darryl joined Kellie, and she felt the heat of his body, yearned for him to wrap his strong arms around her and chase away the chill. She savoured his scent as it unfurled in her lungs, subtle, yet it still unhinged her. She would never forget that smell for as long as she lived.

"That's not even mentioning the businesses he shakes down once a week," Nick added, jarring Kellie from her distracting thoughts. "There's no doubt Coleani feels they belong to him simply because of their locations."

"A man's got to be able to pay his minions some way. Why not employ them in his businesses? That way you get the hired gun and the free labour," Dean said.

"You've thought way too much about that," Amelia commented.

He shrugged, continuing to type up his report, while Nick studied the large map of Harbour Bay pinned to the wall. Amelia had marked Coleani's territory with a red marker.

"I never realised just how much of this city is under Coleani's control," he stated.

She nodded. "I know…and seeing it outlined like that. How can one man exert so much influence?"

"Easy when you start moulding children into doing your dirty work. Kids are so susceptible. Especially when they come from broken homes," Dean said. "He obviously tests the kids, has them commit a crime just so there's no out. No place to turn should something go wrong like having second thoughts. It's a hold on them that gets them to move further into Coleani's lies."

"Start small and progress onto bigger and better things," Darryl finished.

"Like murder," she said, shivering.

Amelia frowned. "Kellie, maybe you ought to think this through before you lay a full attack on Coleani. He will fight back."

She wasn't interested in warnings. "Amelia, get me the names or I'll get them myself."

Raising her hands in surrender, she replied, "Just some helpful advice, Kel. Don't worry, I won't be offering it again anytime soon."

"I'm sorry, Mia, I didn't mean to snap."

"All right then, as long as we're on the same page. You know I'd look out for you to hell and back. So, what are the other parameters for the search?"

Amelia turned her full attention to her computer screen and began typing into the search fields while Kellie mulled over the question. She nibbled on her lower lip as a frown creased her forehead. "Coleani desires loyalty above all else, and you don't get into his pocket until you prove your worth. So focus on the older ones. The men who've been with him the longest."

Amelia nodded and continued to type. The computer beeped as it finished searching and brought up the results. The first picture was the behemoth of a man that had brought them to Coleani at his restaurant. His name was Aaron Huber.

Darryl leaned forward. "That's the man from the restaurant."

She skimmed his rap sheet. The usual offences were there—assault, credit card fraud, car theft, and drug possession.

Amelia kept flicking through the digital files of those within Coleani's employ who were also registered at the youth centre and DoCS.

After five minutes of searching through Coleani's recruits, who each had a record to call their own, every mug shot began to bleed together. Tattoos of every design and colour filled her head until she had to work to see the images.

She yawned. The day had been long and exhausting; the discovery of Lambert's body knocked what little energy she had left out of her. She sipped on a mug of strong coffee, which gave her a zing, evident in her annoying habit of tapping her fingernail against the porcelain mug.

Twice, Amelia glared at her. She ignored her. She was on a mission, along with the collective efforts of Harbour Bay's Detective Unit, and together they would bring Coleani down. She could feel it. Excitement began to restore her depleted energy level, making her edgy.

They were close to being free of him. For all of

Coleani's people to be free, to be able to live their lives without fear. She pulled at the clip in her hair, freeing the strands, placing the clip in her pant pocket as she watched another face flick across the screen.

She blinked, adding moisture to her dry eyes. Around her, voices murmured, and Dean's keyboard clicked as he continued writing up his report. It was one thing she didn't like about the job—the countless reports detailing everything that happened during their shift, from the mundane to the downright bizarre.

The air conditioning unit huffed like an out of shape man running up a steep incline, humming continuously as it pumped out chilled air into the stuffy room.

A photo of a man in his thirties, appeared on the monitor. His brown hair was greasy and his face sported several days' worth of growth. Kellie blinked as Amelia hit the enter button, bringing them to the next photo.

Gripping the back of Amelia's chair, Kellie's breath rushed out and she gasped. "Wait. Go back to the last one."

Something about her voice had Amelia glancing over her shoulder at her. She jerked her head towards the monitor and impatiently waited for her to hit the back button, bringing the picture onto the screen. Kellie studied the image, the sharp facial bone structure with an aquiline nose.

His dark obsidian eyes seemed to pierce her soul as the image seared her while a fleeting memory played across her mind. The face of the man leaning over her in the moonlight as he raised the twenty-two that had almost killed her.

Her heart stopped briefly before beating frantically in her chest.

So this is what a panic attack feels like, she thought as her legs gave out.

Darryl caught her before she hit the ground and held her upright, while Amelia vacated her chair. Together they guided her onto the seat gently as if she might shatter.

"That's the man." Her voice trembled. She hated how weak she sounded.

Years of not knowing, of never believing she would find him, and there he was right in front of her. Where she least expected him. She struggled to regain control of her body.

"You know who that is?" Darryl asked, concern etched on his face. Concern for her. She swallowed hard at the lump in her throat, nodding.

Amelia studied her. "Who is he?"

"The man who raped me."

Darryl's hands tightened around her arms where he held her. Nick and Dean abruptly turned their heads in her direction, the movement drawing her attention. Her face flushed in mortification. She'd forgotten they were there, though she'd always suspected Nick had guessed something of her past. She shivered when she caught the unrestrained anger in their eyes and bodies. They both remained silent which helped her unwarranted embarrassment.

"Wayne Burton," Amelia read from the screen.

The devil has a name.

She recited his list of crimes and was surprised to find no mention of rape. Assault and drug possession made sense; he'd been particularly aggressive with her.

"Kellie, are you sure?"

"Believe me. That's the one face I'll remember until the day I die. Can you bring up my case file?"

Amelia leaned over and typed her name into the case retrieval program. The digital copy of the report filed and photos taken came up immediately on screen. She flicked through them, quickly reading the description Kellie had given to Detective Graham. It fit, that much was certain. But it also fit a lot of other men too.

Kellie frowned. "It's gone. The facial reconstruction I did with the sketch artist is gone. Coleani must have gotten to it."

"He wouldn't want it to blowback in his direction," Amelia stated.

"You two never thought of having the detective check into this before?" Darryl asked incredulously.

Amelia shook her head.

"There was no correlation at the time," Kellie said. "It never crossed my mind that it could have been one of his boys carrying out orders."

She'd never once believed he'd strike out at her, but if Wayne Burton had attacked her, he'd done it with Coleani's approval.

Kellie rose to her feet, fighting a head spin as she stormed off towards the elevator.

Chapter 25

Kellie pulled into her driveway too fast, slamming on the brakes and stopping just inches from her garage door. She jerked in her seat as the safety belt prevented her from flying forward.

Stopping her vehicle beside Kellie's car, Amelia climbed out and waited for her to join her. She was wasting her time. She wasn't interested in anything she had to say at the moment. Her world was spiralling out of control and she fought to make sense of what happened to her one night twelve years ago.

Had Coleani really been behind it all?

She knew he hadn't liked her scaring away business, but to go as far as to remove her from this world into the next? Should she really be surprised? He was a brutal man who would have no compunctions killing anyone if it served him a purpose.

She located her house key on the chain and after several failed attempts finally unlocked the door. She made her way through the dark house, Amelia following behind turning on the lights as she went.

"Kellie, calm down. What are we doing here?" she asked as Kellie opened the door to her bedroom and walked into her closet, pulling at the boxes resting on the shelf above the neatly organised clothes.

She found the box she wanted and dumped it down on her bed which was still rumpled from her sexual exploits. She ignored the rush of delightful memories as she pulled the cardboard top off and stared down into the miscellaneous mixture of photographs she would one day organise into albums. She sifted through the box, moving things aside until she came across the piece of paper she'd been looking for. It was folded down the centre twice, just slightly smaller than a photograph. She unfolded the twelve-year-old paper and looked down at the artist's rendering of the man she now knew as Wayne Burton.

Her stomach churned. Her sixteen-year-old mind remembered everything. Like she had said, it was the one face she wouldn't forget. He'd been drawn several years younger than the mug shot but the likeness was there. He'd raped her and attempted to murder her. Had it not been for two people who'd happened to walk by, he would have succeeded. Her throat constricted as the contents of her stomach fought for freedom. She instinctively placed her hand over her mouth as she ran for the nearest bathroom.

She barely made it, dropping to her knees as she stuck her head into the porcelain bowl and made hacking sounds with her throat as she convulsively threw up. Amelia squatted down beside her and placed a reassuring hand on her shoulder as she removed the drawing from Kellie's clenched fist.

When she started to dry heave, she flushed the toilet and leaned against the cool peach tiles of her bathroom.

"I thought I was over it, you know. That I had finally moved on. I guess I was lying to myself. Here I was lecturing you on the topic. Maybe a little self-examination is in order."

"I don't think you'll ever really be over it. Not until we catch the son-of-a-bitch," Amelia replied as she stared down at the picture. "You were right. There's no mistaking him."

"We can't let him get away with this, Mia."

"*I* won't let him get away." She reached into her pocket and produced her mobile phone, pressing a number on speed dial. She recognised the timbre of Darryl's voice.

"It's Donovan. I want you to get out an arrest warrant for Wayne Burton. He's the guy."

Kellie heard him swear before she hung up.

"I'll let you know when I've castrated the bastard."

"You're not closing me out of this, Mia," Kellie said, outraged.

"Kel, listen to me. Let me do my job, okay? You know I won't let you down. But I can't let you continue on the path of self-destruction. You are too involved in this case, obsessed even. If you don't take a step back, I'll go to Harris and have you removed." She held up her hand as Kellie started to speak, effectively cutting her off. "Don't think I won't do it to keep you safe."

Kellie nodded her consent and Amelia embraced her, crushing her in a bear hug. It had been a long time since she had been held—a longer time since Amelia had shown anything other than contempt or guilt toward her. She hugged her back, feeling the tears burning her eyes.

"I'll leave it with you, Mia, because I trust you to get the job done. No matter the cost."

"There's a change," Amelia replied, grinning before heading back to the LAC, leaving Kellie alone in her house, barely holding onto her sanity and the anger simmering within.

Chapter 26

Kellie screamed, and the sound of her terrified voice woke her from her nightmare. She gasped for air, her breath caught in her throat. Her body jerked into a sitting position, her nightie soaked with perspiration. She trembled as she climbed from the bed and had to grab hold of the wall when her knees buckled. Her heart beat in a painful rapid tattoo. She placed a hand over her chest in an effort to ease the vice like grip.

She could still smell his rank breath and feel his hands upon her skin. Her stomach rolled. She remembered clearly how he'd stroked the chain around her neck down to the golden heart shaped locket she'd worn. A hard yank had the delicate jewellery snapping and in the next moment it was gone, most likely a disturbing keepsake.

She'd never been as terrified as when she'd looked down the long barrel attached to the gun. It had only been a stroke of luck that a noise startled her attacker which ultimately saved her life, the gun jerking in his grasp as he flinched, the bullet missing its target and grazing the side of her head as it exited the chamber. She touched the scar, imagining the acute pain. She'd welcomed the darkness that had surrounded her as the pain swamped her and for the barest of moments she'd thought she would never wake. The scariest part was that she'd been fine with that.

Tears slid down her cheeks, leaving a wet trail in their wake. She'd had the nightmare so many times. She moved into the bathroom and made herself take a hot shower, washing away the sweat and fear. The hot water warmed her chilled blood and helped chase away the remnants of her bad dream. The first few minutes were always the worst.

Soon, she would be fine and fully functional again, she just had to get past the petrifying fear first. She stepped out of the shower and dressed in a clean grey V-neck shirt and jeans. It was late—or rather, early—but there was no way she could sleep now. The adrenaline still pumped through her veins. Car keys in hand, she headed to the LAC.

***

Kellie stepped past the tall stacks of boxes that held decades of cases from all over Harbour Bay and the surrounding areas under their jurisdiction. Each sealed box contained the collected evidence from each case. She sneezed, the dust in the musty air tickling her nose and ignored the sadness that welled up inside her at the thought of so many unsolved cases. She tried to stop herself from thinking about how many people, like her, hadn't found closure. This was the place where murderers went free and hope came to die.

Part of the shared basement, next to the inbuilt gym, had been dedicated to all the cold cases that had gone through the LAC. Chain mail fencing surrounded the main core of the basement where the evidence was kept and continuously monitored by cameras and officers on shift.

Kellie found the M row and using the stepladder from the aisle, climbed up the metal steps and lifted a large cardboard box down from the shelf.

"What are you doing here?"

Startled, she almost dropped the box. She glowered at Darryl. His shirt had come untucked since she'd last seen him, a coffee stain on his red tie. His short light brown hair stuck up in tufts as if he had been running his fingers through the strands. Despite all that, he still managed to look utterly gorgeous and her heart began to race for an entirely different matter.

"How'd you know I was here?"

He smiled up at her. "I saw you park your car and head down." Darryl climbed to stand just a few rungs beneath her. "Amelia said you were obsessed," he added, motioning to the box she held in her hands.

"Wouldn't you be? After twelve years, this is the closest I've ever gotten."

She sat down on the top step and opened the box. Darryl moved to sit beside her. The heat from his body seeped into her own and she almost moaned aloud at the deliciousness of it. Despite the boiling hot shower, she still felt cold. Would she ever be warm again?

Kellie lifted a plastic evidence bag from the box and held the heavy weapon in her hand. Darryl's eyes widened. "Is that the—"

"The twenty-two he used to shoot me? Yes, it is, with my dried blood on the barrel. It was found tossed into a dumpster two blocks over from where I was shot. Wiped clean, of course."

She found the small plastic container with the discharged bullet they'd retrieved from the concrete behind her head where it lodged itself after gliding along her temple. The bullet rattled inside the container.

Darryl clenched his jaw. "We're going to get this guy, Kellie, I promise you that."

Tears spilled down her cheek. The tenderness and utter conviction in his voice was her undoing. She couldn't swallow back the sob that escaped and instead of being horrified over the emotional scene, Darryl simply pulled her closer to him and pushed her head against his shoulder. He wrapped comforting arms around her and held her tight.

Kellie felt raw. For twelve years she had battled her past alone. Had dealt with her nightmares and debilitating aftermath. Had managed to secure a position in the NSW Police Force despite her fear of guns and her inability to touch one. Now Darryl offered to fight her battles alongside her. He'd been her rock since the start of this case. What would she do without him?

She melted into him and allowed him to hold her while the storm of emotions played out. When the sobs subsided, she pulled back just far enough to look into his caring eyes and her stomach fluttered. She touched his stubble roughened cheek with the palm of her hand and caressed him before leaning in to kiss him lightly on his soft and sensual lips.

"Thank you," she said.

Chapter 27

Amelia sat at her desk looking down at the sketch of Wayne Burton. She tried to remember if she'd ever seen the man before, on the street, hanging around Coleani's establishments or even downstairs getting fingerprinted.

He was no stranger to the building, having been brought here ten times over the past twenty years for a variety of crimes. Surprisingly enough, not one of them had been rape. She didn't doubt Kellie's memory and the sketch only confirmed her ID.

She couldn't imagine the emotions that must be going through her friend at the present moment. Amelia recalled seeing her in the hospital bed. Her head had been bandaged, her blonde hair matted with blood. She'd looked so small and delicate covered with the thin blanket, her body hooked up to an array of beeping machines.

Her whole life she'd never needed to cry, but she'd wanted to, and had done so for Kellie when she'd gone home. She knew Kellie wouldn't have allowed her to do so in her presence—just as she wouldn't have if their roles had been reversed—so she'd bottled up her volatile feelings for later.

Never would she'd have guessed it would be more than a decade later before they'd be let loose.

***

Twelve Years Ago
Harbour Bay Base Hospital

Amelia stepped forward, toward the hospital bed. Her heart pounded in her chest and tears threatened to escape down her cheeks as she imagined the pain her friend went through, and continued to go though. From the moment she and Kellie had first met at school, they'd never been separated.

Until now.

Why had she left Kellie alone? Why hadn't she walked her home? All these questions filled her head only to have no answers. She should've been with her, knew that now, and allowed the blame to fall squarely on her shoulders.

Amelia shivered as she took in the sterile room. Clean and empty. There were no flowers or *get well soon* cards bar the Canna lilies—Kellie's favourite—that she was holding.

She moved closer to the bed and reached out to touch Kellie's hand.

"Don't touch me," she screeched as her eyes opened wide, sensing a disturbance in the surrounding air. Her body shook and the heart rate monitor beeped rapidly as her blood pressure shot up.

Amelia stepped back, afraid to set her off. Dark circles marred the soft skin of her face, light purple discolouration dotting her arms, neck, and face.

"Are you in pain?" she asked as she placed the flowers down on the table beside the bed.

"Not anymore. What are you doing here?"

"I'm here to see you. I wanted to make sure you're going to be all right." She stopped, her throat closing and she fought not to cry. Her friend was broken and in pain. Kellie had always been so full of life, until last night, when she had fought for that life almost to the last minute.

"I don't want to see anybody," Kellie informed her, her voice barely audible.

"Except me right, Kel, your best friend? We share everything, why would you think we wouldn't share this too?"

"This is something that can't be shared and I'd rather be alone when I go through it if you don't mind. I don't want anyone to know the details of last night."

"That isn't going to be happen, so get used to me being here." She glanced around the empty room. "Am I your first visitor?"

"They called my mum, but she had to work," Kellie replied and shrugged as if it meant nothing when in fact it meant *everything*. "What can you do?"

Amelia clenched her hands into fists. The rage she felt at knowing Kellie's mother left her only daughter to go through this alone was enough to put murder on her brain. She had never liked the woman but had endured her for Kellie's sake. As far as Amelia was concerned she was an utter failure at everything she did including raising her daughter.

Kellie said it was because of her father, that her mother had loved him so much that after he was gone a part of her left too. But Amelia didn't buy that crap. In her opinion Jules Munroe only cared about one person and that was herself. Kellie was just an ornament, like a plant that gets watered at the end of a long day's work.

The only time Jules spared a moment for her daughter was the first few minutes once she got home at seven in the morning after her shift and ate the breakfast her daughter made for her. But in Kellie's eyes her mother was doing the best she could. It just wasn't the best anyone hoped for.

Amelia never knew her own father. He'd left the same day—the same hour—he'd knocked up her fifteen-year-old mother, who was no peach herself. For the first five years of her life, Amelia moved from one floor mattress to another around the neighbourhood.

She survived on other people's kindnesses until DoCS had stepped in and removed her from her mother's lack of care. A week later, her mother's parents had come and collected her. They were for the most part unforgiving, determined that she did not follow their daughter's dark path, but they loved her. For the first time in years she'd gone to bed every night after bathing, her stomach full.

She didn't even mind brushing her teeth but her childish brain still believed her mother would come for her, that she wouldn't want to live her life without her daughter, and for years, Amelia had continued to believe it. Until one night when two police officers came to her grandparents' caravan with the news that Bree Donovan was dead, a victim of stupidity, and with it went Amelia's dream of her mother returning to claim her.

But the one constant in her life had been her grandparents. They'd fought at times, even drove her mad at their attempts to control her, but they did just about anything for her. She never lacked or wanted in her life, and she knew that should she ever call them, they would be there for her, wherever she was, ready to help her with whatever she needed.

A wave of sympathy went through her, knowing how alone Kellie was. How her own mother couldn't find the time to visit her in the hospital, a victim of rape.

Amelia felt grateful for those she had, but Kellie did have someone who cared—her—and she would do anything for her friend. She was everything to her, the air she breathed, the reason she got up in the morning, the sister she never had and her only friend in the world. She antagonised a lot of people, and Kellie was the only one to stick around after being introduced.

Amelia had always seen their neighbourhood as just another place to live. Moving around in her younger years like a nomad had made her settle in, had her thinking this was as good as it got. Kellie had always been different. She knew there was a better life out there and was determined to be a part of it. Amelia had seen the drug dealers and the prostitutes and thought nothing of it. That everywhere in the world was the same low grade rent, but now she saw it for what it was—human degradation. She knew now of the things that went bump in the night. It had been too late for Kellie.

She couldn't imagine the pain she felt, what she was going through, but it made her ache to know that her friend was hurting. If only she could take it all away. If only she'd been the one to be attacked and not Kellie.

Could she truly heal mentally, or was her friend doomed to remain fragmented? She itched to hold her, to comfort her the only way she knew how. Amelia wasn't the easiest person to love and people in pain weren't usually something she sought out. She had always been unable to tap into that part of her that gave people hope or comfort and she felt out of her league, but her friend needed her, now more than ever. Amelia was determined to give her something—anything.

"But I'm here. So that's all that matters. I'll be with you every step of the way."

Kellie shook her head slightly before wincing. "I don't want you here."

Pain, hot and sharp sliced through Amelia at the words. The voice speaking them didn't sound like the girl she had known for ten years, the tone dead and cool, so unlike Kellie's exuberant bouncy tenor.

"Kellie, please don't push me out. You're everything to me and all I want to do is help you. I couldn't be there for you last night, to stop him from hurting you, but I'm here now. Let me stay. Please."

"I don't feel like reassuring you right now. I'm

the one whose life has ended. I don't care about anyone else. I don't care how you feel. I only have room for me and I don't want you to know what he did to me."

"It doesn't matter to me. You're still Kellie, my best friend. No one can take that away from us no matter how hard they try. Concentrate on getting better but know that I'm here. That I'm not about to let anything else happen to you if it's the last thing I do. I promise you that, Kel."

"Just go away please. Let me deal with this on my own."

Amelia stared into Kellie's watery eyes and saw bleakness. She nodded, telling Kellie silently that she was fulfilling her wish and turned toward the door just as it opened and an older gentleman, dressed in an inexpensive suit, stood just in the entrance.

"Kellie Munroe?" he asked, his smoker's voice filling the room. "I'm Detective Ed Graham and I've been assigned to your case."

Amelia's eyebrow rose. Usually people in their neighbourhood avoided the cops like the plague, and she'd not known any that had willingly helped anyone whose address was in Coleani's territory.

"I didn't realise a girl like me would rank high enough to warrant a detective," she told the cop acidly. Kellie's sharp tongue hadn't diminished in the last few hours.

He moved into the room, closing the door quietly behind him. He brought out his notebook from his pocket and allowed it to tap against his thigh as he approached the bed.

"I don't care about your address or where you come from or what you do. I only care about the crime committed and the person left behind. I'm going to do everything in my power to find the man who did this to you," Detective Graham promised.

Kellie nodded, her hand trembling as she wiped the tears from her cheeks. Amelia had to admit he sounded sincere, like he meant every word. Time would only tell if he was a man of his word, and God only knew how few of those there were.

She refused to budge when he asked her to leave. He scowled before relenting, probably deciding it wasn't worth arguing the case or maybe sensing it might be best to keep her in the room. Kellie wasn't exactly stable and could crumble if left alone with an unknown man. She watched as Detective Graham surveyed Kellie on the bed. His gaze analysed her bandaged head and the few bruises that showed above her blanket. He raised his notepad and pen in preparation to write.

"Can you tell me what happened?" he asked.

"Haven't you people already taken enough from me? My clothes, swabs, photos. I've been poked and prodded and now all I want to do is forget this ever happened." A tear spilled over onto Kellie's cheek, rolling down to be absorbed by the white pillow under her head. Her hands shook slightly as she swallowed convulsively.

"I know this is hard for you, Miss Munroe, but the best bet I have in finding the scum that did this to you is with your cooperation. I need you to tell me everything."

Kellie turned her head away, her entire body

shaking beneath the blanket.

Amelia frowned and stepped forward, closer to her friend. "Must you do this now?" Amelia asked Detective Graham.

Kellie could only take so much, and Amelia was concerned with her state of mind.

"It would be easier to get the questions over with now, while the unfortunate event is still fresh in her mind." He turned back to Kellie. "I wish I wasn't the one to say this, Miss Munroe, but I don't believe you will ever fully forget what happened last night."

Amelia itched to lay her hand on Kellie's, but she sensed it would be of no help at the moment and would only hurt the situation. She crossed her arms over her chest to keep herself from temptation as Detective Graham continued.

"There is nothing to be ashamed or feel humiliated about, Miss Munroe. You are not to blame for anything."

Kellie turned her head slowly, her eyes red and weeping. "You've never been raped have you, Detective?" she asked as her chin wobbled. "Never had someone claim your body without your permission. Never had someone you'd never met before put his disgusting hands all over you, to rip and tear your clothes while he took away the only thing you had control over in life."

Kellie exhaled, shaking, as her hands linked together so tightly her skin paled. "Yes, I feel ashamed. Ashamed that I couldn't stop him, prevent him from hurting me. To save myself and fight back. Humiliated that he could so easily take from me what he wanted without so much as a proper fight, that he used my body, desecrating it, making me feel dirty, like a whore. Yes, I know, it wasn't my fault. But I should've known better. After all, it was Coleani's neighbourhood, and I knew what might be there, so I should've been more cautious."

Detective Graham moved closer and looked down at her in compassion, like a man who was thinking of his own daughter and imagining her in the same position.

"It wasn't your fault, and while you may not see that now, one day you will. Instead of sitting there wallowing in self-pity—"

"Hey," Amelia said, interrupting him. "You're out of line."

"You should help me catch the son-of-a-bitch so that we can hang him up by his balls," Ed continued, as if Amelia hadn't spoken.

Kellie cracked a wry smile. "What is it you want to know, Detective?"

He nodded and Amelia could see the glint of admiration in his eyes as he took in Kellie's small form and fierce personality. "What can you remember about the man? What did he look like? Feel like? Anything you can tell me will help me. There are no wrong answers or stupid insights. Just tell me everything."

Kellie nodded and Amelia could feel the effort she used to stay calm and in control. She bit down on her lip, hard enough to draw blood. After what seemed like an eternity, she spoke with a quaking voice.

"He smelled like smoke and bad B.O. His eyes were dark and his hair was either brown or black. I can't tell much more because we were in the dark but sometimes when he moved a strand of moonlight would hit his head and I could see the grease in his hair."

Amelia rested her hand on Kellie's shoulder. There was no sign that she even realised it was there. She was clearly locked inside her mind full of nightmares. "He was rough and I don't just mean the sex. It was his hands. He was strong. He had me pinned in a matter of seconds and there was no way to break his hold. No matter how much I wanted to."

She dropped her chin, a blush rising from her neck.

"Did he wear a condom?"

Kellie's head jerked up in surprise. "I'm, um...I'm not experienced enough to know the difference," she struggled to say. "I didn't see one but then I wasn't paying attention for that sort of thing, you know."

"That's fine. You did good. I'll check the rape kit for semen. I assume the nurses treated you with the normal after rape cocktail—anti-pregnancy pill and such?"

This time, both girls blushed. They weren't women of the world and didn't try to be. They were both innocents, or at least until last night they had been. More than Kellie's virginity had been taken. Her carefree and trusting nature also went, along with her mental health.

Detective Graham returned his notepad and pen to his pocket before offering Kellie a smile. "You're a very smart and strong girl." He handed her his card. "Any questions, anything at all, give me a call. Days, nights, weekends, public holidays, I'm always available."

"Not much of a life, Detective," Amelia said.

"Nope. Long hours, bad pay, and mean people."

"Then why do you do it?"

"To clean up the streets. It's a big job but someone has to do it. If only to make the world safe. It's not one hundred percent fool proof, but I'm trying. Rest up, Miss Munroe, and heal. I'll be back later with an update, I promise."

He paused long enough to pat Kellie's shoulder before walking out the door. It was a brief, barely there touch, the detective knowing that any longer would most likely send her into hysterics.

"He seemed nice," Amelia said into the silence that followed his departure.

Kellie nodded but didn't say anything. She leaned back heavily against the pillow, exhausted. She closed her eyes. Believing her to have fallen asleep, Amelia pulled the visitor's chair closer to the bed before she sat down.

"They said I'm lucky to be alive." The sound of Kellie's tired voice startled her. She half laughed, half sobbed. "I wanted to die. I begged and pleaded for the end. I just gave up."

***

Amelia jerked as her desk phone rang, pulling her from the horrible memory. She had never heard such desolation in a voice before and the words had rung inside her head for years after. She'd never been so helpless in her entire life then that day. The day her best friend had told her that she had wished to die.

It wasn't long after that day that she and Kellie had begun to drift apart. She admitted now she'd overcompensated, hovering over her friend who hadn't appreciated her protectiveness at the time. It hadn't stopped Amelia from checking on the case. She'd hounded Ed Graham ruthlessly for answers. He'd done his best to bring Kellie justice, but the leads had gone cold and there wasn't anything more he could do. Amelia understood that now but it didn't stop her from raging at the world.

Years later, when she'd joined the LAC, she'd met up with Ed for coffee often. He'd mentored her for years and had helped her cope through the injustices of the world, the crooked legalities that had more than one criminal walk away scot free. He'd been her sounding board, her voice of reason when she'd had none and if it hadn't been for him, Amelia knew she wouldn't have made it this far.

Amelia pushed away the past and answered the phone. Dean Matthews's voice came through. "Donovan, you won't believe what I'm looking at."

"I assume you're not going to make me guess?"

Dean chuckled. "Nope. I'm looking right at the black Honda CRV Prescott said he saw at the LAC when it was shot up."

"How do you know it's the right one?" Amelia sat up straighter, her blood sizzling with anticipation. Dean had her full attention.

"Well, for one, it's here at Coleani's little ghetto. Two, there's a bullet mark on the back. And three, it looks like it's about to be burnt to a crisp. So if you want to catch the S-O-Bs who thought they could attack the LAC and get away with it, you better get down here quickly."

"We're on the way," she said, and hung up. She immediately retrieved her weapon, then grabbed her mobile and called Darryl.

Chapter 28

The Houston building, a decaying dump, caught Kellie's attention as the Commodore pulled up beside Detective Matthews's unmarked vehicle. The man himself was leaning against the chassis waiting, his chest already covered with a bulletproof vest, his gaze never leaving the building even as they approached.

"They're still in there. I only saw three of them exit the CRV but they were real nervous. Then they starting stripping the vehicle until they were interrupted by another man. Older. Authoritative. I didn't recognise him but they all followed him inside."

"Probably one of the lieutenants," Amelia said.

"More than likely," Dean replied.

"How many do you suppose are in there?" Kellie asked as she stared at the building. She had lived in one just like it for years with her mother. Her building had been torn down five years ago, and a new service station stood on the land.

Dean shrugged, merely lifting one shoulder.

"Who knows? I've seen kids coming and going all day. You'd think they were giving out free Xbox games in there, considering the foot traffic."

"How do you want to handle this?" Darryl asked Amelia.

"We take them hard, detain anyone who resists, and find those shooters. I'm sure there will be plenty of evidence lying inside to make charges stick."

Darryl nodded and moved to open the boot of his vehicle. He handed Amelia a vest similar to Dean's then lifted another larger one and slipped it over his chest, securing it. He swung around to face her as Amelia and Dean jogged on ahead. "Stay here. You don't have a gun or tactical experience and no reason to be in there when the shit goes down."

She put up a hand. "Understood."

Darryl nodded as if accepting that she wasn't a complete idiot, and joined the others. Kellie opened the car door and slipped on to the passenger seat. She gripped the radio in her hand as she surveyed her surroundings. If anyone came near the crumbling building, she would let the team inside know.

***

With their weapons drawn, Darryl, Donovan, and Matthews quickly climbed the steps, easily manoeuvring around the broken ones. So far they had found the tenement empty, much to his relief.

The more parties involved, the harder it would be to contain them, and something could go seriously wrong. Together, they cleared each room before moving on to the next one, making sure to keep an eye on each direction so no one could sneak up behind them and blow their brains out.

Darryl couldn't believe anyone actually lived in these rooms. Each resembled more of a squatter's paradise than appropriate accommodations, but then again, these kids probably thought this was the Hilton compared to what they were used to. He could smell the mould and wondered at the damage it did to the kids' lungs on a permanent basis. They would need to do something about this building. He made a mental note to bring it up with Harris.

He tried to imagine Kellie living in a place like this. From what she'd told him, this was as close to her home as he would ever see, and he shuddered to think at how vulnerable she had been. Looking at her now, he never would have guessed at her past. She had overcome so much and he was proud of her for that. She was an incredibly strong woman even if she didn't believe it, but he did, and that was all that mattered.

He reached the end of the hall. It curved around to reveal another set of doorways and Darryl knew they would spend the rest of the day clearing the place. Oddly enough, the only sounds they heard so far were the rodents nesting in the walls, and the creak of the weakened floorboards beneath their feet. His gut warned him to be careful.

A moment later, a loud pop echoed through the apartment complex and shook the thin walls like an earthquake. Darryl glanced at Amelia and nodded. She responded in kind and he took off up the next level of stairs as she continued searching the current floor.

He took the stairs two at a time, wary and cautious, ever mindful of the danger. He moved silently down the hallway, taking a quick inventory of the rooms as he passed. Some doors were conveniently left open for his perusal, others he had to open.

He was halfway down the second corridor when he heard another shot. He quickly and diligently scanned the area as his ears registered the fact that the shot had come from a room not too far down the hall. He could see the open door and the shadows against the wall from a figure moving about the room.

He reached into his pocket and dialled Donovan's number, allowing it to ring once. He knew she had it on vibrate, just like he did, and hung up. She would know he'd found something, and when it was safe to do so, she would join him upstairs.

Darryl approached the room and peered inside. Another *pop* blasted inside the room, piercing his eardrum. A body fell, joking two more on the floor. He had gotten there just in time to see the last body fall.

"Don't move, you son-of-a-bitch," Darryl spat at the tall man holding the gun in a coolly efficient manner. His gaze drifted over to the three dead teenagers.

The man's wild eyes shot daggers at him even as he assessed just how serious Darryl was about squeezing the trigger. He must've seen the anticipated gleam in his gaze since he immediately dropped his weapon, the gun bouncing loudly on the floorboards.

"Kick it away," Darryl ordered, and watched as the man, clearly pissed, kicked his gun away. "Get down on your knees."

The man snarled, and Darryl studied the three bodies. It was clear from the angle that they'd been on their knees before they died, probably begging for their lives. None of them appeared older than eighteen. Darryl turned his dark gaze back at his captive, approaching warily, knowing it was unwise to assume he had the upper hand.

It was always a lesson learnt the hard way.

Darryl made it only a foot away when suddenly the man rose to his feet in one lithe movement, his head bowing slightly as the man rammed into his stomach like a bull. Caught off guard by the attack, he grunted as he took the hit, his feet lifting off the ground at the momentum. Darryl gripped the handle of his Glock tighter it.

Rule number one: *Never drop your weapon*.

His lungs were robbed of breath, the force of the blow sending him backwards onto a broken mirror before his back slammed against the rotting timber floor. He heard it creak under his weight as a white-hot pain shot through his palm.

Glancing down, he cursed as he saw the long jagged line on the palm of his hand and the blood dripping from the wound. He fired his weapon at the retreating man, who upon disabling him, hadn't waited around and took off through the decomposing door that dangled precariously on its hinges.

He cursed loudly. Amelia appeared in the doorway, her weapon at the ready. The three victims drew her gaze first, her expression darkening before turning to his hand.

"I'm fine," he told her. "He went that way." He pointed in the general direction.

"Go get yourself checked, Darryl, you're bleeding all over the place." And with that, she was gone, through the door their assailant had used. He cursed himself again for being taken off guard.

He stood, feeling a few other, smaller cuts on his body and the start of some fresh bruises. Maybe, if he was lucky, he could get Kellie to tend to him.

Unlikely. He had no idea where they currently stood.

He exited the apartment building slowly and made his way toward the Commodore. Kellie was beside him suddenly, surprising him. She must've sensed something was wrong the moment he emerged into the harsh light of day. He blinked as he took in the commotion. The LAC's forensic team were busily combing over the CRV and he nodded at them.

"You're hurt," Kellie said.

"Want to kiss it better?"

Had he seriously just said that?

He must be in worse shape than he'd thought.

Instead of kissing him, she punched him on his shoulder, hard, and his arm went dead. "*Ow.*"

He leaned into her as she took his hand and felt a little lightheaded as she examined his palm. She stared at him with serious blue eyes brimming with worry. Her concern warmed him. Maybe there was hope for them, after all.

"It's deep. I need to get you to the ER," Kellie said, immediately patting him down for his keys.

"Jesus, Kellie," he groaned as she incited him into a much more painful state.

"You're such a guy, Darryl. All you can think of is sex," she admonished as she retrieved the keys from his front pocket. He squeezed his eyes shut as her hand moved against him.

Just great. He was about to be taken to the hospital with a raging hard-on. Talk about uncomfortable.

She led him toward the passenger seat and helped him in as if he were a child. He liked this nurturing side of her.

Then she climbed in next to him and started the car. He ran his uninjured hand up and down her arm. He felt her shiver, then gave him a hard, quelling look.

"I heard some shots. No one else was hurt, were they?"

He shook his head as he awkwardly clipped the seatbelt around him. "Only the kids who shot up the LAC. It appears Coleani sent in a cleaner."

Kellie cursed bluntly, shocking Darryl with vocabulary a sailor could be proud of. The woman had quite the mouth. She peeled out of the parking spot before he could comment and into main traffic. Five minutes later they arrived at the hospital.

Chapter 29

Amelia moved covertly through the maze of broken glass, half rotten walls and the most God-awful stench. It reminded her of home. She would always associate places like this to the tenement Kellie had lived in, and the small caravan she had occupied with her grandparents.

She didn't believe in forgetting where she came from. Her past made her into the woman she was today, and Amelia liked that woman. She was strong, independent, smart, tough, and even though she didn't want to admit it, soft in places. It wasn't as bad as she'd originally believed. She was still a woman. But she was also a cop, and sometimes the two didn't go together and she had to make sure that only one side of her showed at a time.

Amelia rounded the corner. A series of running footsteps thudded up ahead. She didn't follow them, but instead surveyed her location. It would be dangerous to chase him when he could easily turn around and wait for her, leading her into slaughter. Amelia didn't plan on going out that way, or that easily.

She took the next right and then another, making her way through the building, rapidly picking up speed. If she had calculated correctly, she would locate him soon. A shadow appeared in her peripheral vision and she nodded to Matthews as he joined her. Together they listened to the loudly approaching footsteps.

Dean made a series of hand signals and she nodded in agreement. He moved silently away, down a small hallway and out of sight.

Amelia held her position. She didn't have to wait long.

Harsh breathing told her that her mark was almost upon her and she readied herself for the confrontation. A second later a savage curse filled the room as the man skidded to a stop. Dean slipped around behind him and blocked his exit.

Cornered, the man did the only thing he could do. He raised his weapon. He never got a chance to squeeze the trigger.

***

Kellie paced back and forth in front of Darryl, every so often sparing him a glance. He was pale and his forehead held a light sheen of perspiration. The towel the admissions nurse had given them in effort to slow the bleeding had soaked through, and she was beginning to worry.

Where in hell was the doctor?

One would think a member of the police force would be the first patient seen, but forty-five minutes had gone by, and they were still waiting.

"Kellie, calm down. I'm fine."

She glared at him. "You are not fine, Darryl, you're bleeding."

"I've noticed," he said, which only made her narrow her eyes.

She was spiralling out of control. Every time she let her mind wander, she thought of how she'd almost lost him. One wrong move and the world would be a darker place without him in it. The thought became unbearable as she tried to hold back the tears that threatened to escape.

"This is not a joke," she said with sudden calm, her voice eerily soft.

Darryl's smile abruptly faded. "Believe me, I'm well aware of that."

She nodded jerkily and resumed her pacing. A minute later the door behind her opened and she spun around.

"About time," she muttered.

Kellie's mouth dropped open in shock as she stared at one of the most gorgeous women she'd ever seen. Eyes the colour of the ocean on a clear day framed by naturally dark lashes against flawless porcelain skin. The woman's raven hair was pulled back into a messy ponytail, her body unflatteringly hidden beneath a loose uniform.

"Rose," Darryl said amicably. "Glad you could make it."

The nurse—Rose—smiled, showing off straight white teeth. Her dentist bills must have been huge as a child. "Someone is in a good mood," she said.

"I'm offsetting her bad one," Darryl explained,

indicating Kellie.

She glowered at him. How dare he?

When he got better, she'd kick his arse. Then kiss him better like he'd asked of her earlier.

Rose moved gracefully across the room, and Kellie had a sense that she knew this woman. But how could that be? She knew for a fact she'd never met the nurse. Darryl seemed to know her.

A little too well, Kellie thought sullenly.

Someone would be answering questions when he got out of here.

Rose sat down on a small wheeled stool, and rolled closer to the examination bed where Darryl sat. She took his hand in her own small, delicate one.

Kellie took a few steps closer, her teeth cutting into her lip with worry and watched as Rose removed the now red towel and probed at the injury.

"This is deep. How'd you get it?" she asked, and Kellie realised Rose had become a nurse rather than a friend in that short moment she had examined the wound and discovered it to be more than a mild cut.

Darryl shrugged. "Fell into a mirror."

Rose raised an eyebrow but didn't comment. "You'll need stitches," she told him as she moved his hand to hover over a stainless steel bowl resting on the table next to the bed. She retrieved a slender opaque container with a nozzle on the top that Kellie assumed to be antiseptic liquid and washed out his wound, clearing it of smaller shards of glass to keep it from getting infected. "When was your last tetanus shot?"

Darryl winced and Kellie was immediately by

his side, caressing his back to comfort him. He smiled gratefully at her.

"A couple years ago, I think."

Rose nodded. "I'll give you another just in case."

Kellie shuddered. She hated needles.

A short time later, he'd had his shot and Rose finished up with the last of his stitches. Kellie had alternated from comforting Darryl, to pacing, to looking over Rose's shoulder as she worked. If the nurse had minded, she'd been polite enough not to comment.

Kellie occupied her mind during the entire process, switching between concern for Darryl, grateful that his injury wasn't more serious and scouring her memory for when she might've met Rose previously. Although the woman made no sign that she recognised Kellie, the sense of familiarity stayed with Kellie.

Frustrated, she began pacing again. Rose shared a look with Darryl and her blood boiled from jealousy. She'd never once been jealous in her entire life and Kellie hated the feeling, but she knew she was seeing the little green monster when she imagined Rose and Darryl together.

She stopped suddenly and glared at them, hating to be out on the inside joke. "What?" she demanded, and both Darryl and Rose's heads swung in her direction.

"How long have you two been dating?" Rose asked conversationally.

Kellie fiddled with a loose fabric on her shirt. "We're not."

He stiffened. She winced internally. She'd hurt

him with that denial.

Rose glanced at each of them in turn, and her mouth formed a perfect O. "Forgive me, I just assumed…"

Kellie stared at her back intently. The nurse caught her gaze over the curve of her elegant shoulder and cocked her head enquiringly at Kellie.

Her eyebrows drew together in puzzlement.

Rose smiled and turned her attention back to Darryl's hand.

"If you're wondering why I seem so familiar it's probably because I look like my little brother," Rose told her. "He works at the LAC."

Realisation dawned on Kellie and she smiled. "Nick," she said, and Rose nodded. She could see it so clearly now. How had she not noticed it before? Rose had the same midnight black hair, only hers was much longer and pulled into a high ponytail. Her eyes were also the same cornflower blue as Nick's. But that was where the similarities ended. Where her brother was six foot, Rose was closer to her height.

"Yep, Detective Nicholas Doyle, my Nicky. Do you know him?" Rose tied off the last stitch.

"Kellie trains with Nick," Darryl said.

Rose gave her a considering look. "Does he ride you hard too? You'd think being his sister he would cut me some slack, but no."

Kellie laughed and she relaxed, the tension draining out of her with one of the questions currently bouncing around her head answered. She peered over Rose's head and her gaze settled on Darryl. As always, when their eyes met, her stomach fluttered and desire heated her blood. Her body tingled with awareness. She couldn't seem to be able to control herself where he was concerned.

"Yes, Nick's a slave driver but I've come to respect him for it. He only wants the best from us."

Rose nodded and wrapped a clean bandage around Darryl's palm. "Yes, he does," Rose agreed before changing the subject back to the more serious. "Now, change the dressing daily. Don't let it get wet and if you start to feel your temperature rise call me immediately."

"I will. Thank you, Rosie."

Rose hugged Darryl, then squeezed Kellie's arm on her way out.

"He'll be all right," she said soothingly, but in a tone that made Kellie think that if Rose decreed it, then it must be so. "It was nice meeting you."

"You too."

A moment later she and Darryl were alone, and she moved to stand beside him. He shot her look.

"What?"

"I was getting worried there for a moment. You were starting to look very dangerous, Kellie. I thought you were going to slug Rose."

She snorted derisively. "Hardly."

"You can't tell me you weren't jealous."

"Like you were yesterday when you growled at Nick?" she countered. She wasn't proud to admit that she'd gotten a little thrill when he'd snarled at Nick. She remembered his easy exchanges with the nurse. "Do I have a reason to be jealous?"

"No. I've never had carnal thoughts about Rose."

She placed her hands on her hips, not believing

him. "How is that possible? The woman is gorgeous."

Darryl shrugged. "She's like a little sister to me. Besides, Nick wouldn't take kindly to one of us fooling around with his sister. Not unless marriage was our intention."

"Ah, yes, because then it would be all right," she said mockingly.

"We men are simple creatures."

Kellie didn't doubt that. They could be extremely single minded when the occasion called for it. She shivered at the sensual reminder of how intently Darryl could focus on a task. She led him out of the ER and towards the parking lot. His keys jingled in her hand as she walked.

"Come on. I'll take you home and keep an eye on you."

"No," he said, coming to a stop. "It'll be better to keep some distance between us."

Kellie turned around to face him. He looked like a man with his mind made up. Clearly she hadn't been the only one thinking. Sharp pain pierced her heart but she forced her face to be impassive, as if his words weren't crushing her. She had given him the power to shatter her after all, she thought harshly.

"We're good together, Kellie, but that doesn't change the fact that getting involved right now isn't the best idea. I could see how much it frightened you in there and how worried you are about me. It could be dangerous in the wrong situation and I think we both need to take a step back, at least until the case is over."

She had to admit that he was right. She cared for Darryl far too much and it surprised her. She wanted him with every fibre of her being. The night they were together only seemed to whet her appetite for him and every day they spent in each other's company had her falling for him even more. The intensity of her feelings scared her more than looking down the barrel of Wayne's gun. He was kind, considerate, and just plain wonderful. She wondered what the hell he saw in her. She was temperamental, bitchy, and her sharp tongue had the ability to cut a person to shreds if she so chose.

What the hell would she do? They had moved too quickly, jumping into bed without thinking of the consequences, and now they were being brought into the harsh light of day. Not too long ago, she'd had everything worked out and now she was utterly lost.

She wanted Darryl's strong arms wrapped around her comfortingly. How had she become so dependent on him in such a short amount of time? She hated that he had so much control over her and that she had very little. She needed to step back and maybe get some well needed clarity.

Darryl swore and stepped closer. He pulled her into his arms and she realised she must've let her true feelings show on her face. Damn her for allowing that mask to slip. She stiffened her spine and broke the embrace. She had to be practical. Maybe the time apart would be good for them. Make her realise he wasn't as awesome as she believed him to be.

Could they be happy? She wasn't so sure. She

was too damaged to be able to sustain a healthy relationship. Darryl may understand the demons she fought but she'll never be able to share them with him. And they were a very big part of her life. Surely she was just kidding herself. Maybe it was better to make a clean break now before either one of them got in too far over their head. Before he had the ability to break her heart so completely that there would be nothing left but the pieces.

Her mind made up, she smiled sweetly and brushed a light kiss over his lips. A goodbye kiss. Desire sizzled. Passion ignited and she forced herself back even though she wanted to deepen the kiss—to stroke his tongue with hers.

But Darryl had a point. The case they were working was dangerous and if they didn't get their distance they could easily wind up getting one or both of them killed. That didn't mean she didn't hate him for suggesting it.

"You take the car. I'll have one of the guys swing round and pick me up."

Kellie nodded and stepped back. "Goodbye. Take care Darryl. I'll see you tomorrow."

She turned and started quickly away. Usually she wasn't such a coward but she needed space between her and Darryl. Needed it like her next breath. Had he heard the finality in her voice? The pain consumed her.

"This isn't over," he called out to her. "When the case is over, you'd better watch out because I'll be coming for you, Kellie Munroe, and I won't be letting go."

She picked up her speed.

Chapter 30

A few days later, Kellie hit the print button and waited for the printer on her desk to spit out her report. The temperamental beast wheezed sickly before finally relinquishing the paper. She gathered up the pages and signed the bottom of the document before stapling it into to the manila folder resting on her desk.

The siege and corresponding paperwork on the Houston was over and the three bodies belonging to the party who'd opened fire on the LAC—along with their executioner—had been brought to the morgue for identification.

The case against Coleani continued to move slowly. The man had not managed to stay in power for as long as he had by being sloppy. Kellie felt frustration at every turn. She'd hoped by now that they would've been able to build a strong case, but if anything she felt further away from her goal than the day they'd started.

She hadn't seen Darryl again since the hospital despite her weakening resolve, especially at night when the memories of how he felt against her body were the strongest. She longed to be held by him again, longed for more mornings like the one they'd shared in bed, and felt a tightness in her chest and a deep sorrow inside her. She knew she was doing the best thing for them both by maintaining distance but she hated herself for it. Only knowing there could be no future except heartache stopped her from throwing herself at him.

It would be foolish to hope. Sure, the idea had appeal.

Home. Love. Family.

Everything she'd been deprived of in the past. But it was too risky, and she felt hollow inside. Darryl deserved so much better than her. She would never be normal, her issues running so deep they might never be resolved. Kellie wasn't even sure if she had the capacity to love and she didn't want Darryl to end up hating her for never being able to give him what he'd eventually want from her.

She ached knowing he'd never be hers, but she wasn't selfish enough to keep him when she knew nothing would come from their relationship. For a brief moment she'd been sublimely happy, then the world had come crashing down beside her and she was forced to sift through the rubble.

Despite the arrest warrant out for Wayne Burton, he'd yet to be located and she'd been placed on desk duty by her boss. She'd been practically chained to her cubicle, which may have helped her to keep her distance from Darryl, but it made overseeing Mia difficult. Thankfully, her friend had graciously kept her informed on the meagre developments in the case. Carlisle had also insisted she speak with the site psychologist, so she'd spent two hours with the woman. She left feeling raw and in a worse emotional place than when she'd first walked through the door.

Kellie brought up yet another report template and began filling out the relevant information. She was so engrossed in deciphering her own notes that she didn't hear the man approach her desk.

"Such a nice office, Ms. Munroe," he said.

Kellie startled, and found herself staring into the cold eyes of Dick Coleani. She tensed and took a deep breath in an effort to control her outward appearance. Her mind might be wreaking havoc on the inside but her expression remained composed and indifferent. Kellie fought the urge to throw her letter opener at him. The scum had some nerve to sully the LAC with his stench.

"Mr. Coleani, to what do I owe this honour?" she asked, distain dripping from her voice.

He stepped closer. "I'm just visiting the detectives downstairs, trying to help out in Michael's case."

"Come to sign a confession, have you? That would certainly make things easier," she said flippantly, even while her stomach knotted.

He smiled, baring his teeth which were slightly yellowed, a colour that no amount of cleaning could possibly remove. "I've also come to make arrangements for Mikey's body."

She nodded. "Probably would have been easier to have buried him after you shot him, huh? That way you could've bypassed all that red tape."

Coleani grinned as if she truly amused him. "You're nothing like your mother, you know that? She was so pliable. No sense of self-respect. Do you know I punished her every time you interfered with my business? In the end, she enjoyed it."

Bile rose and her throat burned in an effort to keep from throwing up. She'd seen the bruises on her mother's skin, yet the woman had always brushed off her concern. Knowing Coleani had touched Jules gave her the shivers, but to know her mother had unduly suffered at his hands because of her actions gave her pause. Kellie had never expected retaliation. She'd been foolish and her mother had paid the price.

She blinked back tears for her mother, who had tried her best and had taken the brunt of Coleani's anger for her. She wanted to rip this man apart with her bare hands. The letter opener looked extremely good right now.

She remained quiet lest she open her mouth and allow him to see how much his words affected her. He eagerly waited for a response. She would not give him one—at least not the one he was after.

"I never thought a perky little blonde could cause so much trouble," he commented when she didn't rise to the bait.

"Yes, well, we know how you deal with trouble don't we, Mr. Coleani? You're leaving quite a few bodies in your wake."

His eyes hardened. "You may want to take note of who you're talking to, little girl. I have eyes everywhere. Call off the investigation or you'll find you're the one getting buried."

Kellie sucked in a sharp breath. "Is that a threat? Note who *you* are talking to. I am not a little girl. I am a sergeant in the NSW police force."

He snarled. "I don't give a shit who you are. Back away or you'll find yourself in a world of pain."

Her ill-advised temper reared its ugly head. "What will you do? Sic Wayne on me?" she asked tartly even as her heart beat wildly in her chest.

He stepped closer again, his voice dropping an octave. "Oh no, Ms. Munroe, it's not *you* I'll attack. It'll be your friends downstairs. Your buddy Nick, the instructor. How about dear Amelia…or what about your current fuck, Detective Hill? Yes, I know all about you. Do you really want to be responsible for whatever happens to them? Good day, Ms. Munroe. Please take some time to consider what I've said."

He walked out of her office like a king, as if he owned the building and had every right to be there. Kellie slammed a fist against her desk, hard. The sound echoed in the empty room. Her stomach knotted as once again she felt impotent, weak, and unable to defeat one man. She fought for control, breathing heavily in an effort to calm the rage and helplessness she felt. Tears rolled down her cheek.

Days like these she wished she had a bottle of Wild Turkey in her bottom drawer. She yanked a tissue from her purse and dabbed at her rebellious tears, then blinked and took a moment to regain her composure before applying corrective foundation to her mascara streaked cheeks. When she had successfully covered up her temporary loss of control, she stood and adjusted her dark grey pencil skirt and jacket.

For the first time, she felt thankful the elevator moved so slowly to the second floor. She was in no rush, but even so, the doors opened before she was ready and she stood staring out at the Pig Pen.

"Stop whatever you're doing in regards to the Coleani investigation," she told them as she drew near, hoping her voice would remain steady and clear and not broadcast her fears.

"What?" Amelia looked up from her desk, followed by the three other detectives. She felt Darryl's stare acutely and it burned her. She refused to look in his direction, knowing she would crumble if she did.

"Do as I say, Detective Donovan. You have your murderer lying in autopsy."

"And what of *his* murderer? Coleani is up to his ears in this."

"He may well be."

Amelia snorted. "You know he is."

"As far as IA is concerned, the investigation into your conduct is finished. All that's needed to close the case is my report. I will advise you of the outcome. And unless you have direct evidence linking Coleani to the shootings, the LAC doesn't have the manpower to continue looking into it."

Amelia raised an eyebrow, clearly biting off what she wanted to say.

Kellie turned and started back toward the elevator. She passed Nick, who asked, "Has this got anything to do with the fact Dick Coleani just left?"

She ignored him and quickly retreated, trying to

hide her fear. Coleani didn't make idle threats. She jabbed her finger against the *up* button and was relieved when the doors immediately opened. Kellie slipped inside. A moment later, Darryl's large form dominated the small space.

Kellie sank into the corner, careful not to touch him.

The doors closed, trapping her inside with him. She did her best to ignore him even though every breath she took brought his scent deep into her lungs.

"Want to talk about it?"

She didn't bother to pretend she had no idea what he was talking about. "No."

"Dammit," he snapped, and she spun around to face him in surprise. He sounded so pissed, and she'd never seen this side of him before. And it was directed at *her*. "What do I have to say or do to make you trust me?"

"I do trust you," she said softly and meant it.

"Then why do you shut me out? I can help you. I want to help you if you'd just give me a chance. We all do. You're not in this alone."

She had a feeling he wasn't just talking about Coleani. He was frustrated with her just as she knew he would be, only it had come quicker than she'd anticipated. Maybe that was a good thing. Maybe Darryl would stop fighting her and just give up. There could be no future for them. They'd had a good time, enjoyed some fine memories. Now it was over.

Tears pricked her eyes. When had she become so damn emotional?

259

He huffed out a breath and ran his fingers through his hair when she didn't answer him. "I know Coleani said something to you. Is that why you ordered the investigation to be stopped? What was it? Did he threaten you?"

Kellie witnessed a myriad of emotions cross his face—anger, frustration, sympathy, concern, and love.

The last had her heart thumping in her chest.

Her throat started to close and one tear escaped the tight hold she exerted. She shook her head. "No. He threatened Nick, Mia, and *you.* I couldn't live with myself if anything happened to you."

He crossed the short distance and pulled her into his arms. She went willingly and held onto him like a woman drowning, which she supposed she was. She shut off the feelings that rose to the surface at his nearness, and allowed herself this one moment before reality closed in once more. His strong arms enveloped her and warmed her cool skin.

She wanted to bury Coleani but not at the risk of the people she cared about. Hell, she wasn't even sure anymore if it was a need for justice against his crimes or pure revenge that drove her. She cared for Darryl but wasn't sure if she could go to distance. Loving someone left her open to be hurt. One thing she'd promised herself she'd never be again.

"We can look after ourselves," he said.

"He abused my mother because of me." She trembled and pulled back. "He hurt her, Darryl."

He cupped her cheek gently. "That wasn't your fault. Men like Coleani find any excuse to inflict pain. Don't let him place guilt on you. You're an amazing woman, Kellie Munroe."

"You're just angling for more sex," she joked, lightening the mood.

His eyes heated. "Is it working?"

"Yes. Damn you."

"Damn us both." He leaned in to kiss her, but the carriage stopped and the doors opened to the fourth floor. He groaned. "We can't give up. Coleani must be stopped," he said as she stepped out.

No, she had no plans to give up.

Whenever Kellie was pushed, she pushed right back. She admitted to her fear. Being faced with one's worst enemy, a man who placed everyone she held dear on the chopping block, could do that to a woman. But if anyone would be punished for her actions, it would be her.

Now that the adrenaline had left her system and she was able to think clearly again, seeing Coleani here in her office had only made her angry...and more determined than ever to put the son-of-a-bitch behind bars where he belonged.

Chapter 31

Nick moved into enemy territory, otherwise known as Special Crimes and Internal Affairs. Kellie's blonde head was visible behind the partition that provided the wall to her cubicle. He sauntered over and leaned a hip against the wall as he waited for the woman he considered a friend to acknowledge him.

Her hair was loose and hung over her shoulders in messy tendrils. She'd kicked off her heels and unbuttoned the top button on her blouse. A half empty mug of coffee sat on her desk, and one glance told him it was stone cold. Kellie looked as if she'd stayed all night at the LAC. Her grey suit—the same one she'd worn yesterday—was rumpled.

She flicked through several folders, her avid attention drawing his notice. He frowned. What had been so important that it couldn't have waited?

He knew she was determined to put Coleani behind bars and Darryl had told them what transpired in her office. She better not have continued the investigation into Coleani alone.

Besides being dangerous, it would piss off Amelia and—if he'd read the situation correctly—Darryl as well. He was downright protective of Kellie, and so was Nick. Kellie deserved better in life. Better than some scumbag raping her and leaving her to die.

Catching up to Burton would be a race to see which one—Donovan, Hill, or himself—got to him first.

"You'd better not be doing what I think you're doing," he warned, his usual jovial tone gone.

Kellie startled and turned towards him, accidentally knocking a couple of file folders off her desk. Police reports and photos spilled onto the carpet. Her eyes widened and she began to scoop them up quickly. Nick bent and collected a few before she could shove them back into the folders.

He glanced down and frowned. Kellie snatched them from his hand.

"Kellie…"

"What are you doing here?" she demanded, turning the situation around on him in a clearly evasive manoeuvre.

"You missed this morning's session. I came to check on you."

Her gaze drifted down. "I'm sorry Nick. I got distracted and completely forgot."

"I noticed. Is this something Hill and Donovan should be aware of?"

"Not yet. I'm still sifting through this."

"Be careful, Kel."

She smiled and he got a glimpse of the woman she'd been a week ago before the stress and anxiety had gotten to her. He hadn't noticed how much she'd changed until just now.

His phone rang, interrupting his thoughts and putting his fear for whatever she was doing on the backburner. He held her gaze as he took the call. When he was done, he clipped his mobile back onto his belt.

"That was Hill. He and Donovan are working a double down on Charles. He wants me down there. Want to ride along? Charles is Coleani's territory." He turned and started for the door.

"Sure, who are the victims?" she asked, rushing to join him since he was already halfway to the elevator.

She tripped as her heel caught on the steel grey carpet and took a header toward the floor, reaching out and grasped the first thing she could to stop herself from falling...which happened to be him. She caught hold of his arm, pinching his flesh as she stumbled. He caught her before she fell.

"I'm used to women throwing themselves at me, but this is ridiculous," he joked. "Slow down, it's not a race."

"No, it isn't, so *you* slow down. I'm not the one with a six-foot stride."

He grinned and stared down at her. "No, you aren't. You're pint-sized. Are you okay?"

Kellie nodded without checking herself over. She bent down and jerked her caught heel away from the carpet, taking a strand of hard wool lodged between the rubber cap of her stiletto and the heel with her before following him into the elevator.

"So...you and Darryl, huh?" he asked, grinning as he rocked back on his heels.

Kellie blushed. "I'm not discussing that with you."

He ignored the comment. "You two are good for each other."

"We are?" Kellie asked, seeming surprised by his statement.

"Sure. That and every time you're in the same room the heat ratchets up several degrees. Is this a temporary thing?"

"What if it is?"

"I don't think Darryl sees it that way."

Kellie gnawed on her lower lip. "He told me that when the case is over he'll be coming for me."

He wasn't surprised. He'd seen the discreet glances between the two when they thought no one was looking, and he hadn't missed the glares he'd received from Hill when he stood too close to Kellie. One thing was sure, Darryl had it bad for her.

He grinned. Two down…

***

The house on Charles was built in the fifties, the blue paint chipped and faded. The weatherboard rotted and in places missing. The red-orange rust dulled the glint of the iron roof in the sunlight. Unfortunately for the residents on Charles, it wasn't unusual. All the houses lining the cul-de-sac could have used a fresh coat of paint and a good gardener, the grass dry and brittle.

Kellie opened the door to Nick's dark green Holden Commodore and followed him up the overgrown pebble path leading to the front door. He flashed his holographic ID and introduced them both to the uniformed officer guarding the door, who dutifully wrote their names on the sign-in sheet.

"Detectives Matthews, Hill, and Donovan are already in there," the officer told them.

Nick donned a pair of booties and handed a pair to Kellie, who followed suit. When they finally entered the house the first thing she noticed was the smell and almost gagged.

"You okay?" Nick asked her when she felt the blood leave her face.

She waved him off, not wanting to appear weak.

He rolled his eyes at her bravery—or stupidity— and opened a jar of Vicks VapoRub, then dipped his index finger deep in the gel before swiping it under her nose.

"Hey!" she snapped, stepping back.

"There's no shame in admitting the truth. Many a man has emptied the contents of his stomach on a stench like this. Unfortunately, we pros get used to it."

Kellie frowned as she followed him through the maze of empty Domino's pizza boxes, James Boag beer bottles, and what appeared to be a year's supply of TV Guides, some torn into long strips that when rolled up would bear a striking resemblance to a cigarette or something less legal.

"I wouldn't think that would be unfortunate, Nick. You should be happy the smell no longer affects you like it does us rookies."

Nick gave her a sideways glance. "That all

depends on how you look at it. Yeah, it's great I no longer have the need to chuck my guts up but that also means—"

"You've seen too many. I get it," she interrupted, understanding.

They stopped as they reached the crime scene. The LAC's forensic team was already bagging and tagging evidence and taking photos. Dean, Amelia, and Darryl were hovering over the victims, waiting for Doctor Stone to examine the bodies.

Kellie looked about the room and regretted it immediately. Blood pooled beneath the bodies and splattered against the wall. Flies had found their way into the house—or had already been there at the time of death—and had set up shop within the bodies. A large rat had gnawed on their faces, leaving a bloody skull peeking through the muscles and cartilage. The rat itself had been caught and now sat sulking in a cage off to the side.

"Oh God," she said and turned away from the bodies to find more blood and an intestine that had spilled out of a victim's stomach.

"You're looking at the remains of Jeff Carlton and Brian Mitchell. They worked at the local Shell on alternating shifts and as far as we can tell have kept their noses clean," Nick said, reading from his notepad as he motioned towards the room as if she had somehow missed the bloody chaos in front of her.

"In this neighbourhood, steering clear of trouble and Coleani himself is something that isn't done. How old were they?" she asked, keeping her gaze on Nick's face.

"Mitchell was sixteen, Carlton only fifteen."

"Son-of-a-bitch," she muttered.

Darryl brightened, his frown turning into a smile when he found them there. "You made it. Good. We can use all the help we can get on this one. You okay?" he asked, noting what she could only imagine was a green tinge to her skin and a dollop of Vicks under her nose.

"No."

She had hoped to find Wayne Burton by now, though she wasn't looking forward to confronting him. But she wanted this all over and done with.

"Yeah, I know it's pretty grisly."

She spared a glance at the body of Brian Mitchell as he was lifted into the black durable body bag and watched in horror as more of his internal organs flopped to floor, hollowing out his stomach cavity.

Kellie stumbled for the door, her hand over her mouth. Darryl followed her, placing a comforting hand on her hip as he caught her by the exit. She bent down at the waist until she was looking between her legs at the dry fern plant left to die by the door.

"Just take deep breaths. It'll pass soon."

Kellie nodded as she sucked in fresh air. She would never get the sight or smell out of her memory no matter how long she lived.

"Here, drink this," Darryl added, handing her a bottle of water. She straightened as he removed the cap from the bottle and drank deeply until half the water was gone.

"Easy there. It's not a bottle of Jack."

"I wish I had one right about now," she muttered

and laughed as she remembered what she'd thought—God, was it only yesterday? She met Darryl's inquiring gaze and said, "Is it bad when you've wished for a bottle of hard liquor twice in one week? It seems to be becoming a pattern."

"It's been a hard week. That usually calls for the hard stuff and lots of it."

"I wasn't expecting that," she admitted, gesturing to the inside of the house. "After Michael Lambert, I thought I could stomach death. At least in the pure form and not just in photos."

"Yeah, well, bloody gets messy and stinky. The bay washed Lambert clean. It was about as fresh as they get."

Kellie made a face. "Remind me never to go swimming again."

"You want to wait in the car?"

She shook her head. "No I'll be fine, now that I know what to expect."

"All right then."

She followed Darryl back inside, this time taking in her surroundings. The victims had been pigs, which she assumed was typical of teenage boys living together without adult supervision.

"Where are their parents?"

"Dead. Mitchell and Carlton were foster kids. They disappeared from the system a few months ago. Decided to make it on their own."

"It looks like they were doing that. A place of their own, holding down steady jobs. Despite the mess they were more in control of their lives than most adults. How long have they been dead?"

"A couple of days, according to Stone. No more

than week. He's sure."

She raised her eyebrow as they re-joined the others. Both bodies had been bagged, leaving bodily fluids and excrement on the old cracked linoleum.

"No one noticed they were missing or didn't show up for work?"

"Apparently not," Amelia said from across the room as she sifted through some organs with the end of her ball point pen. "Neighbours finally noticed the smell and called it in."

"I can understand that."

"What do we have here?" Her head jerked back as she caught sight of her find. She put on a pair of white disposable gloves she'd borrowed from the nearest forensic kit and picked up the object. A bright flash of gold temporarily blinded her as the metal connected with the sun peeping through the rotting curtain.

Amelia poured water from a bottle onto the palm of her hand, washing away the blood. She examined the piece of jewellery and squinted. She paled and turned to Kellie.

"What is it?"

"This is something you need to see," she told Kellie as she moved towards her, deftly avoiding the dried blood pools on the floor. As she walked she placed the object into a plastic evidence bag, sealing it as she came to a stop before Kellie and Darryl. She could feel Dean and Nick's complete attention on them and a few members of the forensic team as well.

Kellie took the bag from her and frowned. She didn't understand her friend's reaction. "Look inside, Kel."

She glanced at her, somewhat confused by Amelia's expression. She noted that Darryl watched with an expectant yet questioning gaze. Amelia shook her head at him sadly, as if to tell him this wouldn't end well.

Kellie turned the bag over so the outside shell of the locket was rested on her palm. It only took a moment for her to understand. The second she caught sight of the photo she knew exactly what she held in her hand after all these years. She trembled as tears blurred her vision.

"I'm so sorry, Kel."

Kellie shoved the bag into Darryl's hands and turned away, never once looking back as she left the Charles Street crime scene.

Chapter 32

Kellie went straight from the crime scene to her desk. After several hours, she had given up trying to get any work done and had gone home. She despised the silence and she wasn't one for being idle. She'd scrubbed her house, washed and folded her laundry, and even cleaned out the refrigerator.

Now she was back to having nothing to occupy her hands or mind, leaving her to recall the locket and the implications surrounding its sudden reappearance in her life. Once again she felt helpless, a scared girl of sixteen. She'd promised herself she would never feel that way again, but seeing her locket had thrown her twelve years into the past when she'd been an innocent.

She'd let Coleani frighten her, allowed Burton to take her virginity. One thing was for certain, she wouldn't put up with it. She had an idea. She just had to figure out the best way to use it.

Coleani was playing with her. He knew she would get the implications of the necklace—knew Burton was on the fringe of her life again. He thought he could throw her off balance. He was right. She was reeling, and she had to get control over her emotions quickly before she made a mistake that could turn deadly.

A loud banging brought her to the door, and she grabbed hold of the baseball bat sitting in the corner that she used for protection. It would do little against a gun but it was the best deterrent she had. Kellie looked through the peephole of her door and let out a deep shaky breath before opening it.

***

Darryl pushed past Kellie and stepped into the house. He swung around and took stock of her pale skin and white knuckles holding too tight onto the bat.

"I hope you're not planning on using that thing on me."

Kellie frowned, confused. "Darryl, what are you doing here?"

She still hadn't relinquished the bat which he took for a bad sign and immediately stepped forward and relieved her of it, placing it in the corner. He then turned his attention on her, looking her up and down, his brief but thorough survey not missing much. She'd showered and changed since he'd last seen her. She wore a pair of grey track pants and an over-sized *Snoopy* shirt that appeared stretched from years of use. Her blonde hair hung loosely over her shoulders in wavy curls.

He glanced down and noted she was barefoot, her bright pink toenails peeking up at him. Had they

273

had been that colour the night they'd spent together? He couldn't remember but admitted he hadn't been interested in her toes at the time.

"How are you?"

Kellie started for the kitchen and he followed, waiting patiently for her to speak. "I'm good. What do you want?" she asked stiffly.

She poured herself a glass of amber liquid. He couldn't see the label from where he stood, but he smelled it—potent and quite capable of putting hairs on his chest. He noticed she also poured him a glass.

Good. That meant she wasn't planning on kicking him out just yet.

He'd wanted to talk with her since they'd been at the crime scene, but had been unable to get a moment alone with her. Now he had all the time in the world and didn't know what to say.

He gave it some consideration, thinking he must be losing his mind. Once, he'd been so level-headed, but she was spinning him around and around and he couldn't make sense of anything. He looked over at her and his body ached. He took a calming breath before he completely went off track.

"The locket. What does it mean to you?"

Kellie took a deep sip of her drink while she considered his question. "It's nothing...nothing important, anyway."

She was afraid to let him in. He saw the fear in her eyes. She wasn't nearly as good at masking her emotions as she believed. It pissed him off that she was keeping secrets from him. He wanted to protect her, and he wanted *her*. Would he ever get past her defences? She turned to walk away but he reached out and grabbed her arm gently, effectively stopping her.

"Cut the crap. This is my case too, and I seem to be the only one out of the loop here. What does the locket mean to you?"

He was mad and he wasn't entirely sure why.

Glancing around her house, he noticed the cream coloured walls with their chocolate skirting boards. Her furniture resembled her—untouchable. Her sofa, a sandstone fabric, rested on dark stained floorboards. She had a small TV, one that any man would be ashamed of, but he could see it was never used. A huge stack of manila file folders were piled in front of it.

She was also a fan of pictures. None were family photos; instead, they were beautifully rendered landscapes of Harbour Bay and the surrounding areas. The photographer must have been local, since most of the pictures were taken in obscure and out of the way places that no tourist would know about.

Had she taken the photos herself?

He opened his mouth to ask her when she met his gaze and he was lost in her eyes.

Running his finger down her cheek, he heard her sharp intake of breath. She moved away from him abruptly, keeping her back to him as she struggled with her inner demons.

"It's my locket. Mia gave it to me for my sixteenth birthday. The picture inside is her at the same age. I was wearing that locket the day I was raped. Wayne took it off me as a souvenir. All these years, he kept it. He's telling me he's here. He wants me to know what he's capable of."

She peered at him over her shoulder and he could see the tears shimmering in her eyes before she blinked them away.

"I'm sorry, Kel, I didn't mean to…"

She put up her hands to stop him. "It's okay. He was a sadistic bastard. I suspected he'd kept it as a sign of his power over me. But the reality is different. I was just taken by surprise."

Darryl shook his head and drew her into his arms. She resisted at first before the tension seeped out of her body. He never wanted to let her go. "It's not your fault. Those boys were dead before Coleani even came to see you. They probably defied him in some way, so he ordered them to be killed. They knew you'd be involved in the investigation so he decided to shake you up."

He rubbed her back in a comforting gesture. He loved holding her, could go on forever like this. She clung to him and something inside him shifted.

"It's working."

He kissed her forehead tenderly. Emotions so pure and potent spiraled through his body, causing an acute ache. He'd never felt anything so *right* before.

"It's not in your best interest to take the blame for their murders. Especially since you had no control over the matter at all."

Kellie pulled away, discreetly wiping her eyes. "Coleani's a monster. His men are no better. I'm not the only one, you know. There's been at least eight more women that Burton has hurt, all probably sanctioned by Coleani."

Darryl leaned forward and kissed her softly, allowing her to feel the sweetness and emotion in the action, silently telling her that he planned to keep his promise to her. He took her hand and pulled her toward the sofa and sat down before tugging her onto his lap.

She put an arm over his shoulder and placed a hand on his chest as she leaned into him. He stroked her cheek, feeling her softness. He nuzzled her neck and she shivered. He loved how responsive she was to his touch. He placed his bandaged hand on her knee as Kellie tilted her head to give him better access. He took advantage of what she offered and she let out a moan.

He tightened his arm around her back as he slid his hand up her thigh. Her breath stuttered and she melted into him. He'd only meant to distract her from her morose thoughts but he was quickly losing sight of his good intentions. Kellie always had that effect on him. He breathed in her scent. She smelled delicious. He rested his head against hers.

"You drive me crazy, you know that?"

She let out a soft chuckle. Her breath tickled against his jaw and he shuddered. "Right back at you. What am I going to do about you? You're extremely distracting."

He grinned and snuggled against her, loving the feeling of her pressed against him. It reminded him of the other morning. He could get used to lazy moments like these when time seemed to slow down and they were the only two people in the world. When he imagined the future he saw them together curled up as they were now. Maybe a fire burning before them in the winter.

His heart swelled. "I like that it isn't just me.

He felt her smile, her lips moving against his neck. What was going through her mind? Did she regret her desire for him? Would she walk away when the case was over? What would he do if he couldn't convince her to give him a chance?

He pushed away the dark thoughts dampening his mood and focused on the case.

"So, about those women..."

Kellie pulled back to look him in the eye. She had obviously forgotten she'd made the remark but he hadn't. She took a deep breath then started telling him everything she'd discovered.

Chapter 33

Darryl watched as Kellie nervously tucked her loose silky strands behind her ears. It was clear she hated being the centre of attention. Today she had gone for the casual look with blue distressed jeans and a black square cut fitted shirt, her feet in a pair of silver pointed heels. All he could think about was getting her alone and admitting he'd made a mistake by telling her they should keep their distance.

The past few days had damn near killed him. Knowing she was just a few floors above had been a bittersweet torture. The desire to hold her and breathe in her scent had him constantly fighting himself. Even now just hours after holding her he wanted her back in his arms. She needed this time just as much as he did. For them to both to evaluate how they felt. So much had happened in their short acquaintance that even he struggled to understand how his feelings could be so strong.

One week. That was how long he'd known Kellie. Yet, it felt like a lifetime.

Last night had been a turning point in their

relationship. They'd let down their barriers and for a brief time had forgotten about Dick Coleani and the case. He'd told her of his family, of the exploits he and his brothers had gotten into over the years that had turned his mother's hair prematurely grey.

He'd coaxed her to talk about her past, hoping it would be therapeutic for her. He hoped to understand her situation better, to give her the support she required. She told him of the fears she had, the dreams she wished for, and in return he'd done the same. They had fallen asleep in each other's arms and for the first time in his life, he'd felt complete.

And more in love with Kellie than ever.

She cleared her throat and looked at her audience. Donovan, Dean, and Nick all stared back at her with rapt attention.

"After Coleani left the other day, I continued investigating on my own."

Donovan launched out of her chair. "You did what? Are you fucking stupid, Kellie? Have you no regard for your safety? You've already got Burton leaving calling cards at crime scenes in warning. Next time it'll be a personal visit."

Kellie flinched under her anger but held her head high.

"Wait, what's this about calling cards?" Dean asked, his gaze flicking from one female to the other.

"Burton took a locket from her as a souvenir and planted it at the crime scene yesterday," Darryl explained.

Dean raised an eyebrow, and Darryl didn't need

to explain further. He'd been there the day Kellie had discovered Burton worked for Coleani. He'd witnessed her collapse and knew how deeply it affected her. Darryl knew Dean wasn't happy Kellie was still working the case, but he kept his mouth shut.

Nick swore savagely.

"You're playing with fire," Dean told Kellie.

Darryl gave her credit from not wilting under his hard glower. He looked every bit the dangerous man he could be.

"I know. But this is something I've got to do."

"If Coleani doesn't have you killed, I will," Donovan muttered as she sank back down in her chair.

"What'd you find?" Nick asked, obviously in an effort to diffuse the situation. From the feral look on his face, he wasn't taking the news about Burton any better than Darryl was.

Kellie took a deep breath. A weaker woman would've buckled under the weight of disapproval and anger floating about the room. But Kellie had a backbone of steel.

"Several women known to Coleani shared a similar fate to me. All in all, eight cases match perfectly—except I was the lucky one. I survived. I spent the night before last compiling the case files, but I doubt they're the only ones."

"Another nail in Burton's coffin," Nick said. "But not Coleani's."

"No. Once again, Coleani will walk."

Darryl heard the bitterness in her voice. He wanted to soothe her but didn't know how. He knew she'd been trying to use the murders to convict Coleani. She was frustrated at having him once again slip through her fingers. He doubted she would ever be at peace while Coleani and Burton were free.

"Was any DNA recovered?" Darryl asked.

She nodded. "In a few of the cases, yes. In the others the bodies were too degraded to get any viable evidence. The detectives assigned to each of the cases ran the DNA against NCIDD, but no hits were found."

NCIDD was the National Criminal Investigation DNA Database that was used in every LAC and forensic lab across the country.

Nick leaned against his desk. "Do we have enough evidence to compel Burton to provide a DNA sample?"

"Possibly. With my testimony and the similarities in the cases there should be enough probable cause. I can contact Aidan Carmichael with the DPP and have him start on a subpoena."

The DPP was the Director of Public Prosecutions office. They would handle the case when it went to trial. Aidan was the main Prosecutor who had worked for the office for years and had a ninety percent win rate. He was passionate about the cases he worked, and where most people in the role burned out after a few years, Aidan seemed to thrive.

Burton was a small fish compared to Coleani. If only they could get him to roll on his boss. But the first thing Coleani taught his boys was loyalty to him. Burton would probably lay down his life rather than implicate the closest thing to a father he'd ever known.

"He'll never talk," Kellie said, as if reading his mind.

"We can always try," Amelia said.

"Even the Donovan Style isn't going to break Burton. And without a confession naming Coleani, the bastard will walk. He'll find another ten Burtons, and the cycle will continue."

Amelia crossed one leg over the other. "What do you want from us, Kel? We can't pull evidence out of thin air. I'd love to take that man off the streets, but we're bound by the law—something you reminded me of a week ago."

"We're not the enemy, Kellie," Dean reprimanded sharply. "You're losing sight, allowing your vision to be clouded. This isn't a place for personal crusades. If you can't leave it at the door, then you shouldn't be here."

The air surrounding them turned frosty. Dean wasn't one to mince his words. Darryl stood, prepared to defend her. His co-worker may be right, but Darryl didn't like him attacking his woman. He understood her anger. Burton had hurt her but he'd merely been the weapon Coleani used. Kellie stepped forward and placed her hand on his arm, stopping him.

"You're right and I apologise. I was brought in to supervise Mia but no one is reining me in—until now." She nodded at Dean, accepting his criticism and bridging the gap between them.

"We will get Coleani," Dean said firmly. "Maybe not today or tomorrow, but we'll get him.

As for Burton, you did good work. There's no way he'll be able to escape the charges. I know what the bastard did to you. Believe me, we all want him punished."

Darryl nodded in agreement and noticed Amelia and Nick doing the same; they all wanted a moment alone with Burton. Tears glittered in Kellie's eyes at the sentiment.

Darryl wrapped his arm around her waist and pulled her into his body. Dean sucked in a sharp breath, but he was done hiding. He loved this woman and didn't care who knew. He would keep her safe, no matter what, which would be a full-time job in itself.

He kissed her forehead tenderly, soothing her. He let her know without words that he was in her corner. She melted against him, and he felt a surge of triumph. Maybe when this was all over he'd have a chance after all.

Donovan glowered at him. He stared back at her, unrepentant. She'd better get used to the idea of him and Kellie as a couple because he would fight like hell to keep her.

Dean said nothing. Of his team, he'd assumed Matthews would have something to say but instead the man glanced over at Nick. He narrowed his eyes when Dean retrieved his wallet from his back pant pocket and handed Nick a fifty.

Bastards. They'd bet on him.

There'd be a time in their lives when a woman would twist them up. He looked forward to seeing that.

Not for the first time, Darryl wondered what

Kellie was feeling. Was she elated that the man who'd raped her would finally be going to prison where he belonged? Or was she hollow, unsure how to feel now that she was on her way to having closure?

"I'll call Aidan and get the ball rolling," she said. "It may be late, but I bet he'll be at his office. He has less of a life then we do."

Darryl tensed at the familiarity Kellie seemed to have with the prosecutor. He'd never considered himself a jealous or possessive man, but she brought those emotions out in him.

Nick flashed him a grin, as if knowing exactly what was going through his mind, then rocked back on his heels, thoroughly enjoying himself at Darryl's expense.

"Not that a warrant or subpoena is any good without a person to serve it to," Kellie stated, taking Darryl's mobile from his belt, her fingers brushing lightly against him.

Donovan grinned recklessly. "But we do know where he is, Kellie. He'll be with Coleani."

Chapter 34

Amelia turned off the ignition and surveyed her surroundings. Coleani's restaurant was located south of the beach in a prime location along the promenade beside an array of tourist shops, ice-cream parlours, and a fish and chip take-away overlooking the water.

During the day, seagulls waddled along the wharf cleaning up spilled food before flying away, leaving white splats all over the footpath. Children ran, playing, screaming with laughter before they spent a day on a boat with their parents or enjoyed a picnic down on the rocks watching for whales.

At night, the area was deserted.

The only sign of life was the nightclub pumping out a steady beat a few blocks away. The parking lot was dark, the lack of security lights making it difficult to see. Shivers ran up her spine as she searched the square, ensuring they were alone and not about to get an unexpected surprise. A sense of foreboding washed over her. She tried to shake it off.

"So, what exactly is the plan?" Kellie asked as she moved her body to lean between the two front bucket seats of Amelia's vehicle.

"We ask Coleani politely where Burton is and hope he gives us lip so I can haul his arse in on obstruction of justice charges," Amelia replied, a dark edge to her voice.

All she needed was a reason. Just one, and Coleani was toast. He'd put Kellie through so much pain over the years that Amelia burned to punish him.

Above them a thunder clap rolled across the night sky, dark grey clouds blocking out the moon, telling them a weather change was coming and a storm would soon be upon them. She squinted into the blackness. There was no sign anyone had seen them pull up. No faces showed at the windows of the building nor did any lights turn on. She turned in her seat and watched the back door of the restaurant as if expecting a full frontal attack.

A lone light glowed in the back, which she assumed was Coleani's private office. She stiffened her spine and unclasped her seatbelt before making a move to open her door. Darryl grabbed her arm, halting her from his position in the passenger seat. A white van pulled up beside the restaurant and blocked their view. Two young men exited and opened the back double doors. Another man she recognised as Aaron Huber—Coleani's muscle—joined them. They spoke for a bit, but the sounds of the water crashing against the wharf nearby masked their words.

She sensed Kellie freeze between her and Darryl,

as if afraid any movement would make the three men look their way.

Amelia watched as the young men unloaded the van in a few short trips while Huber guarded the vehicle. She didn't have any doubt as to what the packages contained. Coleani was one of the biggest drug distributors in the state.

They waited until the van had driven off and Huber had gone inside before climbing out of the car. Amelia felt the usual anticipation course through her body with every step toward the building. She was eager for a faceoff with Coleani.

As they neared the restaurant's side door used primarily for deliveries, they heard a raised voice penetrate the wall. "That fucking little bitch. She's determined to bring me down. Starting with you," the livid voice fumed.

"What the hell are you talking about?" someone asked.

"The end of you, the end of *us*. A subpoena, Wayne. For your fucking DNA, that's what I'm talking about. What have you done? What evidence have you left behind?"

Amelia recognised Coleani's voice this time. Aidan Carmichael had obviously filed the paperwork in preparation, so they could arrest Wayne Burton. Clearly there was a rat in their house if Coleani knew about it just moments after the fact. She filed away that thought for another day.

"I told you to sort her out years ago," Coleani shouted. "The little bitch should've been bug food. Nothing but bones by now. Instead she's causing me more problems than ever."

A chill went down Amelia's spine and she looked over at Kellie. "One guess as to who they're talking about."

Darryl's expression darkened as he latched onto Coleani's threats. Amelia could see he longed to pull Kellie into his arms and hold her but he was on the job and couldn't afford such distractions.

Exactly why it was never a good idea to hook up with a colleague.

One moment of hesitation could prove fatal.

Darryl's gaze found hers, and she noted his professionalism. Not one hint of inner turmoil showed. Good. She'd have left him behind otherwise. "To me that's probable cause," he said.

She smiled ruthlessly. Coleani's outburst had not only verified that Burton was inside but had given them sufficient reason to search the restaurant and seize any evidence linking to a crime, such as the cache of drugs that had been delivered just a short while ago.

"Let's hope Carmichael is as good as his reputation," Amelia said.

After tonight, it would be up to the lawyers. It would be Aidan Carmichael's job as prosecutor to keep Coleani from walking. With both Coleani and Burton on scene, Aidan should be able to charge Coleani as a co-conspirator, if not an accomplice, to Burton's crimes.

Coleani's ruling days were numbered.

Darryl jogged back to the car and returned, shrugging on his bullet proof vest. He handed Amelia her own before detaching his mobile from his belt and handing it to Kellie. "Call dispatch. Have them send back-up and whatever you do, stay here," he ordered in a tone even *she* wouldn't ignore.

Amelia caught Kellie's gaze. "We're not kidding. If I see you in there, I'll shoot you myself for disobedience."

"Okay." Kellie held her hands up, stalling all further orders. "I'm not arguing with you. I'm supposed to be on desk duty, remember? Besides, I'm at a slight disadvantage being unarmed and all."

Darryl gave her a look that said he wasn't convinced by her easy acceptance. Amelia could well understand why. Kellie wasn't one for following orders. But then, neither was she. Amelia retrieved a small black canister from the belt at her hip. She was always well prepared for any eventuality. She handed it to Kellie, who took it and studied the label in the dim golden glow.

"Capsicum spray?"

"If anyone gets past us, I want you to take that sucker down. No one is getting away without first taking a trip to the LAC, understand?"

"Sure." Kellie studied her hands. In the left she held Darryl's mobile and in the right her capsicum spray. "Well, I'm all set. Be careful."

Kellie's eyes said it all. She was afraid for them. Amelia had missed the idea of someone caring whether she came back or not. She nodded to Kellie, who raised Darryl's mobile and dialled the direct number for dispatch.

Amelia bent down towards the lock on the door and withdrew a pick gun from her back pocket. It was a favourite among thieves as it was quick and easy to use and didn't require luck or finesse. The pick was a long white cylinder that resembled the handle of a torch, except it had a small metal torsion wrench sticking out of the top which she placed into the lock and turned on the device. Vibrations moved from the base to the tip causing the lock to rotate.

She reached the doorknob and it turned easily in her hand as she knew it would. She opened the door an inch and looked through the gap for anyone who may have heard them and were waiting to greet them. As far as she could determine, they were alone. Burton and Coleani must be confined to the office, she assumed. But there was still Huber to consider and any number of unknown felons hiding inside.

Darryl withdrew his weapon from its tan leather holster and nodded to her. She in turn pushed on the door, opening it wide. Darryl entered first while she provided back-up for him. When he found a safe cover he returned the favour and she followed him into the building, allowing the door to close in her wake.

They crossed the room slowly, keeping to the shadows as they used the tall stacks they found in what appeared to be a storage room as protection. The room was dark except for a small streak of light spilling from the office up ahead through the open doors. Using their hands, they signalled to each other, talking silently in a code all police officers knew and lived by.

"You need to fix this," Coleani was saying as they moved closer. "Otherwise it'll be you I put in the ground."

"It won't be as easy now. She's a cop."

Her eyes narrowed. From the angle, she could see Coleani sitting behind his desk. He was dressed in a suit that would no doubt have a famous label sown into the silk lining. His focus was off to his right—her blind spot.

A shadow fell across the wall behind Coleani as the figure moved forward. She caught sight of his hand first, then the cheap creased pleather boots he wore, the soles worn down almost to nothing from overuse. She held her breath as he finally moved into view. Light from the bare overhead bulb shined down on him and she went cold.

Wayne Burton in the flesh. She pushed back the tidal wave of emotions that came at seeing the man and one glance at Darryl told her he was doing the same.

"Have you gone soft, Wayne? I know she's a fucking cop. I don't care. I want her dead. But I want her to suffer first. Kill them all. Doyle. Hill. Donovan," he barked. "Then go after her."

"Police. Put your hands up," she shouted.

Burton turned at that moment and raised the weapon she hadn't seen. A moment later a gunshot reverberated throughout the room.

***

Kellie heard the shot. She dropped instinctively to the ground as Darryl's mobile slipped from her hand and clattered against the pavement several feet away. Two seconds later an answering shot sounded out. She recognised the bang as a Glock 23, the standard weapon for plainclothes police officers.

Which meant it had either been Darryl or Amelia who had returned fire. She shook uncontrollably as she rose to her feet. Fear threatened to swallow her and she closed her eyes briefly as she gained some much needed control over her body. It hadn't mattered how she'd tried to overcome it. The sound of a bullet exiting a chamber had always incapacitated her. She could barely hold a gun without becoming a gelatinous blob and had only just managed to pass her weapons competency test that had been compulsory to join the police force.

Her body refused to move and in the distance she heard the shrill sound of sirens that told her help was on the way. But would Amelia and Darryl survive that long? They may already be injured—or even dead. No. They couldn't be dead.

She hesitated. If she went in she could very well turn into more of a hindrance than anything else. But knowing her best friend, and Darryl, were in there pushed her forward. On stiff legs, she moved toward the door.

She gripped the container of her capsicum spray hard as she slipped quietly inside and stood motionless for a few beats as her eyes adjusted to the unusually dark room. Slowly, she made out shapes. Tall stacks—at least a dozen—of shelves, each filled to capacity with canned items and an assortment of dry goods dominated the space. She was in the restaurant storeroom which made sense since she'd entered through the deliveries entrance. She felt along the cool cylinder, working up from

293

the base to the tip to remove the safety cap. She took a moment to make sure she had the spray nozzle facing away from her.

Kellie moved cautiously when she saw a figure up ahead in the darkness. The shape told her it was neither Amelia nor Darryl. She'd recognise their silhouettes anywhere. She had no idea how far inside they'd gotten but from the multitude of sounds surrounding her, Kellie knew they were dealing with more than just Burton and Coleani.

Blood pounded in her ears and the scent of cordite burned in her nostrils.

Kellie stopped suddenly. The back of her neck tingled and her ingrained survival instincts screamed at her to run. She retreated quickly only to find herself trapped by thick bulging arms as they wrapped around her waist and throat, squeezing hard and cutting off oxygen. Kellie struggled. Her feet dangled in the air as she was lifted up off the ground. Her mind flew into a panic.

Blackness whirled behind her eyes as little sparks of light mingled with the dark. The nails of her free hand dug into her captor's arms as she began to hyperventilate. Within minutes she would be unconscious or dead and considering what lay beyond for her, she welcomed death.

Her brain started to shut down. She knew she should fight back but couldn't get her limbs to move. She had trained for years in case she was ever confronted with this situation but she hadn't counted on the emotional element.

She tried to calm herself, to clear her mind of everything but Nick's instructions. He had taught her all the dirty moves a woman could utilise to disarm a man. All she had to do was remember and use them. She took deep breaths and relaxed her body, going pliant. Instantly, the behemoth loosened his hold on her which she immediately used to her advantage.

Her right leg bent at a ninety degree angle as she sent it in motion, allowing her leg to gain velocity as she brought her knee up as high as she could in the air before sending her leg back, the ball of her stiletto slamming hard into her attacker's knee. Bone snapped and his leg crumpled, almost sending him toppling to the floor, releasing his hold on her. As soon as her left foot touched the ground, she dug the sharp heel of her shoe into his foot, the point of the three inch dagger-like heel piercing the leather of his shoe and stabbing the top of his foot.

He sent out a yelp, distracted. Kellie swung around and sprayed her attacker with capsicum spray. His hands moved from his knee to his eyes as they burned and he screamed, disorientated. He stepped back, knocking into a stack. Kellie glanced around. She hadn't completely incapacitated him just yet and would need something more than capsicum spray and her stilettos. She caught sight of a wrench resting beside a can of creamed corn on a shelf. Obviously someone had been fixing the stack but had been too lazy or distracted to return the wrench to the red toolbox that rested at the base of the same stack.

Kellie snatched up the wrench and before the man could move another inch she'd smacked him hard over the head with the stainless steel tool. The man, who she now recognised as Coleani's bodyguard, Aaron Huber, fell to the floor in an unconscious heap.

She rested her hand over her pounding heart and stepped back, her heels clicking loudly against the floor. She removed her shoes, tucking them beside the toolbox before slipping into the next stack, then the next, as she continued further into the room. She made it around two stacks before she tripped over a large prone figure lying outstretched on the floor. Her fists clenched as she squeezed her eyes closed and pressed her lips together all at once in an effort not to scream.

Darryl?

Pain so acute cut through her as she dropped to her knees beside the body and rolled it over. Relief washed over her as she recognised the man as being another one of Coleani's bodyguards.

A shaky breath escaped her lips. She couldn't wait until this night was over. Kellie's chin jerked up when she saw movement in her peripheral vision. Her heart thumped as Darryl moved around the end of the stack opposite her, his finger poised over the trigger.

She watched, horrified, as yet another of Coleani's bodyguards appeared behind him. Kellie couldn't stop the shout of warning that tore from her mouth any more than she could change the situation. Darryl swung around and had discharged his weapon before Kellie could finish her warning. She'd barely gotten her breath back when another gunshot rang out, the echo ringing painfully in her ears.

Everything in that moment slowed to a standstill as Darryl fell.

She screamed his name, the sound wrenched from her throat, the voice that filled the room nothing like her own, so full of anguish that it was palpable before the world became deathly silent.

She covered her mouth with her hand as tears blurred her vision and rolled down her cheeks. Her body shook violently as she watched the man she loved die, powerless to stop what was already in motion.

Her heart felt as if it had been torn from her chest.

She stopped breathing.

Her lungs burned with the need for oxygen.

She didn't care. Couldn't.

Nothing hurt more than knowing she had failed Darryl in every way possible.

Chapter 35

Amelia stepped out into the open. She scanned the immediate area as she moved toward her partner. She crouched down beside him and without looking at him, felt for a pulse as blood pooled beneath him. She allowed herself a moment of relief when she felt a faint throb beneath her fingertips. The bullet had pierced through his vest.

Her partner was damned lucky. But only if she got him immediate medical assistance.

A sob nearby had her turning in Kellie's direction. She brought her finger up to her mouth, signalling her to be quiet. Her teary friend nodded and covered her mouth with her hand to muffle her sobs.

From her position on the floor she saw the small shadow streak under a stack. She lowered herself closer to floor and caught sight of someone moving toward her. She twisted the gun on an angle to get it closer to the floor. With some satisfaction she lined up her barrel with the man's shoes and squeezed the trigger, the *pop* shaking the nearest stack.

A cry of pain filled the room as Amelia leapt to her feet in a single motion. She raised her arm higher and set off shot after shot through the stack, each bullet finding her target, some through tins of olives, the brine dripping onto the floor.

Dick Coleani's body fell hard and blood stained the concrete beneath him. She didn't spare him another thought and turned back to Darryl. She didn't sense the malice in the air until it was too late.

The bullet hit her hard, biting into her skin and sending her rocketing to the floor with force. She blacked out for a moment and when she came to, she was staring into Kellie's tearful face.

The fear in her eyes told her how much Kellie loved her. She'd made so many mistakes in her life but her biggest regret was allowing her to walk away. She couldn't believe she'd held onto her hate for so long while her friend had almost died. Now their positions were reversed and she was slipping away.

"Stay with me," Kellie whispered desperately, and Amelia could feel her shaking as she took her hand and squeezed hard.

The pain consumed her. She tried to speak, her voice not working. Her mouth opened and closed and nothing but air came out. She tried again, using the last of her energy to warn her friend. She had seen the man who had shot her, knew that Kellie's only chance was to get the hell out of there.

She gripped her wrist, causing her blue eyes to widen.

"Run," she said, before the darkness took over.

Chapter 36

Wayne Burton slipped out from the cover of the stacks. Satisfaction filled him as he saw the bitch cop go down. He stepped forward, stopping a few feet from Kellie. He stared at the golden tresses of her hair, which hung over her shoulders in a wavy mass.

"Hello, Kellie."

Her chin jerked up and he smiled. He inhaled deeply, his nasal cavities picking up the scent of blood, fear, and the flowery smell he always associated with her. It had been twelve years, but he still remembered.

Her moist blue eyes condemned him. "You bastard," she spat.

His smile grew wider, enjoying her rage. Her lip quivered and he could see the force she was using not to cry openly in front of him. Her hand blurred in his vision and something sailed toward his face. Using his arm, he blocked the empty black canister of capsicum spray from hitting his face.

She surprised him.

He'd not been expecting her to have so much fire. It reminded him so much of the younger Kellie, the girl he'd loved. He had watched her for months, not that she ever noticed.

God, how he loved to watch her. Her young athletic body moved so enticingly. He longed to touch her smooth skin, to glide his hand over those creamy mounds, ripe with womanhood. She was a woman now, so much more than she'd been as a teenager, and he longed to experience her. He was already hard as he looked over at her like a starving man seeing a roast leg of lamb.

"Why?" she asked him.

"Because I wanted you. Still do. Coleani's order only made something I didn't think I could have accessible." He took a step toward her, his gun in his hand. He waved it in the air and her gaze followed it. "I will have you again before the night is out. I promise you that. Once, you didn't know I existed...but you've thought about me constantly over the years, haven't you? I like knowing I'm with you always."

Her eyes flashed with hatred and her face distorted into disgust. "You're nothing to me. I used to think you were something to fear, the bogeyman in the closet, but you're not. You're pathetic. I won't remember you, not after today."

Anger ate at him. Once more he was invisible to her. His lip curled with distaste. He aimed his weapon at her, wanting her to feel afraid. To fear him.

Kellie whimpered, tears rolling down her cheek. She closed her eyes as if she welcomed death, shutting him out. Her hand still held Amelia's as if she provided her friend life just by touching her.

"Look at me," he screamed. "Open your eyes and look at me. I want to watch the life drain from your eyes."

"Back-up is on the way. If you're going to kill me, you'd better get on with it. You don't have a lot of time."

The bite was back. She was still afraid of him, he could sense that, but that didn't stop her from going down without a fight. He liked that about her. There was nothing worse than begging and whining. But *his* Kellie would never beg for her life. No…she was taunting him, daring him to kill her.

Wayne flicked the safety off. The sound had Kellie's eyes widening. Her body froze, her movements small as she watched him carefully. "Don't push me, Kellie."

"Oh, get on with it already. You're boring me."

His lips thinned. He didn't like being challenged. He squeezed the trigger, the bullet whizzing past her face to lodge in the wall behind her. He'd purposely let it go wild and delighted in the small jump her body instinctively made that even the coolness she was trying to project couldn't hide.

His finger grazed seductively over the trigger and he lovingly stroked it. By the end of the night, Kellie would truly fear him. He would take the fierce woman before him and break her and once he got that acknowledgement from her, he'd kill her.

Suddenly a sharp pain bit into his skin, followed by another one and then another. He felt weak as a chill descended on his body, creeping up from his toes.

Wayne saw his end as if in slow motion. It wasn't a movie of his life that passed through his mind, a collection of regrets and achievements. It was only the past few minutes that he reviewed, trying to pinpoint where he went wrong, how he'd miscalculated.

Kellie appeared so beaten. He should have known better. She had raised her hand so fast, he hadn't seen it coming. One moment she had been telling him to end her and in the next she had a gun in her hand and she was emptying the magazine into him.

He fell to his knees, his legs no longer able to hold his weight. His vision blurred and he knew he would soon die. He called himself an idiot for underestimating her. He should have known from the past that Kellie was a fighter.

She had beat him.

The last thing he heard was a female voice telling him to go to hell.

***

Kellie's hand shook from the heaviness of Amelia's gun. She would've dropped her arm, but something drove her and it took all her strength to keep the Glock straight and not allow it to push back with the force of each bullet exiting the chamber. Soon the gun clicked over, indicating it was empty but she continued on listening to each click as she watched Wayne, his face frozen in surprise, drop to his knees before his face hit the floor.

She startled at a noise behind her and swung her head and the empty gun towards the sound as the overhead fluorescent lights blinked on. Nick held up his left hand in a surrender pose.

"It's me, Kel. It's Nick," he soothed.

She wondered what he saw. She could only imagine the expression on her face. Wild and feral were the words that came to mind. She had just killed a man and she didn't feel a thing.

"It's all right now," he said.

He watched her warily, determining whether she had recognised him enough not to become a danger to him. Kellie dropped her hand along with Amelia's gun and let out a deep relieved breath as she returned her attention to her bleeding friend.

She watched from under her lashes as Nick moved carefully to Wayne's body, the barrel of his gun aimed at the figure. As he neared, he kicked the man's gun away, the metal sliding noisily across the concrete floor. He glanced down at the blood pooling around the body then looked back at her in surprise.

"Jesus, Kel, I didn't think you had it in you."

She hadn't thought so, either. She had no idea where her courage had come from. She'd been terrified. She'd been frozen since the moment he'd revealed himself. She'd barely heard him in the end. It was like she'd been looking into a swirling tunnel and with barely conscious thought, her reaction automatic, she'd picked up Mia's gun and a force had taken over. Without her usual inhibitions, she'd squeezed the trigger.

Her hands still shook. Sobs welled up inside her and her delicate shoulders shook violently as she began to cry. Somewhere inside her a dam broke and years of bottled up emotions, the fear she felt, the hatred she held for Wayne Burton was released…and she let go.

Epilogue

Darryl shifted on the hospital bed. His whole body ached. He'd been told how lucky he was that none of the bullets had hit an artery or organ. The loss of blood had made him weak and it hurt to breathe, but it was a small price to pay to be alive.

Dick Coleani was dead and so was his first lieutenant, Wayne Burton. Darryl had heard from Dean that the LAC seized all assets belonging to Coleani in an effort to stop his rivals from taking over his business. They would be working overtime to make sure they hadn't just cut the head off the snake, only for another to grow back in its place. A taskforce was already underway, and this would be a major coup for Harbour Bay. Particularly those who resided in Coleani's neighbourhood who were now free from his control.

Matt Murphy had come home from his vacation and had visited, bringing along Hallie, who had handed him a bouquet and a 'get-well' balloon. An intelligent girl, she aced all her classes and took on extra work most kids her age struggled with. Matt had kept him occupied regaling him with stories of their vacation, mainly his attempt at fishing and how they had ended up eating Hallie's catch since neither Natalie nor he could get a fish to bite. He also confirmed that Natalie was twelve weeks pregnant and had practically burst with pride when he uttered the words.

Darryl had congratulated him and couldn't help the ping of jealously he got at knowing Matt was so happy. It brought him back to his own relationship issues with Kellie—if he could call it a relationship. He knew he wanted her. But he had no idea what the hell was going through her mind.

The knock at the door brought Darryl's attention to the person standing in the doorway. He smiled when he saw her.

His dilemma. The love of his life.

His gaze caressed her. Dressed in casual wear, jeans and pale blue t-shirt, she appeared relaxed. Good. The last thing he wanted was for Burton's death to weigh on her conscience. Her blonde hair fell in loose waves, softly framing her face and lilac, painted toenails peeked through her silver sandals. His heart did a happy dance.

She stepped forward into the room, watching his face closely.

"How are you feeling?" he asked.

She smiled at him and his body warmed. "Shouldn't I be asking you that? After all, you're the one who was shot."

Kellie fluffed the extra pillow sitting on the nearby chair. She put her hand behind his back and gently pushed him forward, adding the pillow to the other propping him up. He could certainly get used to being coddled.

"The doctors said I should be fine. I'm barely in need of a Band-Aid. I was more worried about you."

Kellie smoothed his hair back from his forehead. He stared into her eyes, studying the blue depths. She let out a deep breath and played with the edge of the hospital blanket.

"I'm fine, Darryl, thank you. It's really amazing what the mind and body can do given the chance. I've never been more terrified in my life. But it's all over now. At least, part of it is. I have to see a psychologist before I can return to work."

Darryl nodded. It was standard procedure.

"I know just the one if you're looking. Her name is Natalie Murphy. She's good and she'll understand your trauma. Trust me on that."

"Okay, I'll see Doctor Murphy. And I'll see you when you get out, Detective Hill."

His gaze locked on hers. "I'm not going anywhere. The case is over and I meant what I said. When I'm free of this damn hospital, I'm coming after you and I'm not letting you go."

He had to admit, his tone was slightly threatening. But he had to let her know she wouldn't be able to be rid of him. He had waited a good thirty-one years to feel the way he did now and he wasn't about to let that reason walk away from him without a fight.

Kellie nodded, the threat in his voice heard and accepted. She placed her hand in his and squeezed as she leaned over and kissed him lightly on the lips. As she pulled away from him, he put his hand on her neck, holding her in place as he kissed her again, this time deeper. When the kiss ended, her eyes were glazed with desire and she almost stumbled as she stepped away from him. He grinned at her reaction.

"I love you, Kellie."

He swallowed hard at the lump in his throat. He couldn't imagine a life without her. If she walked away from him now, he wasn't sure how he'd find the strength to keep going. Tears glittered and brightened her eyes. His stomach clenched painfully. He'd thought he'd known true fear but nothing compared to this moment.

"I love you too," she said finally. She swiped at a tear that rolled down her cheek. "How could I not, Darryl? You are the best thing that's ever happened to me. I'm not even sure I can describe how you make me feel."

He let out a relieved breath and tugged her back to him. She placed the palm of her hand on his chest.

"When I said I'd never been so terrified," Kellie continued, "I didn't just mean facing Wayne. When you went down and I thought you died, it was the worst moment of my life. I realised all my fears were nothing compared to living without you. Please don't ever let me push you away."

"Never going to happen."

He drew her down for another all-consuming kiss. "Damn, I wish we were alone. The things I'd do to you if I wasn't in a hospital bed."

Her eyes darkened with desire then cleared as

her expression turned sad. "What does it say about me that all my friends are in the hospital?"

"Damned lucky."

Another tear escaped her eye and she dashed it away as she nodded.

The door to his room opened as Rose slipped inside, stethoscope dangling from her neck. She stopped when she saw Kellie and smiled.

"I hear you've had a rough couple of days. How you holding up?" she asked Kellie.

"I'm fine. Thank you. In fact, I have some more visiting to do. I'd better get going and make the rounds."

He sensed she blamed herself for his and Donovan's current states. He'd fix that the moment he was free from this antiseptic hellhole. She kissed him lightly on the forehead and stepped back. Their hands slowly separated and he felt bereft at the loss of her touch.

"Take care of my man, Rose."

Rose smiled more broadly this time. "Will do."

With that, Kellie turned and walked out the door.

***

Kellie wandered down the hall of the hospital. She had always hated hospitals since she'd woken up in one twelve years ago, her head bound with bandages, her body throbbing as she relived the last few moments of her previous life over and over in her head as she lay helpless in the bed. She had endured the rape exams to be told what she already knew, that she'd been raped. The perpetrator had

310

left no evidence of himself behind and he'd probably used a condom. Thank God for small favours, she'd thought at the time. She wouldn't have to worry about an STD or pregnancy.

At some point during her reflection she wished she had died. She'd felt humiliated and used. Her virginity gone. It wasn't much in this day and age, but it was hers and it had been brutally taken from her. It should have been her decision to make when and where she lost it and with whom. She had dreamt about rose petals and champagne and instead had gotten a dark alley and garbage.

The hardest part had been remembering the feel of the gun pressed against her temple, knowing that was the end. That she would die. Feelings she never expected to feel, that she would remember for the rest of her life, boiled inside her. She'd been powerless to do anything and had meekly prepared herself for death. Never again would she give up. Life was precious and no matter what, meant to be lived.

Kellie opened the door to Amelia's room and walked in. Memories swamped her, only this time, their positions were reversed. Would Amelia treat her with disdain? After all, it was Kellie's fault she was in the hospital. How could she have let her go? It hadn't just been her, though. They'd both given up. She placed the bouquet of flowers she was carrying on the table beside the bed.

Amelia looked up from the bed, her face pale. She frowned at the flowers.

"What's this?"

"Flowers. The usual gift when visiting someone

in hospital. How are you doing?"

Kellie poured a glass of water for Amelia and handed it to her. She took a grateful sip before leaning back in her bed.

"Better."

"I'm glad. I wouldn't want to lose one of my only friends."

Amelia smiled. "Relax. I believe Nick would be happy to take my place. In fact, I've been watching myself around him. I think he's actually been trying to knock me off."

She was obviously feeling better. Not even a bullet wound could bring her down.

"Well, he should know better. No one can replace Amelia Donovan."

"Damn right. So how's everything going down at the LAC?"

"You mean is everything falling apart without you?" Kellie asked. "Sorry, I hate to burst your bubble, but everything is fine. The boys are handling it."

Amelia snorted.

"Anyway, I just wanted to come by and make sure you're okay. Also I wanted to tell you that I've filed my report on the investigation today."

Amelia gnawed on her lower lip and Kellie could see the apprehension etched into her face. The job was everything to Amelia and what she wrote in her report would affect her entire career.

She smiled warmly. "I'll be proud to call you boss one day."

The tension left Amelia and she sank, boneless, back onto the bed. "Thank you."

Kellie shook her head. "I didn't do anything. Your record speak for themselves. I only confirmed what they and your colleagues have to say about you."

Amelia turned her head but not before Kellie saw the glistening of tears in her eyes. Who knew Amelia Donovan had tear ducts? She wanted to tease her friend but knew now was not the time. Not when she was clearly so emotional.

When she composed herself, Amelia asked, "How's Darryl?"

"Good. He'll make a good recovery." They fell into silence. A moment later, Kellie blurted, "I love him."

Amelia nodded. "I know. He's damn lucky. You could do better," she joked.

"You know?" she asked, bewildered. She'd only worked it out when the real possibility Darryl had died filled her with such emotional agony that her whole world shattered.

"Sure. We all felt the heat between you two."

She blushed. Nick had mentioned something along the same lines.

"You don't mind?"

Amelia shook her head. "I want you happy."

Kellie sank into the chair beside the bed. "Well, I am."

"He and I will have words if that ever changes," Amelia said seriously.

"Still protecting me, I see."

"Always."

"I'm glad we got a second chance."

Amelia gave her a pointed look. "Me too."

Kellie leaned back against the chair and placed her feet on the side of Amelia's hospital bed. She started talking about inconsequential stuff at first—shoes she'd seen on sale that she was thinking of getting, who she thought would win the State of Origin later that year—just to keep the uncomfortable silence away. Then the conversation turned to personal and suddenly the years melted away and it was like they'd never been separated, their friendship stronger than ever as they shared their histories from the time they'd parted and about Detective Graham who'd been so inspiring and led them both on the path to their calling.

Hours later, their conversation eventually fell upon Coleani.

"With Coleani gone and his business deemed illegal and repossessed, his boys have scattered to the winds. They'll be back to try to reclaim his territory."

"That's just what we need," Amelia said.

"When the time comes, we'll stop it. Today, tomorrow, next month…they're not taking back this city. It's ours now. It's a whole new world out there. Hell, maybe I can finally get the closure I need."

"Well, you know what they say. Open wounds never heal."

"That's true. Very true."

Her own wounds were certainly open and seeping. Maybe now with Burton and Coleani dead, they would close and she would heal. She couldn't change the past, only accept it and move on. Like Darryl had told her, it made her who she was today…and she kind of liked who she'd become and what she'd accomplished.

She'd come a long way. Now she had Darryl and Amelia and an even brighter future than she could've imagined.

Acknowledgments

Thank you for reading Open Wounds. This story has been part of my life for years and I'm happy it is out in the world. I'd also like to thank the team at Limitless Publishing, I'm forever grateful for your support and help in bringing my stories to life. A big thank you to Rosa who made this book great, I appreciate all your input.

About the Author

Camille Taylor is an Australian author who resides in the Nation's Capital with her small dog. She was the typical 90's kid and was raised on Goosebumps, Roald Dahl and Paul Jennings. In her teens she began reading the Queen of Crime, Agatha Christie and in later years found Christine Feehan, Janet Evanovich and Julie Garwood.

She started writing at sixteen and enjoys spending time with her family, doting on her nieces and nephews, writing the many stories floating about her head and working on her genealogy where she can trace her heritage to England, Scotland, Ireland and Russia.

Her other interests include, anything creative— such as scrapbooking and drawing and has travelled across Western Europe, New Zealand and the UAE, after spending a year living in London. She's also dabbled in tae kwon do.

Facebook:
https://www.facebook.com/CamilleTaylorAuthor

Twitter:
https://twitter.com/CamilleTaylorAu

Website:
https://camilletaylorbooks.wordpress.com/

Goodreads:
https://www.goodreads.com/author/show/7791241.
Camille_Taylor

www.ingramcontent.com/pod-product-compliance
Lightning Source LLC
Chambersburg PA
CBHW030527120726
47904CB00005B/1655